"This book is exceptional
love story unfold. The C
touching, and Mary develo

I want to read again, this is a great reminder that God is always by our side, guiding us, gently prodding us to do His will so we can experience His perfect plan."

Paula McGrew
Author of *My Heart Beats for You*

"*Winter's Past* is a beautiful story of love and 2nd chances. The characters were so endearing and real in the struggles they faced. I found myself experiencing their emotions as they did. The hurt, the frustration ... the love. There was an interesting connection for me with Winter, the heroine, since I am also a missionary kid who grew up in the Philippines. The book will make you laugh and cry and root for these two people."

Kimberly Rae Jordan
Author of *Faith, Hope and Love*

"*Winter's Past* will leave you feeling warm and assured of God's unfailing love for His children, even when we need a 'second' chance at love and life."

Katherine Pasour
Author of *Sheltered by an Angel's Wings*

Only You

Change my heart, make it new,
Until my life is filled with you.
Open my eyes so I can see,
Your righteousness at work in me.

Chorus:
Only You are righteous and holy.
You are faithful and true.
Only You, by Your grace and Your mercy,
Change my life so all can see
Only You.

Bridge:
Search me O God.
Know my heart.
I surrender all I am to You.

Tag:
Change my life so all can see
Only You.

For sheet music for "Only You," visit:
www.LanceSimmonsMusic.com/OnlyYou.html

Winter's Past

Second Chance 1

Mary E Hanks

www.maryehanks.com

www.LanceSimmonsMusic.com/OnlyYou.html

Suzanne D. Williams Cover Design:

www.feelgoodromance.com

Cover photo: © goodluz

Author photo: Ron Quinn

Visit Mary's website and sign up for her newsletter at

www.maryehanks.com

can write Mary at
hanks@maryehanks.com

For Jason

The man who shares my dreams.

You are my hero!

Thanks for believing in me.

For Deborah

You used to watch over my shoulder,

reading every word.

I hope you like how it turned out.

See! The winter is past;
the rains are over and gone.
Flowers appear on the earth;
the season of singing has come,
Song of Solomon 2:11-12

One

Forgive Without Second Thoughts

Winter Cowan read the title of her conference topic, and the words thudded in her heart like rocks tumbling down a hill and landing in a pile at the bottom. Could she even speak on forgiveness when a day rarely passed that she didn't remember what Ty did to their marriage? To her?

A few minutes ago, she escaped to the motel lobby to find a quiet spot away from her ministry traveling companions, to think and pray. Praying came easily. But pondering forgiveness?

Ugh.

Had she forgiven her ex-husband? She hated to admit even to herself that she might not have.

I forgive him—she recited as she had a hundred times over the last ten years. She waited for a comforting peace to wash over her. Instead, one word pulsed through every sensor in her brain.

Forgive.

But that's what she—

Wait. Ty was the one caught in the wrong. She was doing her best to live for God. She went on with her life, trying to forget the past. Even now, she was involved in ministry. While Ty was … well, who knew what he was doing?

Just then, Neil Quinn, her ministry adviser, rushed across the lobby, his face ashen.

"What's wrong?" She stood to meet him.

"The receptionist from First Community Church in Seattle called. The pastor's wife had a heart attack last night." His voice softened. "She died."

"What? Oh, no." Only a few days ago, Winter spoke to Pastor Leslie, and he told her that he and his wife recently returned from a cruise to celebrate their fiftieth anniversary.

"The church board canceled next week's conference." Neil stroked his forehead as if he were feeling ill.

"I can understand that." Compassion rushed through her. "What sorrow the pastor must be going through."

"I know."

"I'm sorry, Neil."

He shook his head like he didn't want her to mention it. Of course, he wouldn't. Six years ago, he lost his own wife to cancer. Added to that, he carried the scheduling and financial weight of their ministry. A week without a conference meant extra living expenses for the team of five. Where would the money come from?

But, then, didn't God always supply their needs?

"Things will work out. They always do."

"I know they will." He stared at the floor, out the window, anywhere but at her face. "Ever since I got the call, Molly's passing has been on my mind."

Just like she thought.

He swiped moisture from beneath his eyes as if batting away a bit of dust. He cleared his throat, collecting himself. She'd seen this heartsick look on his face dozens of times. The man was like an older brother to her, and she knew he still pined for his wife.

All business again, he took a deep breath. "I've been trying to figure out what the team should do for the week. Then I remembered my old college roommate, David Michaels." His eyes brightened. "He pastors in Coeur d'Alene, Idaho. So I gave him a call and explained our situation. He's interested in hosting Passion's Prayer at his church next week, even on such short notice."

His words hit her like a tennis racket across the face. "You didn't say *Coeur d'Alene*, did you?" A gulp, like swallowing cotton, choked her.

"Yes, I did. It's five hundred miles west of Billings, off I-90."

She knew exactly where Coeur d'Alene was.

Lord, why this? Why now?

"I'll send David an email attachment of our flyer." Despite the tragic news and the unexpected turn of events, her co-leader for Passion's Prayer was handling the next event with his usual diligence.

She didn't know what to say, what to think. A decade had passed since she left Coeur d'Alene. She had no desire to revisit that city. The chance of running into Ty there was too great.

"I'll pull the car around in front." Neil pushed open the glass door of the lobby. "We're expected at the church in fifteen minutes." His shoulders looked more relaxed as he walked away.

She, on the other hand, felt a headache coming on. She sank into the hardback chair with a groan as thoughts and pictures of the past careened through her mind.

Coeur d'Alene.

She couldn't go there. Why didn't she speak up? Why didn't she tell Neil what she thought about this new plan of his? Why not just take the week off?

Glancing at the ceiling, her gaze followed a crack line in the paint, its zigzags reminding her of country roads they traveled in Montana. Roads that seemed to lead nowhere, but always ended up taking them right where they needed to go. Kind of like life.

What if I haven't forgiven Ty? So she was back to that.

She nibbled her lip between two teeth, wishing for a different outcome other than going to Coeur d'Alene and possibly seeing him.

She groaned. *I'm being silly.* What was the chance of her running into Ty in church, anyway? One in a thousand?

For several seconds she almost convinced herself. Then doubts ransacked her calm. How could she speak at the conference if she was stressed about seeing him? How could she walk the streets of the town where she fell in love with him without picturing his face? And if he happened to show up at the gathering—heaven forbid—what would she say to him?

Another concern kicked her in the gut. How would she explain him to her team? She should have done that before now. Yet she'd avoided the discussion for five years.

Of course, Neil knew of her brief, disastrous marriage a decade ago. But he didn't realize Coeur d'Alene was the last place she saw Ty.

If she explained everything, would Neil decline his friend's invitation? Not likely. Her team leader would be the first to tell her to face her past. Not to hide from it. And there was the problem. Reopen the hurts that broke her heart and tore apart her marriage just for full disclosure with her team? No, thanks. She wanted to forget that time.

Lord, I want to do what's right, but I'm struggling. She hated to ask, but she had to. *Is this Your will?* In the silence, she remembered the word *forgive* she felt God whisper to her. Did speaking in Coeur d'Alene have anything to do with that?

Standing, she paced across the tiny lobby, her red heels clicking a rhythm against the patterned floor. She pictured Lake

Coeur d'Alene. The trails and beaches she and Ty had hiked. Their little apartment.

Stop! No thinking about those things.

Instead, with every step, she cried out to God. She'd need His strength to get through the days ahead.

Images of her ministry team brushed through her thoughts—Deborah leading worship songs, Neil praying for the sick and discouraged, Jeremy leading young people to the Lord, and Randi assisting them. As she thought of each person, she found herself focusing more on their journey together, less on her past. Which was a relief.

If God wanted to use her in a town that she never imagined stepping foot in again, so be it. She wanted His will.

However, one question unbalanced her. If going to Coeur d'Alene was in God's plan for her life, what else might He have in store for her there?

Two

Boom!

The loud sound awakened Winter from a restless sleep. "What happened?" She groaned and uncurled herself from the front passenger seat of the station wagon. She'd barely slept, thanks to her agitation over where this car was taking them.

"The Old Clunker backfired." Neil sat behind the steering wheel, his forward gaze intense. "We're six hours west of Billings." His fingers raked through his graying hair. He reached for his stainless-steel coffee mug and took a sip.

"Sounds like a tank back here." Jeremy, her twenty-year-old nephew, stretched and yawned. "You should have warned me I'd need earplugs before boarding this beast."

Glancing back to where he sat between Randi and Deborah, she saw him shaking his head like he couldn't believe they were riding in such a decrepit vehicle. At least they were moving forward.

But then, the car made another odd sound.

"Should we do something?"

One of Neil's eyebrows had the uncanny ability of arcing high on his forehead. It pulsed upward, now, nearly touching his hairline, before plunging down, a sharp charcoal dash between his eyes. "When I joined Passion's Prayer, I told you I knew diddly-squat about car engines. Still can't distinguish between the transmission and the radiator. Or how the distributor differs from the alternator, or—"

"I get the picture." They'd had this discussion at least twenty times in the last five years. She didn't know anything about cars, either.

"What's h-happening?" Deborah's voice croaked from behind her.

"The Old Clunker's up to its usual antics." Randi, Winter's personal assistant, mumbled something about "the horrible car."

"I get the *Old Clunker* reference." Jeremy chuckled. "But I'd suggest something more like *Old Rattle Trap* or *A Breath from Death*."

"Jeremy." She gave him a warning look.

"You'll get used to the car. We all did." Deborah coughed.

"You all right, Deb?" She turned around to better see her team musician.

"I can't seem to kick this cold." Deborah curled up against the door and covered her head with a blanket.

Winter said a silent prayer for her, then faced Neil again. "Should we stop at the next town and get the Old Clunker checked?" Did she sound too eager? If the car had a major breakdown far enough from Coeur d'Alene, they might have to cancel the conference, right? A lighthearted feeling rushed through her. Followed by guilt. Was it selfish to wish for such an outcome? The pastor had scheduled Passion's Prayer on short notice. He might not even mind if they backed out.

But was that God's will?

She sighed, torn by her inner conflict.

"If we didn't have an engagement in Coeur d'Alene tonight, I'd say yes, we should stop and get the car checked." Neil shrugged. "But David is expecting us by seven. You two are going to get along amazingly well, you'll see."

Anxiety rippled up her spine. Here they were barreling toward a place she didn't want to go, and he had to bring up the fact they would be eating dinner with the pastor—a single friend. And he was teasing her about it?

Not that she had anything to worry about. She didn't date—ever.

Hopefully, they wouldn't regret not stopping to check the car. Going to Coeur d'Alene? *That* she already regretted.

She scooted lower in her seat. The firm cushion beneath her didn't offer much comfort, but she was glad for the pillow she carried with her from motel to motel. She bunched it against the window and pressed her cheek into the soft fabric. But as much as she tried, she couldn't fall asleep again. After several minutes, she lazily watched as the Montana landscape flashed by her window, the terrain changing from flat prairie grasslands, stretching forever, to mountainous forests with sharp, rocky peaks reaching vertically to the sky.

What would Ty look like? He'd be thirty-five. Ten years since she saw him. Was he married? Handsome as ever?

Ugh. Any thoughts besides those would be welcome. Maybe she could recite Bible verses. Or go over her notes. Anything.

But she didn't move, and slowly her mind danced back in time, to six years ago, when Passion's Prayer was nothing more than a possibility. Everyone in her Practical Mission's class was given the same assignment—create a plan for evangelizing an area of the world. Most students chose places far afield, like China or Africa. One girl planned to serve in the Philippines, Winter's childhood stomping ground where her parents were missionaries.

Unlike her classmates, she didn't want to cross any seas. Instead, she chose home missions.

The task began like most school projects. She wanted to do a thorough job and get a good grade. Her idea was to travel across the U.S. as cheaply as possible and share the gospel in as many locations as she could in a year. She charted out how to establish contacts with ministries in different states, what fundraisers would be needed, and how to serve the communities her team would visit. Cutting out pictures of people from magazines, she made a display board of an imaginary team—herself, a co-leader, a musician, and someone in charge of PR. She even thought about buying a big yellow bus to travel in.

Her assignment came together nicely. An "A" would surely be hers. However, something inside of her began changing. During those days of finalizing her report, an idea grew bigger than her anticipation of a good grade. Could the ministry she envisioned for a college project become her life's work? She started praying about becoming a motivational and evangelistic speaker.

For weeks after her report was finished, she worked on ministry ideas. Whether in her studio apartment, campus chapel, or shopping in the grocery store, the inspirational thoughts of traveling and sharing God's love across the United States wouldn't leave her.

What would she call her team? Who would she ask to join her?

Neil Quinn, a young-adult leader at a church near the college she attended in Tennessee, drew her attention as a possible co-leader. Six months before she met him, Neil's wife, Molly, had passed away. Winter remembered his brokenness, his sad eyes, his weight loss. But even through that awful time, his compassion for others and his leadership abilities stood out to her. Like a compass pointing true north, she found in him the perfect adviser for her team. When the time was right, she asked him to join her new endeavor. He willingly vacated his apartment, choosing to serve with her across North America with no other worldly goods than what could fit in a suitcase.

A pastor-friend donated an old station wagon, and despite its peculiar noises, it had carried them from coast to coast, border to border. She considered it a blessing, even after five years of travel.

Following a gas fill-up near Missoula, Montana, Neil pulled back onto the freeway. "She sounds better. Maybe I picked up some bad gas earlier."

"Bad gas, Neil?" Randi muttered.

"You never know." He chuckled. "At least we're closer to our destination."

The car did sound better. *Thank you, Lord.*

"If the car has trouble in the mountains, what then?" Randi's doubt-filled question, like a pebble in a shoe, couldn't be ignored.

"Then we'll face the music together." Neil peered into the rearview mirror. "For the record, I know Someone who supplies all our needs."

"Amen." Winter smiled at the reminder.

"I'll keep my fingers crossed," Randi said in a grumpy tone.

Winter glanced at her assistant, puzzled by her skepticism. What had it been, seventeen years since she met Randi Simmons in eighth grade in Manila? Randi's dad was stationed in the Philippines with the military. Her mom died the year before, and Winter, filled with compassion for the girl who endured such a loss, befriended her, despite Randi's sometimes prickly behavior.

Over the two years Randi lived there, she got into several fistfights with the locals to protect herself, a military brat, and the missionary kid who tagged along but refused to engage in her scuffles. They made an unlikely pair, she and Randi.

When it came time for Randi and her dad to leave the islands, she and Winter made a pact—someday they'd find each other again and always be friends. Time and distance almost erased their promise. But years later, Winter ran into her at a missions' conference. When Randi heard about Winter's ministry plans, she offered to serve as her personal assistant and protector. Since then, her diligence in seeing to Winter's personal needs, and in keeping men at arm's length, had proven invaluable. Although her edgy disposition occasionally tried the team's patience, Winter hurt for the girl who lost her mom at such a young age.

What would Randi say if she found out Winter had kept a secret about being married, then divorced, during college? She hated to consider how upset the other woman might get. But she had her reasons for keeping the story to herself.

"There's not enough room for my legs." Jeremy moaned.

She turned to see him leaning his knees in one direction, then the other, bumping into Randi in the process. Randi glared at him.

"Sorry, Jer." Winter snickered. "When your dad didn't want you tagging along with us, didn't want you wasting a year of college on a traveling ministry team, what did I promise?"

"Don't bring that up. My legs are cramped. That's all."

"I said I'd send you packing when the road got too difficult and the quarters too tight."

"Yeah. I know."

"And now you say …" She knew he was twenty. Still, she longed to hear him say it.

"Sorry, *Auntie*."

A muffled giggle erupted from Deborah.

"For this year, if you last that long, call me Winter. You're part of the team now." She meant the ribbing as a joke, but she knew her brother, Judson, was displeased with his son's choices. Jeremy hoped to be a pastor, and ever since she started Passion's Prayer, he begged to travel with her and experience the ministry firsthand. His dad wasn't convinced a year with her team would benefit Jeremy's goals. He said his son should finish school and get on with adult life, instead of traveling around with no income and no way to pay off his college loans.

Had her brother told Jeremy about her unsuccessful marriage? If not, would Jeremy be disappointed in her when he found out?

"Are we almost there?" Deborah croaked.

Winter leaned around the headrest to better see her. "Your voice doesn't sound good."

Jeremy touched Deb's forehead. "A fever too."

"No wonder I'm shivering." She pulled the blanket over her head and moaned.

"Don't fret. Jeremy can sing in your place tomorrow night."

"What?" His face portrayed his horror.

"That's right. We all cover for each other." Neil chuckled. "Before the year's over, you'll be speaking too."

"Sure, but singing?" Jeremy groaned. "Deb's the only decent singer in this car."

"True." Winter recalled the first time she heard Deborah McBride sing. *Amazing* was the only way to describe it. At a women's conference in Austin, Texas, the most poignant message she ever heard came through a song Deborah wrote about God being a refuge during life's difficult times. Not only did the song move Winter to tears, it stirred her faith in God's provision for her future team.

Because of Deb's heart for worship, her cultured singing, and her professional piano playing, Winter begged the younger woman to join her fledgling group. After a week of prayer and consideration, Deborah said yes.

Not long after joining the team, she wrote a song called "Only You," a tribute to the Lord reverberating with dedication and passion. Upon hearing the lyrics "Change my life so all can see ... only You," Winter thought, *What a passionate prayer.* Then it hit her. Her team would be called *Passion's Prayer.* Their heartfelt prayer would be for the Lord to change them and make them more like Him.

Together, the four of them—Winter, Neil, Deborah, and Randi—had been traveling and ministering across the continent for five years. Now Jeremy had joined them. As a team, they were eager to share God's love and be willing to pray, *Change my life so all can see only You*, wherever that promise took them.

Even if it meant to Coeur d'Alene, Idaho.

Three

When the Old Clunker crossed the last rise of the mountains west of Missoula, everyone in the car cheered. The climb up Lookout Pass kept Winter on the edge of her seat, wondering if the vehicle could reach the mountaintop. She didn't whisper a word of doubt as semitrucks passed them like they were standing still. But once they made it to the downhill side of Fourth of July Pass, she exhaled a sigh of relief.

However, her peace was short-lived. As the Old Clunker rounded the final curve before Coeur d'Alene, she needed more air. Her throat felt parched. Empty. She sucked in a deep breath, hoping the panic would vanish. It didn't. "Stop the car!"

Neil slammed on the brakes. "Why? What happened?" He kept the car moving, but slower. "We're not far from town. Can't it wait?"

"No." She noticed that raised eyebrow of his. "Please. I need a couple of minutes to myself."

They all faced her, but she met their inquiry with silence. How could she explain without telling them everything? And how could she tell them everything without there being misunderstandings over her keeping her past a secret?

"Neil, let's pull over."

Winter appreciated her assistant's take-charge tone as the car bumped to a stop along the gravel shoulder. She pushed open the door and hopped out.

The chilly air let her know fall had arrived in Northern Idaho. She buttoned up her trench coat, then trudged up the hill they just descended. Vehicles sped past her on busy Interstate 90, but she barely noticed. As she hiked, her gaze raked the tree-lined hillside opposite her, then skimmed the blue shimmering lake reflected below where a few hearty fishermen's lines were extended—all familiar terrain.

For a decade, she dropped this city from her personal road map as if it didn't exist. As if she never lived here with Ty. But the truth remained—she had called Coeur d'Alene home. Had loved it, even.

She sucked in a ration of air, then released it. Her mind churned in muddy waters of the past, her memories filled with troubling thoughts staging a coup on her. She stared at the lake below, felt her heart thud to her shoes.

Why did she agree to come here? Facing her past was overwhelming. But after ten years, why should it bother her at all?

Ty.

He was the reason her confidence was melting like butter in a hot frying pan. Did he still live in Coeur d'Alene? Did he ever think of her? Even a little bit?

She forced her arms and legs to go faster, climbing uphill against the wind. Her body balked at the exercise, but she lunged forward, pushing herself harder. The hill was a demon she had to conquer, just like she'd conquer the mental battle waging war inside of her.

Another matter also concerned her. Ever since Neil scheduled the meetings in Idaho, he kept dropping hints that she and David Michaels would make a perfect couple. Why would he say such a thing? He knew she didn't date. Didn't want to start a romantic relationship. Of course, Randi would roadblock unwanted suitors, pastors included. But Neil's encouraging her toward his friend was something she couldn't ignore, either. Not when she respected his advice in so many areas of her life.

She charged farther up the hill, letting her lungs feel the burn. She thought she already came to terms with this stop on their tour.

Apparently not.

Air. I need more—

She bent over, dragging in gulps of cold air. *Why am I letting old feelings control me? My past is forgiven.* She looked up at the sky. "Why can't I forget?"

She stood, hands on her rapidly beating heart, staring at the magnificent expanse of lake water below. A gust of wind grabbed her long hair and tossed it crazily in the wind. She snatched at the strands whipping around her face and stuffed red tendrils inside the trench coat. *I should cut my hair like Randi keeps pestering me to do. A short style would be easier.* She focused on that, appreciating the distraction. But, then, she shook her head. Ever since her dad called her *Princess* twenty years ago, she'd kept her hair long.

Recalling her eighty-year-old dad's endearment brought a smile, but as quickly as one thought warmed her another crept in, snatching away the fond memory. The image of a different man rose in her mind. A man with startling brown eyes who whispered tender, beautiful things about her hair during the most passionate moments of her life.

Don't go there.

Still, she pictured his smile. The way he—

A car door slammed, jarring her introspection. Her assistant jogged up the hill toward her. "You okay, Captain?" Randi called from a distance.

Winter groaned at the nickname. She was doing her best to co-lead this ministry team, but she didn't feel like a captain. "I just needed a walk." With her hands deep inside her coat pockets for warmth, she strode down the slope, breathing easier.

"You should take time for yourself more often," Randi hollered.

They approached each other, and Winter saw the curiosity in her assistant's expression. This flight of self-preservation was unlike her. She knew it. Her whole team would know it.

"You okay?"

"I am. Something's bothering me, that's all."

"I'm here, if you want to talk."

"Thanks." They walked in silence for a few moments. "Hey, if Pastor Michaels is overly attentive, you'll take care of it, right?"

Randi guffawed. "That you can count on." She grinned. "I'm studying martial arts. I could use some practice."

Winter assumed that was said in humor. But knowing her assistant had her back gave her a sense of relief.

In many ways, her team resembled a family. Randi mirrored the bossy mother. Neil was like the dad, providing for needs and lending a sympathetic shoulder to cry on. Winter was like the older sister, and Deborah and Jeremy the kid siblings. However, as she approached the car and saw how close the two were sitting, she had to reassess that idea. Might they be feeling something more than friendship?

She glanced at Randi, hoping her assistant didn't notice the duo. By Randi's glare, she saw and didn't like it one bit.

The week ahead could certainly get interesting.

Four

"Why is this a problem?" Neil stood at the ladies' motel room door. "We've eaten dinner at parsonages across the country."

"Pastor Michaels is single." Winter hated causing friction in the group. But dining at an unmarried pastor's house, with a man who Neil had teased her about, didn't seem wise. The team was in Coeur d'Alene for one reason. Prayer was a better way to spend the evening. Boy, did she have the urge to pray.

"I'm sorry." He sighed. "I shouldn't have teased you about David. Just treat him like any other pastor we've worked with, and everything will be fine."

She wished his words made her feel better.

"Is Randi coming?" His eyebrow quirked up.

"Yes."

"Then what's the problem?"

He was right, of course. Her assistant would create a diversion to any attempt at romance, if there even was one. She might as well relax and enjoy the evening. Meeting the pastor might be just what she needed to keep her thoughts off Ty.

Deborah's cough had worsened, and she opted to stay at the motel. The rest of the team arrived at Pastor Michaels' house at seven o'clock. The pastor's housekeeper and cook, a jolly woman in her late sixties or early seventies, answered their knock. She wore a big white apron with the words "Bake My Day" displayed boldly in red.

"Come in!" She smiled and her warm hospitality encompassed the group. "My name's Marie. One, two, three, four." She pointed at them as she counted. "Are we missing someone? I heard there were five of you."

"One of our team members isn't feeling well," Neil explained. "I should have called to let you know."

"That's okay. No problem-o. Easy to remove a plate. Here, let me take your coats." She collected Neil's jacket and hung it on a hook in the hallway. "Pastor Dave!" she yelled. "Your guests are here ... and pretty as a picture she is." She clucked her tongue as she took Winter's coat and leaned in close. "Have you met Pastor Dave? Eligible women within a hundred miles are crazy about him."

The heat of a blush burned Winter's cheeks. "No, I, um, haven't met him." She cleared her throat, smoothed her hands down her cream-colored dress, and waited with a nervousness she rarely felt anymore, even when speaking in front of a packed auditorium.

"He's a handsome one." Marie winked. "Wouldn't the two of you make a splendid couple?"

Uh, no.

"Pastor Dave!" Marie called in one breath, then she was all attentive to her guests again. "I don't know what's keeping the man. He gets phone calls all the time. Come in, dinner's ready. Have a seat. Sit right here, Deary." She clasped Winter's hand and led her to the chair near the head of the table.

By the woman's actions, Winter concluded Pastor Dave's seat was next to hers. Could she switch places with Jeremy seated at the opposite end of the table and not offend Marie?

Probably not. She glanced across the table to where her assistant took a chair. Randi's expression said she'd jump in, if needed.

"Here he is now." Marie waved toward the door. "Pastor Dave!"

A tall man entered the dining area, and the room seemed to brighten, like a spotlight hitting the stage at the precise moment of an actor's entrance. All at once, the man was shaking everyone's hands and welcoming them as if they were long-lost relatives. Winter felt herself relaxing in the man's exuberant friendliness. When he clasped her hand in both of his, she met the warmest hazel eyes, which sparkled with delight—or good old-fashioned mischief. At the same moment, they seemed to notice each other's hair color. David Michaels was every bit the redhead she was.

"Now I see why Neil says we'll get along famously!" He laughed, and she found herself chuckling too. His gaze leveled to hers. "Does your temper ever get the best of you?"

Caught off guard by the personal question from a man she just met, she shrugged. "I suppose, at times. And you?"

He guffawed. "Most definitely." He released her hand. "Winter. A unique name."

"I was born in the winter of my mother's childbearing years. To my fifty-year-old mom, I was quite the surprise."

"A blessed surprise." He grinned, then moved toward Neil.

She let out a sigh of relief. The man was a gentleman. Nothing for her to worry about. Now, if she could keep her thoughts in the present, the evening would be enjoyable.

"How long has it been, Neil? Five years?" David clapped Neil on the back.

"Six. Since Molly's funeral." His answer brought solemnity to the otherwise jovial atmosphere. Neil brushed a wayward finger under his eye as if a stray lash caused his eye to water.

Winter knew better, and she felt a compassionate tug on her heart.

Tears glimmered in David's eyes. "You must miss her terribly."

"I d-do." Neil's voice wobbled.

"She was one special lady. I'll never forget her."

"Thank you."

"Everyone be seated before the food gets cold," Marie scolded, then fluttered around the table, adjusting dishes.

The pastor's large frame folded into the seat next to Winter's, and she found her hand engulfed in his as a prayer circle formed. After David asked the blessing, she released the breath she'd been holding. Obviously, she overreacted where David was concerned. Neil's teasing, combined with a previous experience she had with an overly-interested, unmarried pastor, was the cause of her skittish feelings. David was handsome in a rugged way, but he was Neil's friend, a fellow minister, and that's all.

Neil's and David's stories from their college days soon had everyone chuckling. Her team leader's involvement in practical jokes surprised her, but it was wonderful to hear Neil laughing and enjoying himself. In fact, the banter brought so much ease, she indulged in a second helping of Marie's famous—or so she said—scalloped potatoes, and she barely refrained from taking another one of the cook's delicious garlic-topped biscuits.

Between bites, she noticed the timbre of David's voice alter. Suddenly serious, the conversation pivoted to spiritual things as the pastor shared his heart for the youth of Coeur d'Alene. With tears in his eyes, he expressed how he longed for them to see the power of God as something real and meaningful. Her breath caught in her throat, so intent had she become in listening to him, seeing how his heart burned with a fire for people to know God's love. In this matter, their callings were matched.

"I see you, Jeremy, a young man standing for the Lord and working in ministry. Your example renews my vision that God will do a great work in Kootenai County. Will you pray for that too?"

"I certainly will, Pastor Michaels."

"They call me Pastor Dave around here."

"Pastor Dave it is." Jeremy grinned.

"You know, Jeremy's our intern." Neil nodded toward him. "He wants to learn the ropes of pastoring. If you have anything you'd like help with this week, he's available."

"Absolutely," Jeremy agreed. "I'd be honored to do hospital visits, work in a soup kitchen, clean your office, whatever."

"Sounds perfect."

They finished their meal with Marie hovering over them like a hen with chicks. "There's more apple pie. We can't let it go to waste."

"Thank you, Marie. The meal was delicious, and the pie crust was out of this world." Winter pushed her chair from the table.

"It was nothing." But Marie's wide grin showed she was beaming over the meal's success. "I'll bring coffee into the living room."

"First, I'd like to show Winter the church." Pastor Dave stood and extended his arm as if in invitation.

He appeared to be an outgoing person who meant no harm by offering her his arm. But she felt compelled to draw easy-to-read boundaries. Those, and Randi's watchful eye, usually kept her from erring when it came to working with men in ministry.

She stood and pushed her chair in, stalling.

As if on cue, Randi stepped between them. "I'd love to see the church. Thanks for asking, Pastor Dave. Tour time, everyone." Her scheme worked to include the whole group.

The auditorium, situated across the parking lot from the parsonage, displayed colorful inspirational banners on the walls. The wooden pews were separated down the middle by a center aisle, with plenty of room for seating on both sides. Pastor Dave had mentioned the sanctuary seated three hundred people comfortably.

She pictured the room filling with people eager to worship God and excited to deepen their relationship with Him. With a sense of expectation, she approached the green-carpeted platform. She walked up the steps and strolled across the raised floor. She could never cross a stage where she'd be speaking without feeling an urgency to commit the upcoming conference to God.

Lord, heal and revive hearts. Show the people Your love. Touch our team. Use us for Your glory.

After a while, she glanced around the chapel. Neil was on his knees by the front pew. Randi stood near the altar, her eyes closed. Jeremy sat on the piano bench, and Winter imagined him praying for Deborah.

Where was Pastor Dave? Perusing the room, she found him standing near the back door, wearing a melancholy expression. Was something wrong? Or did he, perhaps, have a lot on his mind?

She could imagine David Michaels might be a lonely man. As a pastor in his forties, he'd no doubt find dating within his congregation nearly impossible. She didn't envy him there. But that didn't mean she wanted to get involved with him, despite Neil's nudges after dinner.

Five

"Thanks for the tour." Winter strode toward the pastor. "I'm eager for the conference to start."

"Me too." David's eyes looked misty with tears.

Impressed with his sensitive spirit, and despite her resolve, she found herself wanting to spend more time talking with him about his ministry. "How long have you been pastoring in Idaho?"

"Ten years."

"What would you say is your biggest challenge?"

He laughed like she asked something funny. "I could talk your ear off about that for hours."

David was certainly charming.

"Why don't you come back to the parsonage for coffee?" His gaze included the whole group.

Randi shook her head discreetly, but Winter agreed to Pastor Dave's invitation. Something intrigued her about his heart for people.

Back at the parsonage, Marie served coffee and oatmeal cookies. Winter listened to David's stories of starting a church from scratch. His storytelling pulled her in, as if she were right there praying for people in the hospital, serving in the soup kitchen, and painting senior citizens' fences.

Later, when she glanced at the clock, it was almost midnight. Where did the night go?

David leaned toward her. "Could I speak with you privately for a moment?"

She noticed her teammates' restlessness. It was quite late. "Well, okay."

Pastor Dave escorted her from the room, his hand at her elbow. Before she stepped into the hallway, she glanced back and saw an alarmed expression cross Randi's face. If David tried anything, her assistant would have his head. But surely, he only wanted to discuss something of a spiritual nature.

Overflowing bookshelves dominated the small office where he led her. She hurried to the opposite side of the room, beyond a desk covered with stacks of papers, and fingered several titles.

"I've read this one many times." She pulled out an old hardback copy of *In His Steps*.

"My all-time favorite." He chuckled, not far from her.

"My dad gave me a copy when I was twelve and wondering what I would do with my life. This book influenced my decisions even then." She pushed the book back into place and faced the pastor, wondering what they were doing in his private office.

He fidgeted with a paperweight on the corner of the desk. "Everyone will think I'm up to something."

"Especially Randi. I must warn you, she'll be joining us any minute." She edged a little closer to the door.

"I thought as much. By her dour expression, she's out to get my hide."

"You can count on that." She chuckled.

Uncertainty crossed his face. "I don't mean to put you on the spot, but would you go out to lunch with me tomorrow? I know you travel as a group. Do you think it would be possible for me to steal you away for an hour? I'd like to get to know you better."

"You mean, as a minister?"

"Certainly. And as a friend?" His smile was inviting.

Could she go out with him, alone?

A knock sounded, and Randi entered. "Ready to go?" Her falsetto alerted Winter to her irritation.

David's smile disappeared.

For the space of a heartbeat, Winter wished things might be different. That she could allow a man into her life again. To be able to relax and have fun and date. But then, her plan to remain single splashed through her thoughts. And while she felt a tad annoyed at Randi glaring at the pastor, she appreciated her interference. For the next few days, the conference at Mercy Fellowship was all that mattered. Beyond that, Neil had an eight-month schedule planned for Passion's Prayer.

She shook Pastor Dave's hand. "Dinner was delightful. But lunch won't work. Tomorrow, my team will be canvassing the area, passing out flyers and talking to folks."

He held her hand a second longer than she should have allowed. "You're really something, Winter Cowan."

Noticing Randi's glare, she released his hand.

Outside, as they walked toward the Old Clunker, Randi grumbled. "Why didn't you tell the man 'No, thanks, I can't retreat to a private room with you?'"

"He's the pastor. There might have been confidential matters to discuss."

"And were there?"

"No."

"He asked you out, didn't he?" Her assistant's eyes widened. "And you considered it?"

"For one tiny millisecond, I did." The admission startled her too.

"That beats all, Winter."

"I know. But didn't you see?" She lowered her voice so Neil wouldn't hear. "We were perfectly matched, like Neil said."

Randi groaned.

Winter walked faster, eager to reach the car. "We both have red hair. We're in the ministry. He's super friendly. The idea of him and me seemed like a possibility, given other circumstances."

"There's the key—other circumstances. Where's your focus, girl?"

Good question. Her prayer time tonight had been partially for herself. To forget the past. To rededicate herself to staying single and following God's call on her life. And although she wouldn't admit this to Randi, sometimes she struggled with being content as a single inspirational speaker on the road with a team year-round. How could a romantic relationship ever fit into that lifestyle, if she wanted one?

David's attention had been nice.

But a relationship wouldn't work for her. Not now. If ever.

Before falling asleep, she'd pray for Pastor Dave. Her earlier thoughts about him had been right. He must be lonely. Surely God had someone special in mind for him.

Even if it wasn't her.

Six

"Can you picture the father waiting for his son?" Winter asked the crowd as she stood behind the podium in David's church. "His eyes are focused on the bend in the road as he waits for a glimpse of his second-born, his prodigal, who's drifted far from home." She walked to the edge of the platform. "When the man's son steps into view, the father thrusts out his arms. 'My son!'" She spread out her arms, acting like the father. "As he rushes to meet his son, tears drip down the man's weathered cheeks. 'My son is home,' he says with a broken voice. 'My son.'"

After a pause, she returned to the lectern. "There was no condemnation. The father's heart overflowed with love for this son who wandered far. Such amazing love." She felt a wash of God's love pour right through her.

"Though the son squandered his father's fortune and had been living in sin, he was welcomed home." Her voice softened. "Can you picture our heavenly Father waiting like this father? His arms wide open? No condemnation. Just simple, undisguised love."

A quiet settled over the room.

"I can see Him." She fought back tears. "Even though I was a missionary's daughter and had heard the gospel, I wasn't serious about my relationship with Jesus. Rebellion took over my heart. It was me who wandered far from home. I broke my father's heart."

She gazed over the congregation.

"When I finally came to my senses, two fathers welcomed me home. My earthly dad, who called out to God on my behalf night after night, wept grateful tears. And my heavenly Father welcomed me with such open arms of love that even now it touches my spirit. Oh, my f-friend"—her voice cracked, but she forged ahead—"do you know my Father's love?"

She bowed her head, praying quietly about how to end the meeting.

The creaking sound of people rising from wooden pews surprised her. She glanced up. Many in the group, of their own accord, were moving toward the prayer area at the front of the church. She spotted the members of Passion's Prayer and Pastor Dave moving forward also.

Touch them, Lord. Heal the brokenhearted. Let them experience Your love.

Deborah made her way to the piano. Before the musician sat down, her fingers played the familiar melody of the team's theme song. The first words out of her mouth crackled with cold symptoms, but she poured forth the love song to Jesus that had become a battle cry for Passion's Prayer across the nation.

With the familiar lyrics running through Winter's mind, the commitment she made to God ten years before resonated through her. She recalled the night she accepted Jesus. How she vowed to follow Him and seek His will her whole life. The remembrance scattered the crumbs of uncertainty she experienced since coming to Coeur d'Alene. She was right where she was supposed to be.

Her voice rose and she joined Deborah's in song.

"Change my heart, make it new,
Until my life is filled with you.
Open my eyes so I can see,
Your righteousness at work in me.
Only You are righteous and holy.
You are faithful and true.
Only You, by Your grace and Your mercy,
Change my life so all can see … Only You."

Her gaze traveled across the people gathered for prayer. Jeremy talked with two teenage boys. Randi spoke with an elderly woman. Neil and Pastor Dave were praying for others.

Stepping down the platform stairs, she heard Deborah beginning the lyrics to a different worship song, and she wondered whom she should pray with first. A man near the center aisle caught her attention. His head was bent at an unusual angle as if he carried a heavy weight. By the way his shoulders shook, he was sobbing. Something compelled her to draw closer, whether curiosity or the Spirit's leading, she was uncertain.

"Sir, is there anything I can pray with you about?" Her head tilted closer, their shoulders almost touching.

With a shudder that reverberated through her, the man's shaking ceased. In slow increments, his gaze lifted to meet hers. Time stood still. Chocolaty-brown eyes searched hers with a jolt that bore into her like a sword ripping away every covering of self-preservation.

"I've lost my wife." Tears dripped down his unshaven cheeks and disappeared into a full, dark beard.

Ty.

But she hardly recognized him.

He reached out and touched her right cheek with a fleeting stroke of familiarity. "Can you help me find her?"

She stared at him, disoriented between a young handsome man in his twenties and this man in his mid-thirties sporting a beard and wearing grease-stained coveralls. She could hardly compare the two.

But his touch, his fingers on her cheek? *That* she remembered. For a moment, she forgot her surroundings. That she just finished speaking fled from her thoughts. That others might be watching and wondering why she was allowing a stranger to touch her cheek didn't matter. Her eyelids lowered, and ever so slightly, her cheek came to rest against the man's palm. A perfect sense of belonging that had evaded her for a decade washed over her like an incoming tide bathing parched beach sand.

Then, as if a horse kicked her, she came alert. Why was she allowing Ty to touch her? She backed up two steps. Three. Searched for Randi. Her assistant would take care of this. But instead of finding Randi, her gaze collided with Pastor Dave's. Now she had some explaining to do. She nodded in his direction, hoping to dispel any concern.

Against her willpower, her gaze trailed back to Ty's face. His dark brown hair fell in soft waves below his ears, its length blending in with his beard. She took in the dirty coveralls, and how his fingers appeared etched with dark lines. Strange. They never looked like that before. Recalling the feel of those manly fingers upon her cheek sent waves of heat rushing up her face. When she met his compelling gaze again, panic stole the breath right out of her.

She had to get away from him. Now!

Without pondering who might be observing or what anyone might think, she rushed up the platform steps, snatched up her Bible, and marched straight out the side door. From a hook in the hallway, she grabbed her coat.

Then she ran from the building.

Seven

In the dark parking lot, one light flickered and cast eerie shadows around the stationary vehicles. Winter dodged around one automobile and then another, using her hands to guide her through the maze. Where did Neil park the Old Clunker? During a flash of light, she caught a glimpse of the station wagon's shape, and she hurried in that direction. Once she reached the car, she slipped inside. To quell her shivering, she plunged her hands deep into her coat pockets.

In five years of ministry, she never left a meeting before her team. Usually, she was the last person to leave, besides the resident pastor.

Tonight, the other members of Passion's Prayer would carry on without her. They were capable, but what would they say? What would Randi think?

What possessed her to run out of the church like that?

Ty.

Seeing him that close, that broken, and feeling his hand upon her cheek, was more than she could handle. Why did he come to the conference? Coincidental? Or did he come to see her? Wasn't that what she feared? And what did he mean by saying he lost his wife?

She clamped her eyes shut as memories flooded her. She tried to hold back a rush of tears, but they squeezed from her eyes.

She sank lower in the car seat, trembling.

Ten years.

He changed so much. The man she saw tonight was someone she wouldn't recognize if she passed him on the street. What had become of the impeccably dressed, stylish man she knew? Nothing about him seemed familiar, not his uncut hair and dirty clothes, not the thick, full beard, and not his sad demeanor.

The only exception was his eyes. His dark, beautiful eyes were still the enchanting windows to his soul she experienced as a young woman. Those brown orbs never failed to draw her in. They spoke of love and promises, of secrets shared between the two of them. Tonight, his eyes filled with tears.

She only saw him cry once before—the day she left.

* * * *

At the end of her second year of college, Winter had just celebrated her twentieth birthday when her roommate, Lacey Williams, invited her to spend the summer with her family in North Idaho. Winter, eager to remain in the States instead of returning to the Philippines where her aging parents served as missionaries, knew Lacey had an agenda. She said so often enough. She wanted Winter to meet her twenty-five-year-old brother, Ty, and fall madly in love.

"Ty would be perfect for you," Lacey gushed. "He's handsome and romantic, or so I've been told." Then she giggled as only a plotting girl can do.

Winter laughed and doubted Lacey's matchmaking plans. But Ty Williams was amazing! From the beginning, the two of them hit it off. And a month later, he was pushing for more from Winter than she was willing to give.

"Thanks for dinner. I had fun," she whispered into the kiss she knew was coming. Ty's ardor had become more demanding, and she pulled away from him on Lacey's front porch. "Ty—"

"What, Sassy? Don't you want me to kiss you?" He leaned in close to her again.

She turned from him, troubled by his look that said he could read her mind. Of course, she liked his kisses … a little too much.

She changed the subject. "Why do you call me that silly name?"

"Sassy? Because you are." His forefinger drew circles around her lone dimple. "Remember the first day we met?"

She nodded, distracted.

"You were talking on the telephone, sassing your parents. Missionaries even. Then you got off the phone and smarted off to me. You didn't even know me." He leaned in to kiss her neck, his breath hot against her skin, but she drew away. "What?"

"I'm sorry, Ty. I don't feel comfortable with this."

"You don't like it?" He gave a throaty chuckle.

"I don't want things getting out of hand between us. I don't want anything ruining our friendship."

"Friendship? Is that all we have?"

"I want to be friends with you." She touched his arm. "And more." His eyes widened. A grin lit his face. "But—" She put up her hand to stop him from moving closer. His smile vanished. "How can I explain without making you mad?" She took a deep breath. "The thing is, I'm saving myself for the man I marry."

"Oh." His eyebrows dipped in a frown.

Then silence.

Disappointment plunged through her like a free-falling elevator. The crash almost crumbled her resolve. Why did she say a word about it?

His gaze met hers. She read his doubt.

In truth she hadn't been living the way she was brought up. But on the issue of purity, she wasn't budging. Too many girls she knew in college went all the way with some smooth talker and were buried in regrets afterward. She helped pick up the broken pieces for too many friends to have a simpleton's view now.

Ty shuffled to the edge of the porch. "I'll call tomorrow." With his hands stuffed in his pockets, he trudged down the steps.

"Don't be angry, please?" She had strong feelings for him and didn't want to lose him. A list of his good qualities fluttered like songbirds through her mind—the way he brought her flowers, sent love notes, the way he took her for long walks and held her hand, listening while they talked.

Why did he have to ruin things by pushing their relationship too far physically? She knew her parents would complain he wasn't a Christian, but she hadn't exactly been living like one, either. Ty would go to church with her eventually. He'd do anything she wanted.

He stopped on the sidewalk by his Jeep, his back toward her, his hands deep in his pockets, his shoulders hunched. She knew him well enough to know he was brooding. He stood that way for several minutes, then he pivoted toward her. They stared at each other through the dark. Finally, he let out a soft groan and trudged back up the porch steps.

When he reached her, he leaned over and kissed the dimple in her right cheek. He looked embarrassed, and she longed to erase the last few minutes from their minds. His fingers fanned through her hair. He held out a strand to the light. "Did I tell you I love your hair?" She shook her head, feeling miserable. "Don't worry. I'm not mad. You've given me something to think about, that's all." He kissed her briefly on the lips, then walked away.

Would she ever see him again?

A week later he called and asked her for a date. But she thought he might use the opportunity to break up with her.

After a quiet dinner, they walked along a secluded beach at Lake Coeur d'Alene. When he sat down on the sand, she sat beside him. He cupped her cheek with his hand and stroked his thumb across her skin with a gentle caress that had become familiar, a soft circling of her dimple. He wouldn't treat her so sweetly and then end things between them, right?

"Sassy," he spoke his pet name for her with a grin. "I listened to what you said last week. Thought about it long and hard. Only one solution comes to mind that will solve our problem."

"We have a problem?"

"Yes. You know, your reluctance for 'things to get out of hand.'"

"Oh, that." Embarrassment scorched her face.

He chuckled. "Want to hear my solution?"

She nodded.

His hands surrounded hers. "Will you marry me?"

"What?" Did she hear him correctly?

His laughter vibrated with the sound of the waves lapping on the beach. "Will you, Winter Cowan, woman of my dreams, marry me? Live with me forever?"

She gasped, then laughed, then cried, all in about ten seconds. "Are you sure, Ty?" She gazed deeply into his brown eyes.

"That I want you with me for the rest of my life? Absolutely. Please say yes."

"Yes. Yes. Yes. I can't believe it!" Without her usual inhibitions, she initiated a passionate kiss.

Soon she was going to be Mrs. Tyler Williams.

* * * *

Sharp pounding on the windshield brought her back to the present.

"What are you doing out here alone?" Randi demanded as soon as Winter popped open the lock on the driver's side. Her assistant slid onto the front seat and glared at her. "I've been crazy with worry ever since Pastor Dave said you ran out of the church. He mentioned something about a guy touching your face. Is that true?" Her words tumbled over each other, showing her agitation.

"I'm all right. I'm sorry I made you worry."

"What's going on?" Randi felt her forehead with the back of her hand. "Are you sick? You always wait until everyone leaves."

"I know. I needed time alone. A little space."

"Next time tell one of us. We were all concerned. Even Dave. I almost felt sorry for him." Randi gave her a withering look. "Did some guy touch you? Who would be so presumptuous?"

"For goodness' sake, he didn't hurt me. Let it rest." She didn't want Randi making a big deal out of Ty touching her. Besides, it was over.

How did he find her? Had he seen a flyer? An ad in the *Coeur d'Alene Press*?

Soon, the others were climbing into the car, ranting about how starved they were. What would they think when they heard the whole story about her and Ty? Would they understand her reasons for silence on the subject? Would they get that she committed herself to him before she rededicated her life to Jesus? And way before she started Passion's Prayer? Was it wrong that she chose to live in the present as if the past never existed? As if she never had a man in her life. A husband, if only for a short while.

Maybe it was time to tell her team everything.

I need wisdom, Lord. Remembering that time digs up old feelings I don't want. I know You forgave me and helped me move on with my life after Ty and I broke up. But seeing him again. Gazing into his eyes. Feeling him touch my face. It rips me apart.

How could she explain that to anyone?

Eight

The next day, Pastor Dave invited the team to go sightseeing. He said no one should visit Coeur d'Alene without seeing the lake. After some prodding, Winter agreed to go along.

The area surrounding Lake Coeur d'Alene was an amazing work of art, with green hillsides and well-built houses lining the shore. Nearby, resort buildings and little shops bespoke a happy blend of tourists and locals. The group strolled through the city park, admiring the playground created out of wood. They meandered around the dock that formed a giant C in front of the towering resort building, talking and laughing. The dock took them beyond the boat harbor, out to where the wind created churning whitecaps on the lake. Here, the group paused to enjoy the scenery.

David extended his hand toward a bench near the wooden railing a short distance from the others, and Winter accepted his invitation. Tired from the walk, and the emotional roller coaster she'd been on since last night, she dropped down on the seat with a sigh. David joined her on the bench and regaled her with tales of his adventures as a volunteer carpenter for church members building on the opposite side of the lake. His stories of mistakes he made were entertaining, and she laughed so hard she nearly cried.

Nearby, Jeremy and Deborah sat at one of the small tables arranged on the dock for guests, talking and pointing at a parasail above the water. Neil rested on a bench and closed his eyes. Randi remained standing, her back against the rail, her gaze intent on David. Winter tried intercepting her pointed look, but Randi either didn't notice her head shaking or chose not to acknowledge it. That she didn't approve of David sitting beside Winter, laughing and telling stories, was apparent. Within a few minutes, she could tell Randi was trying to run interference. Out came her camera, and she took rapid-fire shots in their direction.

"This way, Winter." Randi waved. "Over here, Pastor Dave."

David smiled at Winter, his rolling eyes telling her he planned to ignore Randi's intrusion. "This is my thoughtful spot. I come here often to think and pray."

"I can see why. It's perfect." Just then, a gust of wind off the lake blew her hair crazily. She grabbed the messy strands and bunched them into a twist to stuff under her coat collar.

But David grasped her wrists. Surprised, yet intrigued, she watched him pry her fingers loose until her hair flew about again. "Don't restrain your hair, please." She met his gaze. "I love the way it dances with the wind."

Now, how was she supposed to respond to that?

"Uh, Winter"—Randi's voice sounded tight—"maybe we should get going." She seemed ready to grab Winter and drag her back to the motel if David dared touch her again.

David's kindness was endearing, and his interest in her was obvious, but she didn't have the time or desire for romance. Not today. Maybe not in the next decade.

Randi grabbed her hand and tugged her to the railing, positioning her for a photo. "This scenery is just right for you.

The coloring. The lighting. I'm going to replace your old picture on our flyer with this one." Her toothy smile belied the tumultuous undercurrents oozing from her like sweat on a marathon runner.

David stood and dusted his pants. "How about a little hike?"

Hadn't they been hiking?

"On to Tubbs Hill." He pointed toward the hill beyond the resort building.

Tubbs Hill. The name whisked shivers up her spine.

"What exactly is Tubbs Hill?" Neil frowned.

"An easy stroll with a great view." David grinned like it was all a great adventure.

"Maybe we should head back." Winter didn't want anything to do with Tubbs Hill and her memories there.

"I agree." Randi nodded.

"And miss this golden opportunity to capture the best view of Lake Coeur d'Alene? Not on your life!" David thrust out his arms as if embracing the whole lake.

"I'm game," Jeremy chimed in.

"Me too," Deborah added.

"Tubbs Hill it is then." But her heart wasn't in it as the group ambled toward the two-mile nature trail.

Soon, the sights of downtown Coeur d'Alene faded away, replaced by trees and bushes on one side, the gorgeous lake view on the other. Jeremy and Deborah quickly outdistanced the rest of them. Neil and David strolled along, laughing and teasing each other about old times. They never seemed to run out of topics. In contrast, Randi and Winter walked side by side in silence.

When they approached a spot where a well-worn path veered off in a perpendicular direction toward the water, memories from a decade ago overpowered Winter. The beach below had been Ty's and her special place. Where he first kissed her. Where she won that never-to-be-forgotten rock-throwing contest. Where he asked her to marry him. And the place she ran to after finding him with another woman.

Now, like that last time, she should flee and never look back. But a desire to visit the past compelled her to hike down the trail. "Let's go down and check out the beach."

"What beach?" Randi peered over the edge of the cliff.

"What about our shoes?" Neil complained.

"Do you know the way?" David stared at her.

She could probably traverse the path blindfolded, but she didn't answer his question. "I'll explore a little then catch up with you guys." She moved toward the trailhead leading to the beach.

A step behind, Randi muttered, "Good job getting away from David."

"I wasn't doing that." A twinge of guilt arced up her middle. "I wanted to see the beach. If you'd rather not come, wait at the top. I'll only be a few minutes."

"Girl, I'm not taking my eyes off you."

"Okay, then."

They followed the path around the side of the cliff, beyond the large boulders, to a cove below. The secluded beach still looked like it might have come out of *Treasure Island.* A place pirates could lurk. The gigantic boulders were worn by weather and water, and the cliffs seemed mysterious, like secret outlaw hideaways from another time. Or a place for young sweethearts to steal away and be alone.

Sigh.

Randi pulled out her camera and aimed it toward the lake. A perfect opportunity for Winter to stroll down the beach by herself. Everything looked the same, even after ten years. Beneath her toes, a flat stone caught her attention. Unable to resist her childhood fascination with skipping rocks, she snatched it up. Pulling her hand back, she threw a sidearm toss and watched the rock jet through the air and skim the calm waters of the cove.

Eight skips.

She could still do it.

Her thoughts leapfrogged back to that day she strolled barefoot beside Ty, her hand in his, feeling playful and flirty.

"I challenge you to a duel." She grinned.

"A duel?" Disbelief showed in his eyes.

"A rock-skipping duel."

"I'm game. Best of five?" Leaning over, he grabbed the first rock his fingers touched. "Ready?"

"No!" She plopped her sandals on a fallen log. "Give me a minute. I need to find the perfect rock." She raced down the beach, not stopping until her gaze caught several smooth stones. She picked up one rock and then another, turning each one in her hand for inspection.

"You don't need a perfect rock." He grumbled. "Pick any old flat piece."

"That's where you're wrong." She gathered a pile of weathered rocks. "You have to find the perfect rock for the perfect throw." She walked toward him.

"Like the perfect guy for the perfect girl?" At his husky tone, she met his gaze. He stepped closer and their lips met.

She leaned back. "Are you trying to distract me?"

"Maybe. What does the winner get?" His face looked innocent, but she knew his words were far from innocent.

"Nothing."

"Nothing? You've got to be kidding." His dumbfounded expression was comical.

"The winner gets nothing, except for the pure joy of watching the loser get soaking wet."

"Huh?" He frowned.

"The loser will jump off that log, right over there, into the cold water with all his clothes on." She couldn't hide her laugh. "Notice I said *his* clothes."

"That's not nice."

"Better win, then."

"You're serious?"

She nodded, eager to get started.

"You're on, Sassy." He scooped up a few more stones. "Hurry up or I'll start without you."

Feeling like a child on an adventure, she searched for one last rock. "Okay, I'm ready."

Ty threw first.

She counted each splash. "Six. Ouch."

"Six is good." He lifted his chin as if daring her to disagree.

"Watch and learn." She leaned back and sidearm tossed hers. "Ten!"

"Beginner's luck."

"I've been throwing rocks like this all my life. It's the one skill my big brother taught me. That and tossing a football."

He chuckled and shook his head like he couldn't believe a girl could skip rocks, let alone throw a football. He tossed his next rock. It plunked against the surface, rolling as if it had square edges.

"Five skips." She muffled a snicker. "Ah, too bad."

He frowned, and she could see the challenge was not proceeding as he expected.

Her next rock skipped eight counts.

"Losing your touch?" He smirked.

"Eight is still better than six." She winked at him.

After four throws, Ty's best was six and Winter's was ten. Both of their first tosses were their best shots. He kissed his last rock and sent it flying.

"Seven." She danced a little victory boogie.

"Eight." He crossed his arms.

"Still not enough." The rock she saved for last, the smoothest and flattest of all, sailed through the air, touching the water with the briefest kiss, then skimmed the surface like a hydroplane. "Twelve!"

He shook his head and groaned. He was about to get all wet. "I can't believe it. Do I have to?" he asked like a naughty boy sent to tell his sister he was sorry.

She nodded and grinned.

He leaned over to untie his shoes. "How about without clothes?" He undid his belt.

"No! Clothes stay on. You have to follow the rules."

"But you made up the rules."

She glared at him.

"Okay, okay." As if the waterlogged tree sticking in the water were a gangplank, and he the mutineer being tossed into the drink by pirates, he trudged down the log from the place it was stuck in the bank out to its farthest edge. He was obviously hoping she'd change her mind. He tossed her one of those smiles that melted her to her toes, but she wouldn't relent. She waved for him to hurry up and take the plunge. Sucking in a deep breath, he jumped through the air and performed a cannonball. A wide arc of water splattered around him. She laughed until her sides ached, but then an impish idea struck. Before Ty had a chance to rub the water from his eyes, she grabbed his sandals and dashed behind a boulder.

"Sas?" He splashed toward shore.

She hid her giggling beneath her hands.

"Where are my sandals? Come out if you know what's good for you." She heard the slosh of his wet jean shorts as his legs rubbed against each other.

She didn't consider what he might do to her when he discovered her hiding place. Suddenly, Ty stood beside the rock, dripping wet, his hands on his hips, his hair poking out in odd clusters. He looked like a pirate as he came after her.

"Ty, no!"

He scooped her up against his soaking wet clothes and held her like a sack of potatoes over his shoulder.

"Put me down. Please?"

Despite her squeals, he marched out to waist-deep water and dumped her unceremoniously into the lake. She gasped when a cold wave sloshed over her head, filling her nose and mouth. Finding her footing, she scrambled to a standing position, coughing and wheezing, water pouring down her face. As soon as she drew a clean breath, her fists clenched, and she raised them, ready to punch him. They faced off, glaring at each other, until the whole thing became hilarious. Laughter and a water fight ensued.

Later, soggy and shivering, Ty retrieved his shoes from behind the boulder. A giant rock became a chair for them to dry off in the summer sun. He peeled Winter's lake-drenched hair from her cheek, and his finger traced circles around her dimple before he kissed her. Then kissed her again.

The brisk wind off the lake snagged Winter's attention back from her memories. Her palm skimmed her cheek, reminding her of Ty's soft touch last night. The gentleness of his caress was so familiar. But the comparison of yesterday's bearded man with the youthful Ty she was remembering confused her.

In front of her, a rocky outcropping stopped her, and gazing the way she came, she saw Randi seated on a log at the far end of the cove. Once again, she'd kept people waiting. As fast as she could, she jogged through the sand toward her assistant.

"Isn't this beach amazing?" She swallowed hard, hoping Randi wouldn't ask her any personal questions. "We better hurry or the guys will worry."

Randi shook her head. "Are you coming down with Deb's bug? You've sure been acting strange."

"Sorry."

"I'm here if you want to talk. I'm your assistant, but I hope you know I'm your friend too."

"I know. I'm just mulling over some things. Nothing to worry about." A lump hitched in her throat. One of these days, she needed to tell her the whole story. But today wasn't that day.

David and Neil were chatting at the edge of a rocky overlook when the ladies caught up with them. David's face lit up. "Glad you could join us."

Winter smiled at him, but for the rest of the hike she didn't say much, her thoughts still in turmoil.

Would Ty come to the conference tonight? Would he try talking with her? Did she want him to?

She had to admit, in some small way even she didn't understand, she wanted to see him again. Maybe talk with him.

To find out how his life turned out for him—without her.

Nine

Diner chatter had a soothing effect on Ty as he sat in a booth at Maude's Place, a local eatery he often frequented near his work. The restaurant, known for its old-fashioned cooking, rumbled with conversations, an oldie's radio station blaring in the background, and a couple of waitresses barking orders to the cook. Besides the great food, he enjoyed coming here because the owners, Larry and Maude, made him feel welcome, like he was part of their family. He figured that's how they treated everyone.

Pushing the last bite of his hamburger into his mouth, he gulped down the remaining coffee. He scrubbed the back of his hand across his lips, then rubbed both hands over his beard. Maybe it was time to shave the whole thing off. He let it go too long. What did Winter think of his appearance?

Man, she looked great! How he'd missed her.

He closed his eyes, remembering last night when he went forward for prayer. Sure, he attended the conference hoping to see her. But her words on the Father's love touched him and filled him with a longing to experience a closer walk with God. When he heard Winter's voice near his ear asking if she could pray with him, he couldn't believe it. He took a risk touching her cheek. But man, oh, man. The thought of her skin beneath his fingers didn't travel far from his thoughts all morning. The way her gorgeous green eyes widened when she realized it was him, followed by that sweet smile of hers, was branded to his heart.

All this time, all these years, he ached to see her again. To have the chance to apologize for his past mistakes. To tell her he still loved her. Never forgot her. He expelled a breath.

How many years had he been praying to be able to talk with her? So much had happened since they split up. He'd love to tell her about it. Especially the part about finding Jesus in a place she'd never believe he'd been—prison.

He glanced at the wall clock. Almost one. Time for him to head back to the mechanic shop. Not that his brother-in-law, Kyle, would care if he was late. Not when they were partners, and Kyle kept urging him to take time off. Said he worked too hard. But Ty believed in pulling his share of the load. He'd been working on cars for five years now, thanks to Kyle's tutelage. He liked the business of taking an engine apart, putting it all back together, and then having the vehicle run again, almost like new. Sort of like what God did in his life. When his world tilted out of control, God took the worst parts of him, did a major overhaul, then put him back together with a grace that changed him. *Praise God.*

Standing, he dug his wallet out of his pocket. When the door chimed, he glanced up. A vaguely familiar, clean-cut young man entered the diner with a short stack of papers in his hand. Where had he seen him before? The guy waved at a waitress as if he needed to talk to her. And Ty realized where he saw him—at the conference last night.

He dropped back on the bench, watching. He felt uncomfortable eavesdropping, but he wondered if maybe the Lord would give him the opportunity to talk to this young fellow.

"Hello," the man said to the waitress. "Could I put up a flyer about some meetings we're having at Mercy Fellowship this week?"

"Sure." The waitress Ty had heard called Annie pointed toward the community bulletin board on the wall near the door.

"Thanks." The young man grabbed a thumbtack off the board and posted his flyer. Ty heard him telling Annie about the conference and inviting her to attend.

"Maude!" Annie strolled behind the counter. "Come and meet a guy who's here about a conference down at Mercy."

Ty always thought with Maude's wide grin she favored Julia Roberts enough to be mistaken for her older sister. The owner hurried over, wiping her hands on her apron. Her mile-wide smile broke across her face. "What's this about?"

"We're having special meetings at Mercy Fellowship."

"I have friends at Mercy. I know Pastor Dave too. He comes in here once a week for lunch. What's your name?"

"Jeremy Cowan. My aunt is the speaker."

His aunt? Ty sat up straighter.

"Hey, Larry," Maude bellowed to her husband. "They have a woman speaking down at Mercy tonight. I think I'll go."

Larry turned from where he was chatting with an old-timer and waved at his wife.

"Let me have one of those." Maude pointed to the stack of papers in Jeremy's hand. "How about you give a shout out and tell these customers about your meetings." She shuffled to the center of the diner. "Everyone, this young man wants to invite you to hear his aunt speak at Dave's church. We know Pastor Dave's a good guy, so let's give this fellow our attention for a minute."

Ty saw the surprised look cut across Jeremy's face. While he obviously wasn't prepared to invite a whole restaurant of people, Ty had seen things like this happen before in Maude's

Place. The owner was a character, but people loved her. Ty felt anxious to hear what Jeremy had to say about his aunt.

A few people called out hellos.

Ty gulped a drink from his lukewarm water.

"Go ahead, son," someone in the back yelled.

Jeremy coughed. "Uh, the conference begins at 7:00 p.m. You're all invited."

"How about a song?" Maude poured a man's coffee.

"A song?" Jeremy's face paled.

"You got a theme song or something?"

"Um, y-yes." Ty recognized panic when he heard it. Jeremy glanced toward the door. Was he thinking of bailing? After a false start, and clearing his throat a few times, he sang the chorus Ty heard last night. "Change my life so all can see … Only You."

When he finished, the crowd broke into applause.

Jeremy feigned wiping sweat off his forehead.

Ty glanced around the diner and noticed a few folks wiping their eyes. Even though Jeremy's tune wasn't quite the same as Ty recalled from last night, his efforts sounded sincere.

"Thanks for letting me share." Jeremy waved.

"Come back and see us again." Maude hurried to another table with her coffeepot in hand.

Ty stood, hoping to reach Jeremy before he walked out the door. When he tapped him on his shoulder, the younger man glanced back with raised brows.

"Could we talk for a minute?" Ty nodded toward his booth.

"Okay."

"Do you know who I am?" He asked as soon as they were seated.

Jeremy stared at him so intensely Ty wondered if he might think him crazy or harmful. "No, sir. Should I recognize you?"

Ty leaned against the booth's cushion, trying to appear more relaxed than he felt. "I suppose not." He rubbed his hands over his face, stroked his fingers down his beard.

"Who are you?"

"Ty Williams." He glanced away, then met Jeremy's gaze again. "I wanted to ask you about your aunt. Winter." Her name crossed his lips like a whisper. "Is she married? Engaged?"

Jeremy sat up stiffly. "I'm not comfortable talking about my aunt with you." He stood. "Why don't you come to Mercy Fellowship tonight? The important thing is for people to draw closer to God." He slid a flyer across the table.

Ty glanced at the sheet—a replica of the one Kyle brought to the mechanic shop yesterday. "I'm thankful to be able to say I know God."

"That's good." Jeremy extended his hand. "Will I see you tonight then?"

"Definitely." Ty stood and returned Jeremy's handshake. He had more questions, but he figured Winter's nephew wouldn't answer them.

Jeremy walked toward the door, and when he glanced back with a look of compassion, Ty had the feeling the younger man was praying for him. A comforting thought.

He pulled a few bills out of his wallet and walked to the counter to pay Maude for lunch, more eager than ever to hear Winter speak tonight.

Ten

The church filled quickly, and Winter found herself searching the pews. Would Ty return? Was she ready to hear what he had to say?

A man with a dark beard entered the doors at the back, and her heart beat a rapid cadence. When she realized the guy appeared to be in his sixties or older, she relaxed. Besides, Ty might not even attend tonight. If he didn't, would she be disappointed?

Inwardly, she groaned. Why the mixed feelings? It wasn't like she wanted them to get back together. Goodness' sake, no. But she couldn't help being curious. What had he been doing for the last ten years? Did he think of her sometimes, as she thought of him? Did he have regrets? And what was with the beard?

Part of her longed to glimpse—if only for a moment—the tenderhearted man from her beach memory. To see the guy who'd loved her for such a short time.

She closed her eyes.

Father, how do You want me to feel toward Ty? You see how mixed up I get when I think of him. How I remember things I shouldn't. For tonight, please help me focus on You and Your Word. Fill my heart with love for Your people. I need my mind clear of everything but You. Only You, Lord.

When David introduced her from behind the pulpit, and she approached him, they smiled at each other like old friends. But to her surprise, his fingers clasped hers and held. That was only a greeting, right? Yet, the way his hazel eyes sparkled in her direction, she interpreted his actions as something else.

Oh, dear.

He left the platform, seating himself on the front pew, but for a good twenty seconds she couldn't think of one word to say.

She gazed at the congregation, took a deep breath, and forced herself to focus. "Welcome to Mercy Fellowship. Please open your Bibles to—" A cough tickled her throat. "Excuse me. Open to Psalm f-forty-six." Suddenly she was stammering like she'd never addressed a large crowd. Three pews from the front, concern sliced across Neil's face. His eyebrow angled high on his forehead.

Lord, help.

"'God is our refuge and s-strength.'" Clearing her throat again, she glanced at the floor near the pulpit where she usually set her water bottle. She'd forgotten it. "I apologize. I'm having vocal technical difficulties." A second later, Randi handed her the water bottle she left in the pew. "Thanks." Winter took a big sip of water. Randi hurried off the platform.

"I think I'll pray first." She closed her eyes. "Dear heavenly Father, speak to us through Your Word. Touch our lives. You have a good plan for every person under this roof—children and adults, men and women. Heal us, change us, and use us for Your glory. Amen."

After the prayer, she felt better. She didn't know what came over her. Most likely it had to do with concerns over Ty—and now, David. She needed to have a heart-to-heart conversation with someone. Probably Neil. Or maybe she'd call Mom.

But right now it was time to share her heart. "'God is our refuge and strength, an ever-present help in trouble. Therefore we will not fear.'" She would not fear the past. Nor the future. The Lord would help her get through anything.

Please let that be so.

* * * *

Following the closing prayer, Winter gathered her coat and Bible, and a man in his thirties walked up to her. He had short-cropped blond hair and big blue eyes. An awkward pause followed, making her assume he was shy.

"May I help you?"

He thrust out his hand. "My name is Keith. I wondered, or I was thinking, maybe you'd like to go out for coffee? I know it's late. What do you say?" He looked so hopeful.

"Thank you for coming to the meeting." She shook his hand and glanced around the mostly-empty auditorium. That's when she saw Ty near the back of the room. Was he watching her? She faced Keith again. "I'm sorry, but I don't date."

"Not even for coffee?" He stared at her as if she'd lost her mind.

"Not even then."

"That must be a bummer."

Sometimes. She smiled and shrugged.

"Well, okay." He stared at the floor, shuffled back and forth on his feet. "Uh, great meeting."

"Yes, it was. Praise the Lord."

Randi suddenly stood beside her. "We've got to go." She eyed the stranger coolly.

"Yes." Winter nodded at Keith. "It was nice meeting you."

"Yeah, sure." He trudged away.

Randi's gaze followed his departure. "Definitely not your type." She shook her head. "You ready to go? I'm starving."

"I'm more tired than hungry." Winter glanced toward the back. Had Ty left? She watched Keith leave the auditorium and noticed the slump to his shoulders. "That never gets easier."

"Don't worry. Like I said, he's not your type."

"And who is my type?" She pictured Ty on their wedding day.

"Let me get back to you." Randi handed Winter her purse. "Don't worry, you haven't missed the boat with Prince Charming. I'll let you start dating, say, when you're sixty."

"Sixty? So soon?"

"Maybe. Now, come on. Let's find a restaurant that's still open."

Randi linked their arms and pulled her toward the exit, but all Winter wanted to do was head back to the motel and sleep. Why was she so exhausted?

Eleven

Even though it was after eleven p.m., and despite her fatigue, Winter accompanied David and the team to a twenty-four-hour restaurant for a late dinner.

Jeremy cheered when the waitress set a huge plate of food on the table in front of him. "I'm going to eat every bite of this, and I'm not ashamed to admit it." Everyone laughed as he dug into his two hamburgers, a giant mound of fries, and a strawberry milkshake. "Maybe I'll have room for dessert."

"We have great pies." The waitress hurried to another table.

"You have some appetite." Deborah coughed.

"I know." Jeremy stuffed several fries into his mouth and grinned.

Hearing them giggling and chatting, Winter leaned toward Randi. "I think you have more work cut out for you."

"Tell me about it." She rolled her eyes. "One full-time job running interference in someone's private affairs keeps me busy enough." She leaned forward and glared at David, seated to Winter's left, as if he were the cause of all her troubles.

Winter elbowed her in the ribs. They were enjoying a relaxed meal as friends and coworkers, that's all.

Then she turned to tell David about a woman who said she received inner healing during the meetings and found his gaze locked on hers. Oh, um.

He leaned toward her. "Your hair is quite lovely. Like spun gold."

What was she supposed to say to that? She glanced at Randi, her self-proclaimed man-fighter, and saw her assistant was engaged in a conversation with Neil.

Winter sighed. She didn't feel like being on guard around Pastor Dave. Even though she liked him more than a lot of single men in the ministry she'd met, she wanted to be friends. *Only* friends. How could she break the news without weirdness developing between them?

Ignoring what he said seemed like the higher road. She gazed across the room and noticed the pie case near the front of the restaurant. A slice of chocolate cream pie sounded divine.

"Hello, are you home?" Randi pretended she was knocking on a door in front of Winter's face. "You've been zoning out a lot lately."

"Just thinking." She made the mistake of glancing at David. A smile ignited across his face. "I think I'll stretch and peek at the pies." She stood.

David stood also. "Tell me what you want, and I'll see if they have the flavor."

"I need to stretch and force myself awake." She yawned. "Sorry. Fatigue is a friend of mine after I speak."

"That's because you give your whole heart." He stepped from the booth to make room for her.

His insight touched her. "Thank you, David."

She walked toward the front of the restaurant. When she glanced back, Randi was talking to him with a stern look on her face. The pastor nodded like he was listening, but all the while his gaze followed Winter. She turned away and sighed.

The scrumptious-looking pies in the case made her want to taste every flavor. She had a sweet tooth but eating pie or any other sugar-laden indulgence this late was a recipe for disaster. Smoothing her hand over her waistline, she turned from temptation. Still wanting a few more minutes to herself, she strolled down the short hallway to the restroom.

When she reentered the main part of the eatery, a man standing at the counter captured her attention.

Ty?

He looked up. His gaze drifted lazily over her. Since the first day she met him, his dark eyes had a dramatic effect on her, as if their magnetic line of force could pull her to him. For several moments, she returned his stare. *Why are you here? What do you want?* She didn't realize she mouthed the last inquiry until she saw his lips purse into a single word.

"You."

He's here because of me?

The waitress handed him some change and placed two giant blueberry muffins into a paper sack.

"Thank you." With a slight nod in Winter's direction, he left through the glass door.

Her gaze followed his exit, then she pressed her fingers against her tired eyes. Was he an apparition created by fatigue? Because, if he was real, and if he purchased muffins from the waitress, she was tempted to chase him down and demand what he meant by the word "you." Her face flushed at what his answer might be.

In a daze, she returned to her table and sat down.

"Do you know that guy?" Jeremy questioned.

"Who?" If Jeremy saw him, then Ty must have been real.

"The guy by the cash register." Her nephew nodded toward the entrance. "I met him at a diner this afternoon. He asked the strangest question."

"Like what?" Randi frowned.

"He wanted to know if Winter was married." Jeremy took a slurp of his milkshake.

Randi gasped.

Why would Ty ask Jeremy that?

David picked up her hand. "Could I speak privately with you?"

"Uh, Dave, let's tone it down," Randi said grumpily. "We're here on a mission, and *this*"—she jerked Winter's hand free from his—"is not part of the plan."

That's for sure.

"How do you know?" David stared at Randi. "We all have our lives to live. Winter's entitled to her own."

Also true.

"Well, see here—"

"Please, Winter?"

Apprehensive, but wanting to be respectful, she stood. Her gaze met Randi's shocked expression. Jeremy and Deborah watched her. Neil stood as if to state his opinion, then sat back down. Winter shrugged in an unspoken gesture of compliance and followed David to a booth a couple of tables away.

Behind her, she could hear Neil's and Randi's hushed arguing. Neil seemed to be telling Randi to give them a few minutes of privacy.

"Winter, I realize we haven't known each other for very long." David stared at her from across the table. "And you're leaving in a few days."

"Yes, that's true." She'd let him have his say. Then this had to be finished.

David's eyes were bright, his ruddy complexion heightened. "What I wanted to ask is could we go on a date—without your team?" He chuckled as if nervous. "I'd like the chance to get to know you better. For us to see if the Lord might have a plan for us ... together."

Since he put it that way, it would be harder for her to get out of this conversation gracefully.

A glance toward the booth where her teammates waited confirmed that, while they couldn't hear him, they probably guessed his intentions. By the look of angst on Randi's face, Neil might be restraining her, giving Winter the time he thought she needed.

Let her go, Neil.

But David deserved an honest answer. He'd probably put a lot of thought into his request. And he was a nice man.

Just then, she heard a familiar laugh at the front of the restaurant. Ty was back?

She swiveled around to see him.

The waitress handed him a cup of coffee to go. He turned with the cup pressed against his lips, and his gaze searched the room. The instant she was in his visual spotlight, she knew. His head tilted like he was trying to make sense of the scene before him. She pictured him questioning why she and David were seated at a table alone, away from the rest of the team. For one breathtaking moment, it was as if she could see into his heart. Was he pleading with her not to agree to date the pastor?

But that was silly. How could she know what a man was thinking when she hadn't been with him in ten years? Even if that man had been her husband.

David cleared his throat, drawing her attention back to him. "What do you say? Would you go out to lunch with me tomorrow?"

She paused before answering. "I'm sorry. I can't." Her gaze darted toward the doorway.

Ty was gone.

"I'm sorry." David blinked slowly. "I've experienced such strong feelings since I met you, I thought maybe you felt the same way."

"I have a personal rule about not dating." She shrugged, hoping not to offend him. "I plan to remain single and focused on the ministry."

"I'll wait then."

"Please don't." She stood and smoothed out her dress. "I'd like us to be friends."

"Friends." He sighed.

"Yes." She smiled at him, then moved from the booth, needing distance.

"I'm beat." Randi stood as soon as she reached their table. "Anyone else ready to head for the motel?"

"I am." Winter grabbed her jacket.

Neil paid the bill. And as they left the restaurant, Randi slipped behind Winter, creating a barrier between her and Pastor David Michaels.

Twelve

During the afternoon of the last day of the conference, Winter decided to go shopping by herself, without Randi. She needed a distraction, but she didn't want her assistant tagging along. Ever since David asked her out the other night, and with Ty making no attempt at further conversation in the last two days, she felt a strange melancholy. Not that she understood why. She should be relieved he didn't speak to her. Glad, even. And yet?

She wasn't.

Tomorrow she'd be leaving Coeur d'Alene. Might not see him again. Which was probably for the best. So why did she feel troubled?

Perhaps, if she went to a store and looked for a new souvenir for her collection, she'd feel a semblance of normality. Not that she bought something at every location, because she didn't. But when a town held special significance—and Coeur d'Alene did—she liked to purchase an item to help her recall the wonderful things that happened there. But maybe that was silly. How could she ever forget seeing Ty again? Or even meeting David.

Sigh.

Randi offered to join her on her shopping trip. But Winter grasped for a polite way to decline. "You can enjoy some quiet time without any of us around. Deborah and Jeremy said they were going to lunch after volunteering at the soup kitchen. They won't return for a couple of hours."

Randi groaned. "That's another thing that shouldn't be happening. We don't need relationship problems messing up our team. What's Deborah thinking?" She rolled her eyes. "Doesn't she realize she's five years older than the kid?"

"They're just friends. No need to get worked up about it."

"Friends exploring possibilities." Randi pulled on her ankle-high boots. "I think I will go with you." She grabbed her jacket. "I'd feel better if somebody went along."

Winter took the spare key out of her purse. "I'm going shopping alone, and that's final." Realizing she spoke harshly, she softened her tone. "The mall isn't far. Plus, I haven't driven the Old Clunker in ages. We'll bond. Don't worry."

"It's my job to worry."

Eventually, Winter convinced Randi to allow her some time by herself, after she promised to call if anything delayed her.

At the intersection of Highway 95 and Hanley, the Old Clunker stalled, and Winter wished she chose the city bus instead. It took five attempts to get the rambling vehicle started. Apologetically, she waved at the white-haired man in the red convertible revving his engine behind her. "You're due for a checkup, old girl." She patted the dashboard. "We neglected to see to that in Coeur d'Alene, but soon we'll get you all fixed up. I promise." When she pulled into a parking space at the Silver Lake Mall, without further mishap, she sighed in relief.

As she entered a clothing store, a lighter feeling than she experienced in days settled on her. She missed outings like this—going where she wanted, no time limits, not being accountable to anyone. With Passion's Prayer, people were around her constantly. Good friends, and a great support network, but people, nonetheless. Rarely did she get the chance to be alone. Today would be different.

At the women's department, she paid special attention to the earthy colors that complemented her red hair and green eyes. They were a penny-pinching ministry team, but in the not-too-distant future, she'd forgo frugality and enjoy her once-a-year Christmas splurge. Then she'd buy herself a couple of new outfits as "gifts" during the holiday season.

With a sense of adventure, she browsed through the dresses and slacks. Having a fondness for accessories, she located the belt rack and held up a chunky gold one to her waist.

Where would the team be this Christmas? She put the belt back on its rack and meandered toward the winter coats. Hopefully, in the southern states, somewhere like Florida or California. Trying a black peacoat on, she shivered just thinking about how cold it was in Montana during the last conference. Fortunately, Neil was conscientious about scheduling them in warmer climates during the coldest part of the year. She couldn't fathom how her parents, after living in the hot temperatures of the Philippines, could endure the chilly Alaskan winters like they did.

After looking through the dresses, coats, and shoes, she noticed her stomach growling. Lunchtime had come and gone, and the aromas lingering in the mall enticed her to prolong her independence a tad longer. She moved in the direction of the food court.

Randi's worrywart tendency nipped at Winter's conscience. Her assistant would nag her later if she didn't check in. She pulled out one of the cell phones the group shared and called the motel. Randi's anxious response sounded like she'd been parked by the phone. After assuring her of her well-being, Winter ended the call.

En route to the food court, she saw a gift shop and decided to stop for a minute. On one of the endcaps, she spotted a glass plate with etchings of Lake Coeur d'Alene. The artist had captured the beauty of the lake's surrounding hills with such pristine detail she felt awed over its craftsmanship. She stroked the slight grooves, pleased by the texture beneath her fingers. This was the exact type of item she enjoyed finding—a souvenir expressing the beauty of the area and, at seventy-five percent off, was affordable.

She'd just left the store with a wrapped package in hand when a strange uneasiness crept over her. Like a spider inching up her leg, something felt weird. Was someone watching her? She scanned the mall corridor. A middle-aged man directly behind her smiled. She looked away, trying to ignore the unusual feeling that washed over her.

She hurried to one of the ordering lines where the spicy aroma of taco meat stood out above the other delicious smells. After paying for her food, she dropped into a chair at a small table near the vendor. Behind her, some senior citizens clustered around two tables, drinking coffee and chatting. When she overheard one of the men guffawing about a bear who kept ransacking his compost pile, she glanced over her shoulder to see the animated storyteller.

Still smiling over his tale, she shuffled in her seat and found Ty standing right next to her table. She bit back a gasp. "What are you doing here?"

"Hey." He dropped into the plastic chair across from her like he belonged there.

Like they belonged together. Which was ridiculous.

Even so, her mouth went dry. Her stomach turned over a time or two. And her gaze consumed him and the changes he'd made since she last saw him. Nice changes, she admitted. The Ty she saw at the restaurant and at the conference, the guy with the scraggly beard and longish hair, had vanished. Clean-shaven, he now had short, damp, freshly-styled hair. His green polo shirt appeared new, his jeans crisp. This handsome man sitting at her table was the spitting image of the Ty she knew ten years ago. The man she'd loved, only a tad older.

His presence took her breath away. And just like when they were young, she was completely unnerved.

"Your tacos, ma'am? I called your order three times." A fast-food worker set the tacos on the table and rushed back to her counter.

"Oh, sorry." Distracted, Winter felt twenty again, sitting at a downtown cafe with Ty, the two of them lost in a world of their own, making plans for their future. She stared into his chocolate brown eyes, feeling the familiar pull.

"I see you still like tacos."

"What?"

He pointed at the two paper-wrapped tacos and grinned.

"Oh, yeah."

His chuckle washed over her, meshing the past with the present. She'd always loved his laugh.

Then she remembered how she felt a little while ago. Like someone was watching her. "Were you following me?"

"When?"

"A few minutes ago. Down that way." She pointed in the direction of the shop where she purchased the plate.

"I guess. When I walked out of the salon"—he ruffled his newly-cut hair—"I saw you and hoped we could talk."

"I see." Nothing sinister. But he was following her. "You look great, by the way." She stared at his chin instead of meeting his gaze. His skin appeared red from where the beard had been removed.

"Thanks." He scrubbed his hand across the lower part of

his face. "I let the beard grow too long. I've let too many things go lately."

"Ty, what do you want? Why are you here?"

He smiled that heart-stopping grin of his. "I told you what I want." He splayed his hands in her direction.

He told her? *Oh.* The other night at the restaurant he said he wanted *her.*

"The reason I'm in Coeur d'Alene? I still live here." He nodded toward her food on the table. "Don't let me interrupt your lunch. You should eat before it gets cold." He handed her a napkin.

How could she eat in front of him? The hard tortilla would probably choke her. She could escape out the main doors behind her. But an idea popped into her mind, and without rationalizing her thoughts, she slid the second taco toward him. "Share with me?"

A last meal together?

"That would be great. Thanks." He unwrapped the warm taco and took a bite. "Mmm. This is good."

How many times had they sat like this, across from each other, eating a meal? The next thing she knew, her thoughts traveled to another time and place.

* * * *

At an outdoor cafe in Coeur d'Alene, not far from Ty's apartment, they were having dinner. Two days remained until their wedding, and they still had important things to discuss.

While Ty was aware that she grew up in the Philippines, he didn't fathom her parents' commitment as missionaries, or the way her own life, up until a few years ago, was one of service to Christ. Her moral character remained a mystery to him, as well. But there would be time for him to understand those things later. And he would, she assured herself.

Ty bit into his roast beef sandwich. "I'll be glad when the wedding is over."

His words stung. "Why?"

"Because you're driving me nuts!"

"I am?" What was he talking about?

He leaned across the circular table and gazed deeply into her eyes. He cupped her cheek and ran his thumb along the right side of her face, drawing ticklish heart patterns down her skin. "You're staying with my sister, aren't you? When I'd rather have you at my place? I mean, we're getting married in two days. I want to be with you, Sas. Don't you want to be with me?"

His husky tone did funny things to her insides. Made her wish for things she shouldn't.

"I miss you. For weeks, you've been entrenched in wedding plans. You haven't even had time to be my girl."

His touch melted her, made her question her resolve. She stared into his shining gaze, wondering how she could deny him anything when he looked into her heart like that. Those deep brown eyes were dangerous. "I'm yours forever."

"Starting now?" His hand brushed over her shoulder. In a gentle skid, his fingers trickled down her arm. Pausing at her engagement ring, he twirled it slowly.

"Two days until our wedding. Then I'm all yours." She leaned closer to him so he'd hear her whisper. "I've kept myself for the man I marry. For you. It's hard on both of us, but I'd like to wait. It's my wedding gift to you. Maybe you should be thankful and quit pestering me."

He withdrew his hand and stared into the distance. She knew a keen disappointment.

She'd been raised in a missionary's home in another country and had lived the Christian life for as long as she could remember. Even though she wasn't active in a church right now, she hadn't forgotten the things she learned from her parents about a marriage that could last a lifetime. About starting their journey together pure.

A Bible verse her parents made her memorize when she was a teenager came to mind. *Do not be yoked together with unbelievers.* But she shrugged off the words. Ty would come to church with her after they were married. He'd do anything she wanted.

* * * *

"Can I get you anything else?" Ty's eyes gleamed toward her.

With a jolt, she returned to the present, her taco only half eaten. Her hunger vanished. "I should be going. Randi will worry."

"Randy? Who's he?"

"She. My personal assistant." She stood and tossed the remainder of her taco in the trash can. Getting involved in a conversation with Ty hours before she had to speak didn't seem wise. She'd better head back to the motel.

"Wait." He stood also. "Could we talk?"

"Why?"

"This may be our only chance." He pulled out her chair. "Please?"

She had hoped for such a chance, right? Once again, she noticed the changes he made. Did he go to this effort to impress her? Her heart beat faster. Maybe she could talk with him for a couple of minutes. She was leaving tomorrow. This would be their last chance to talk. Ready to bolt, if need be, she lowered herself to the seat's edge.

He sat down too. "I've dreamed about this moment a hundred times. I've rehearsed what I'd say to you if I ever got the chance." He folded his hands on the table. "Now, with so much to share, I'm at a loss to know where to begin."

"Don't trouble yourself. We don't have anything we have to say to each other." When he didn't respond, she gulped. Was that too harsh? He was a fragment of her past. Someone she got over a long time ago. She had a right to protect her heart, didn't she?

"You're not going to make this easy, are you, Sassy?"

"Don't call me that!" How dare he! "You gave up that privilege a long time ago." Talking with him was a bad idea. She should leave.

But she didn't move. Their gazes locked and time seemed to stand still.

"I've missed you." His soft voice was like a song.

A song she didn't need or want.

She had to get away from him. Away from the past that stirred up like a fog every time she was in his presence, clouding her thinking and messing with her memories.

"I've had a long, miserable ten years without you." He sniffed as if he were near tears. "I never … got over you."

Why was he saying this now? "It's a little late for this, Ty." He was the one who took their marriage for granted. He betrayed her. "I have to go."

He reached across the table and laid his hand over hers, detaining her. He brought her fingertips to his cheek and rested them there.

For some reason, she watched, wary, yet mesmerized as a tear trickled down his smooth face and dripped over her knuckles. Since when was Ty so emotional? He cried at the church the other night, too.

She pulled her hand free of his. He shouldn't be touching her.

"I'm so sorry, Winter."

His words lanced her heart.

Forgive.

Didn't she work through the layers of forgiveness ten years ago? Didn't she encourage others that God had the power to wipe slates clean? Of course, she did.

What about Ty? Did she forgive him?

She stood abruptly. "It was nice seeing you. But I've got to go." She walked toward the doors.

"Please, don't walk out of my life again." His hoarse plea stopped her.

Her temper ignited. "I didn't walk out of your life." She pointed at him. "You waltzed out on our marriage with … with her!"

She couldn't get through the glass doors fast enough. Her heart thudded to a wild beat as she ran across the parking lot. If she were a man, she would have slugged him in the face. How dare he accuse her of being the one to leave their marriage.

Almost to the Old Clunker, she heard steps pounding the pavement behind her.

"You forgot your bag."

She whirled around and yanked the store bag with the glass plate from Ty's grip. His eyes widened.

"Look. I'm sorry." He held out his hands. "I didn't mean to hurt you. I've done enough of that. Please. We need to talk."

"There's nothing to discuss. We're not involved with each other anymore." She averted her face, knowing that thanks to her outburst there would be a telltale flush of red splayed across her cheek. She wished she could control her temper better. And her tears. Wet drops trickled down her nose. She swiped at them, embarrassed. A hoarse sob broke out of her, one she tried to subdue.

Suddenly, he moved forward and surrounded her in a hug. She stiffened. But when she sensed his embrace was one of comfort and nothing else, she relaxed a little. The hug was awkward, somewhat brotherly, and she found a remembered calm in his arms. In that second, she thought only of how she once loved this man. A lifetime ago.

He patted her back, and she cried. Her nose, burrowed against his chest, sniffed his familiar, manly scent. And in the next second, the intimate knowledge of him dislodged her from his embrace.

"I've got to leave. People are waiting for me."

"Pastor Michaels?"

"That's none of your concern."

He cleared his throat. "Looked like he was declaring his feelings for you the other night. Right?"

Anger resurged. "Our relationship was over too many years ago for you to be doing this. I'm a single woman. I can date, or marry, whomever I choose. You got that straight, Tyler Williams?"

He shook his head like he didn't agree with one word. Then he grinned, which infuriated her. "But you don't want to date David Michaels, do you?" He took a step closer. "I think you've been waiting for me, like I've been waiting for you."

"That's not true!" Backing away from him, she bumped into the car behind her. Explosive waves frothed at the surface of her emotions. How conceited he was to think he knew what she'd spent her life doing. "I have not been waiting for you." She dug the car keys out of her purse. "I'll have you know I've been busy pursuing God's will for my life."

"My point exactly."

"What is that supposed to mean?"

"The Bible says I should enjoy life with the wife whom I love." His voice softened. "That means you."

She gawked at him.

"It also says I should rejoice in the wife of my youth." He smiled at her. "God's Word encourages us to be reconciled. That's what I want for us more than anything."

Reconciled? He had to be kidding.

She jammed the car key toward the lock, but missed, leaving a scratch. On the second attempt, she unlocked the door and yanked it open. How could he talk this way after ten years apart? She dropped into the car seat, but his hands kept the door from closing.

"I have one request." He squatted down, meeting her at eye level.

She refused to make eye contact with him.

"Look at me. Please?" His begging tone, and the fact he wasn't taking the hint and moving away from the car door, forced her to face him.

"What do you want?"

At his masculine grin and raised eyebrows, heat flooded her cheeks. He already told her what he wanted, didn't he?

"We need time." He nodded. "Time to look into ourselves and see how we feel about each other. Or rather, how you feel toward me. Because, sweetheart, I know exactly how I feel toward you. And it's all good."

She sputtered in protest.

"My request is this—let me come with you."

"Where?"

"Wherever you go on your next road trip, let me come with your team. I'll do anything—cook, do laundry, be a mechanic, hand out flyers, whatever. Just let me be near you."

"Be near me? Ty, my team doesn't even know about you. About us."

He looked taken back, but he recovered quickly. "That's okay. I just want to join your team. Please?"

Unbelievable.

More frustrated than she'd felt in years, she jammed the key in the ignition and got no results. Several tries later the Old Clunker rumbled to life with a rattling commotion. When she jerked the car into reverse, the engine nearly stalled, but she managed to shut the car door and back up without looking at Ty or backing into him.

In loud protest, the tires squealed as she gunned the car out of the parking lot.

Thirteen

"May I speak with Winter?"

"Whom shall I say is calling?" a female voice—not Winter's—answered the phone.

"Ty Williams."

"And your business with Winter is—?"

He hesitated. "I need to talk with her about something."

"Maybe I could help. I'm Randi, her assistant."

Ah, that Randi. "I'm an old friend. I wanted to say hello." He called several hotels and was glad to finally locate where Winter's team was staying.

"I'll see if she returns the sentiment."

After the way she left him standing in the parking lot earlier, he doubted Winter was thinking favorably of him. Still, he hoped for something good to happen between them. Prayed for the chance to make amends.

"I'm sorry." By Randi's clipped tone, she wasn't a bit sorry. "Winter's preparing for this evening's meeting. She sends her regrets."

"Will you ask her if she'll go out for coffee with me afterward?"

Randi snorted. "That would be inappropriate."

Winter's PA was starting to get under his skin. "And why is that?"

"A single woman out with a stranger. Need I say more?"

"I said I was a friend. Hardly a stranger." *We were married!* "If you'd just ask her—"

"She already told me—"

"Please!" He gritted his teeth to stop himself from saying something he might regret. "She's a grown woman, hardly in need of your smothering." *Lord, some help here would be greatly appreciated.*

He half-expected her to slam down the phone. Instead, he heard a muffled conversation going on in the background.

"The guy won't give up. Wants to know if you'll go out for coffee. Says he's a friend. Like I believe that."

Garbled sounds came across the phone, most likely caused by Randi's hand sliding over the receiver.

Words shifted again on her end.

"Tell him no."

Oh, man.

Randi came back on the line. "She says no."

The connection ended.

He set the phone down and heaved a sigh. What else could he do? Tonight was the last night he had to convince Winter to let him travel with Passion's Prayer. He'd talked to Kyle about taking time off from the mechanic shop. He even packed a bag. All that remained was changing Winter's mind.

* * * *

"I can't believe that guy, can you?" Randi marched across the room and grabbed a hairbrush off the bedside table.

Oh, yes. Winter knew Ty well enough to be certain he wouldn't stop trying. Why did he want to join her ministry team? How weird would that be? Just seeing him today was gut-wrenching enough.

After the way she responded to him earlier, she'd spent some much needed time praying. Of course, she overreacted. But picturing him traveling with Passion's Prayer was too impossible to imagine. How could he suggest such a thing? He was her ex-husband, for goodness' sake.

One thing was for certain—Ty was not joining her team.

Deborah burst through their motel room door. "Sorry I'm late." Her hair dripped with rainwater as she scurried toward the bathroom. "The sky broke open in torrents while Jeremy and I were walking."

"Getting soaked isn't the greatest idea since you've been sick." Winter grabbed a travel blanket to wrap around her shoulders.

Deborah's teeth chattered as she dried her hair with the thin motel towel. "I d-didn't think about what the w-weather was going to do, or I w-would have brought an umbrella. J-Jeremy put his coat over our heads, but you can see how well that w-worked." She laughed.

Randi crossed her arms and frowned. "How is the lovebird?"

"There are never enough towels in these motel rooms." Deborah rummaged through her suitcase and pulled out a red-striped beach towel. She bent over until the top of her head was pointing toward the floor and rubbed her hair briskly. "That's better."

"I asked—"

"I heard you." Deborah's voice sounded muffled through the towel. "I chose not to answer." Turning toward the closet, she grabbed a dress off the hanger.

"Because I referred to him as a lovebird?" Randi taunted.

"I think you should drop the subject." Winter picked up her jacket from the chair.

"I'm not trying to start a fight." Randi grabbed her purse and flung the strap over her shoulder. "I didn't realize this friendship was serious enough for people to be so sensitive. The situation is going to cause a crisis." She walked to the window and drew the curtain aside.

Deborah, always the peacemaker, went straight to Randi and hugged her. "Don't worry. Everything will work out. I'm not a teenager."

"But he is!" Randi stepped from her embrace. "Don't you realize Jeremy is a kid? Five years younger than you? He was a newborn when you were in kindergarten. He was reading Dr. Seuss when you had your first crush on a boy. GI Joes were his favorite diversion when you were on your first date. Get the picture?"

Deborah smiled that peaceful smile of hers. "I know. For now, we're just friends. You'll still be my friend either way, right?"

Winter loved how Deborah pushed Randi for support. She watched to see how her assistant would respond.

"Of course. But in the meantime, Deborah McBride, be warned I'll do anything to keep you from making a fool of yourself."

Deborah chuckled. "I knew I could count on you."

"I don't want to lose you."

"Why would you?" Deborah picked up a wide-toothed comb off the dresser and straightened her hair.

"Jeremy's going back to college next year, right?" Randi stepped toward the door. "If things get serious between you two, what then?"

"I'm not worried about that. Like I said, we're only friends."

"Let's get going." Winter nudged Randi along so she wouldn't continue her line of questioning. Besides, she didn't want to think of Deborah possibly leaving the team. And she was pretty sure that's the direction Randi was headed. "You know how Neil gets if we make him wait too long."

Randi didn't say anything else.

When the team gathered at the Old Clunker, Jeremy stood in front of the car, his gaze intent on Deborah. In his outstretched hand, he offered her a pink rose. "Hey, beautiful."

Deborah blushed as she accepted his gift. "Thank you."

Randi groaned.

Maybe Winter should divert her attention. "Could you help me pack up my souvenirs for mailing to my parents' house tomorrow? I picked up something today that's going to max out my trunk."

Randi just stared at Deb and Jeremy. "Sure, Captain. Whatever you say."

* * * *

From the opening song on the last night of the conference, to the minute Winter stepped to the pulpit, the building resounded with joyful singing and worship. Two topics had been volleying in her mind. One about joy, the other about faithfulness. Feeling the joyful excitement in the room, a lighthearted topic seemed the perfect choice.

"Serving God is fun!" she called out. Then she read seven verses on joy. This theme was one of her favorites because it encouraged people to let go of their guilt and worries, and to experience joy and grace in serving the Lord. As she shared, she felt her own spirits lifting.

After she finished speaking, Deborah went to the piano and led the congregation in praise songs. People responded, but the tone of the prayer service was different from what it had been on any of the other nights.

Winter and her teammates moved through the group, praying for needs. A mom wanted to be a better parent. A doctor felt called to the mission field. Teenagers prayed to be better witnesses at school.

There was Ty.

She gulped. *Help me, Jesus.*

Still feeling awkward about today's interaction with him, she hoped Neil or David would talk with him. She continued sharing with others, but something inside nudged her to speak with him herself. Remembering her promise to follow God's will, she hesitantly approached him.

Jesus loved Ty, and He died for his sins as much as for her own. No matter the hurts of the past, God loved him unconditionally. And she had to also, right?

Her heart thumped in her ears. "Can I pray with you?"

His face lifted until he met her gaze. His look was one of surprise. "Sure, I'd like that."

She waited, wondering where to begin. "Is there anything you'd like me to pray about? Or to explain? Have you ever asked Jesus into your life? He loves you very much."

Tears flooded his eyes. "Yes, Jesus is my Savior."

When—how—had that happened?

"I've been following Christ for six years." He cleared his throat. "Although, I've struggled in my Christian walk lately. Just—" He shrugged.

She could only wonder what person or circumstance had helped him come to know the Lord. Her mind wandered, remembering times he refused to attend church with her. Back then, she boasted she could change his mind anytime she wanted. That idea fizzled. Here stood living proof of God working in his life without any help from her.

"Maybe I could explain over coffee?" He tipped his head.

"We were going to pray." Not talk about personal stuff.

"Would you mind if I prayed for you?"

"Oh, okay." Occasionally, people prayed a blessing over her. Was that what he had in mind?

He stepped closer, their faces nearly nose to nose. His eyes filled with tears again. He was obviously having a difficult time composing himself.

"Heavenly Father," he prayed, and she closed her eyes. "I want to thank You for bringing Winter to Coeur d'Alene. Thank You for Kyle showing me the flyer."

So that's how he found me.

"I've missed this woman in my life so much."

She swallowed back a tidal wave of emotion.

Gently, he placed his right hand on her shoulder. She felt warmth where his palm rested. "You've moved in her life in amazing ways, used her over these years we've been apart to minister to others. This week she's touched my life." His voice broke. "Father, please, help her, um, help her to forgive me … for the sins I committed against her ten years ago."

She opened her eyes.

Tears trickled down his cheeks. A tug of compassion raced through her. He had changed, hadn't he?

"I botched both of our lives."

She shut her eyes again, feeling his words echo in her heart.

"Selfishness and pride controlled me, but You've turned everything around. Made me new. And now, my heart longs to be the man You've called me to be. To be the man Winter needs me to be."

What I need?

What she needed was to run from Ty's words. To escape his touch. But when she opened her eyes again, she couldn't pull away. Not considering the raw brokenness etched on his face. His eyes spoke of an ache too awful to tell. "Winter, I need to confess to you how sorry I am for hurting you."

Oh, sweet Jesus.

"A-and—" His words came to a halt as his hands covered his face. His shoulders bent low. Broken sobs shook through his body.

She bit her lip, holding back tears. While part of her wanted to race out of the building and never see this man again, a longing rose within her to comfort him. To soothe his pain. Tentatively, she reached out and touched his hair. Silky strands eased between her fingertips. The texture felt the same as before. The familiar sensation of his hair against her palm sizzled through her, and she yanked her hand back.

At that moment, in a remote nook of her brain, the tiniest possibility ignited a spark. Did she still care for Ty Williams? Might she even … love him? Even though he'd stomped her heart into a million pieces.

She couldn't breathe.

"Forgive me?"

The desire to put distance between them almost overpowered her. But stronger still was God's tender voice urging her to do what was right. To follow His way, instead of her own.

Forgive.

Yes, Lord.

Forgive.

Heal my heart.

Hadn't she recently talked about being merciful to the one who did the wrong? To love no matter the cost. Could she do that?

She leaned closer to his ear. "I forgave you many years ago. I admit it hurt for a long time. But I did, and do, forgive you."

"Thank you." He dropped forward, his right knee catching his descent to the floor. With his head bent, he appeared to be praying, thanking God.

Years ago, after they separated, she longed for an apology from him. But never had she expected one as dramatic as this. His brokenness and remorse, his tears, the way he prayed for her with such caring, ripped at her heart. Tears trickled down her cheeks, and she didn't pause to sweep them away.

She knelt beside him. "You said you're a Christian now. That means God forgave you. And I forgive you too. From my heart, Ty, you are forgiven."

He clasped her hand and pressed his lips against her knuckles. She didn't pull away. Later, she might be sorry. For now, being close to him and participating in his healing felt right.

"You'll never know how much those words mean to me."

Someone else knelt beside her. "Winter?" Randi's voice held alarm. "Is everything all right?" Her gaze zigzagged between Winter and the man kneeling in front of her with tears streaming down his face.

Taking in Randi's concern, and wondering who else had noticed what transpired between Ty and herself, Winter pulled her hand free from his. "I'm fine. Thank you for checking."

Randi helped her stand, then drew her toward the opposite side of the auditorium.

Away from Ty.

Only once did she glance back to find him still kneeling in prayer.

Fourteen

As the crowd dispersed, Ty waited for a chance to speak with Winter. Standing by the front pew, he watched for an opportunity, but she remained preoccupied with the team, David Michaels, and the people who lingered to say goodbye.

Would she come over to him if he waved?

That he got the chance to apologize to her, and the way she said she forgave him, lifted a huge burden from his shoulders. Now, if only she'd listen to his request with an open mind.

Glancing around the room, he wondered what he could do to make himself useful. He walked down several aisles, picking up forgotten bulletins and Bibles. He was glad to do something productive for a few minutes while he waited.

A woman approached him. "Hey there, I'm Randi Simmons." She thrust out her hand toward him. "I'm Winter's assistant."

Ah, the woman who kept him from setting up a coffee date with Winter. He cleared his throat. "I'm Ty Williams." He shook her hand. Her current friendliness made it easy to assume his name didn't register from his phone call.

"Are you from around here?"

"Coeur d'Alene is home."

"We walked Tubbs Hill the other day. Lovely place."

Tubbs Hill. The name pricked his heart. He hadn't been down that trail since Winter left him.

The conversation stalled.

"Nice meeting you." She smiled and walked away.

He continued straightening the front part of the sanctuary, glancing up every few seconds, watching for any sign Winter might be ready to leave. He moved to one side of the aisle, then the other, hoping to make eye contact with her, but she never glanced his way. Was that on purpose? Was she sending him a message that she forgave him, but she didn't want any further contact with him?

He had to try one more time.

As he approached the ministry team, he heard David Michaels taking charge. "Marie has pies and a veggie tray chilling in the fridge. How about if we head to my house for a snack?"

Ty's cue. "Winter?"

She glanced at him.

"Could I speak with you privately?"

Randi stepped forward. "May I help you? Would you like a Passion's Prayer brochure?"

"Uh, no, thanks." He turned to Winter. "Please? Just a moment of your time."

Her expression said she'd rather he took a hike. But she walked several feet away. He followed her, but he couldn't escape Randi's curious stare.

"What did you want to speak with me about?" She sidled between two pews. Sensing her need for distance, he positioned himself on the opposite side. He noticed how she kept glancing toward the team. Or David? Did she have feelings for him?

"Could we go somewhere and talk? Get a cup of coffee?" His words came out more desperate sounding than he intended. But the opportunity to convince her of his plan was slipping through his fingers.

"That would be impossible. My team and I spend time together after the meetings, recapping and planning for the next conference. Tonight, Pastor Dave invited us to his house."

"I know. But he's going to—" He swallowed. Nothing he could say would convince her not to go to David Michaels' house. But the idea of the pastor asking her to date him, and her accepting, tore at his resolve to remain calm.

"He's going to what?"

"Nothing. But I would like to talk with you."

"We spoke at the mall."

And that didn't go so well. He sighed. She said she forgave him. But welcoming him into her life? He had to try to convince her. "Please, let me go on the road with you." He hated begging, but he'd crawl on his knees if it meant she might allow him to travel with her. The greatest desire of his heart was for her to realize how much he loved her, how he still wanted her for his wife, how he'd do anything for her. Ever since he saw her on that flyer back in the mechanic shop, he'd thought of little else.

"Ty—" She dragged out his name. "This scheme of yours won't work. You and I are the past. I've worked with Passion's Prayer for five years. You have your own life separate from mine."

"My life is nothing without you." He stared into her green eyes, willing her to believe him. "My work schedule is flexible. My bag is packed. I'm ready to leave with you tomorrow, if you'll let me."

Her eyes widened. "As what?"

He doubted she'd think kindly of him if he blurted, "As your husband." He swallowed hard, giving himself time to collect his thoughts. "As anything you need—businessman, mechanic, dishwasher, whatever. Please. I just want to be with you."

"Why? After ten years apart, and all that happened between us, why are you saying these things now?"

"Because"—his heart hammered like a bass drum—"I still love you."

Her face blanched.

Saying the words to her after such a long time of imagining himself doing so felt amazing, even though she stared at him as if he'd lost his mind. "I believe we belong together. Despite everything. You're the wife of my youth. I want you with me forever, like I said in our wedding vows."

She glanced over her shoulder toward her team. "Ty"—her voice went quiet—"you and I are not married. I'm *not* your wife." Her words rang with finality.

"In my heart, you still are."

She shook her head. "I need to get back to my team. It's been nice seeing you again. Take care of yourself. Tell Lacey hello for me, okay?" She rushed back to her team and Pastor David.

He'd lost his chance.

An unbearable ache ripped through him. How could he stand by and watch her leave, not knowing if he'd ever see her again?

He couldn't. He had to do something.

* * * *

Winter's focus should have been on the fact that tonight was her last night in Coeur d'Alene. Her last chance to visit with David, a man she considered a friend. Instead, she kept replaying Ty's words when he said he still loved her.

Why tell her that now? If he loved her, why didn't he contact her in all these years?

Instead of experiencing turmoil over the past, she should be feeling overjoyed at the week's accomplishments. She'd faced her fear of speaking with her ex-husband, even prayed with him, assuring him of her forgiveness, and inner healing had begun within herself.

She could move on now, right?

But, if that were the case, why was uncertainty making her question every word she exchanged with him? The idea of him traveling with Passion's Prayer really was too bizarre.

On the other hand, could it be within the realm of possibility—like he said—that they still belonged together? Married?

No way. Too many years had passed. Ty didn't even know the person she'd become, and she didn't know him.

She turned, hoping to catch one last glimpse of his face. To tuck away a mental picture of him where she could draw it out in the future when she was lonely.

His gaze met hers, and she smiled.

Goodbye, Ty.

Fifteen

Winter strode into the parsonage dining room and her footfall staggered to a halt when she saw Ty standing there talking with Randi. What was he doing here? Her ex-husband was invading her world like a conquering king, and she was determined to get to the bottom of this invasion. She grabbed hold of Randi's elbow and propelled her down the hallway toward the bathroom. "What is Tyler Williams doing in this house? Who invited him here?"

"You mean Ty?" Randi's voice lifted.

"Yes, Ty. Explain what the man's doing here. And be fast about it." She didn't try to hide her frustration as they stood at opposite sides of the powder room.

Randi's eyes widened. "You rode with David. Ty came over in the Old Clunker with me."

"With you? Why?"

"He looked sad." Randi grinned sheepishly. "I felt like being spontaneous, so I invited him. He's kind of cute, don't you think?"

Cute? Winter groaned. "Why would you invite him? You don't know him."

"He seems nice. What's the big deal?"

"Do you mean he's your date?" This couldn't be happening.

"Not a real date. Besides, we're leaving tomorrow." Randi winked. "What's the harm in a little flirting?"

Don't get me started.

How could Ty flirt with Randi after declaring his love to her such a short while ago? If her assistant only knew of her marriage to Ty, and how he treated her, Randi would be back-pedaling at lightning speed. Considering Ty's apology tonight, she didn't feel justified in blabbing about their past right now. But still.

"Pies are ready!" Marie's voice startled her. "Everything okay?" The housekeeper glanced back and forth between them. "You two need anything?"

"We're fine, Marie. Thank you." She tried to sound more self-controlled than she felt.

"Saved by the pies." Randi dodged around her.

Groaning, Winter followed her back into the dining room where Ty was introducing himself to David. Randi rushed to his side, her eyes sparkling up at him. The way her hand landed on his arm and lingered sizzled jealousy right through Winter.

But she had no ownership over Ty. She didn't want anything to do with him. Good thing Passion's Prayer was leaving Coeur d'Alene tomorrow.

She moved to the table. "Marie, this food looks amazing." She eyed the blackberry pie, avoiding Ty's gaze.

"Everything all right, Winter?" David pulled out her chair.

Sitting down, she glanced up at him. She could tell he was waiting for her answer. "The meeting was a blessing." She hoped to divert his attention from her.

"Absolutely." He smiled, then sat down and prayed for the snack. "Mmm. Marie, this is fantastic."

"Really great." Jeremy stuffed a forkful of pie into his mouth.

Marie grinned and shuffled back into the kitchen.

Winter tasted the berries and her gaze met Ty's, across from her. Time, and her longing to leave Coeur d'Alene, stood still.

* * * *

Lacey, Ty's sister and Winter's maid of honor, had walked down the aisle lined with white tapered candles and mint-green bows. Winter followed in her friend's steps, with fragrant rose petals lifting and fluttering beneath her sandaled feet.

She gazed down the long aisle and met the gaze of her handsome groom decked out in a dove gray tux. When he grinned at her like he was besotted with her, so in love, her heart did somersaults. She was going to enjoy a lifetime of meeting his gaze across a crowd. Knowing she was his.

But something felt wrong. Why was Dad stopping halfway down the aisle? She tugged against the crook of his arm, attempting to pull him forward without making a scene. Despite her father's gaunt frame, some inner strength became his ally. He refused to budge. What was he doing?

"Dad?"

He leaned his balding head toward her. "Princess, your mother and I love you." His lips quivered.

"I love you too."

"We want what's best for you. God's best. Even now, it's not too late to change your mind."

"What do you mean? I'm getting married."

Dad patted her hand and leaned closer to her veil. "Are you certain Tyler Williams is the right man for you? The man God has chosen for your life's partner?"

"Of course." She tugged on his arm again.

"This is forever. If you say 'I do' to him, you're vowing to stay true to this man for the rest of your life." Dad's hand shook. "No matter what."

"Daddy, I do love Ty." Her hand slid into his wrinkled one and she gave it a squeeze. "Come, celebrate and be happy with me." She coaxed him forward with the music still playing.

Embarrassment made her shudder. Did any guests overhear Dad's line of questioning? Of course, she was certain about Ty. He was everything she dreamed of in a man. He was kind, gentle, romantic, and faithful. What more could a girl want? Running down the aisle wouldn't get her to him fast enough.

When she reached her groom, he smiled his heart-stopping grin, and she winked at him. Later, she'd explain the delay. He pulled her right hand to his lips, kissing it softly. This was their day—the picture in time they'd remember for as long as they lived. His chocolaty eyes met her gaze, making a lifetime of promises.

Promises. Promises. Promises.

* * * *

"Winter? Did you hear me?" David patted her hand.

"I'm sorry. What were you saying?" She turned her chair toward him, severing the rope-like connection binding her to Ty.

"I was saying the conference was amazing." David's face seemed to glow. "I'm sorry for Seattle's loss in not having you there, but my congregation has reaped blessings. I hope you'll plan another conference here next year."

"Sounds good," Neil chimed in. "I'll check the schedule and get back with you."

"You do that." David's gaze returned to Winter's.

Did he regret his question the other night about dating? She hoped they could both forget that and part as friends. Now more than ever, she wanted to keep romance out of her life.

After they finished dessert and chatted for a while, Neil stood and extended his hand toward David. "Big traveling day tomorrow. We'd better get going."

The men shook hands and clapped each other on the back.

Winter stood to receive her coat from the housekeeper. "Marie, you've been a wonderful hostess."

In the hallway, the other woman clasped her arm. "You come back and marry my Pastor Dave." Her voice lowered. "He's a God-fearing man, and he's powerful in love with you. Never seen him act as peculiar as he has this week." She winked.

Winter glanced at David and was relieved to find him preoccupied in his goodbyes with Neil.

He stepped toward her and shook her hand. "Email me? Or call? Maybe things will be different the next time we meet."

She could only smile. Time did have a way of changing things.

Sixteen

Most of the team and Ty stood beside the Old Clunker, looking as if they weren't sure where to sit.

Neil took charge. "Tyler, why don't you sit in the front, on the other side of Winter?"

"Thanks." Ty opened the front passenger door.

Randi looked grumpy with the arrangement.

Not that Winter was happy about it. She slid to the middle of the seat next to Neil, aware of Ty moving in beside her. Their shoulders touched. She uselessly tried to create more space between them, wedged as she was between the two men.

What would her team think of her past relationship with Ty? Few outside of her family, Neil, and the Commissioning Board knew of her brief marriage. Would Deborah and Randi understand her reluctance to elaborate on her past? Maybe they would if she explained how her father counseled her not to discuss her divorce. How he told her people in ministry have a higher standard to live by. A divorce could be the death of her ministry, being a female preacher would prove difficult enough. "Stay single and focused on God's will," he admonished.

But, now, she wondered. Had she done the right thing? Full disclosure may have been the better choice, the more honest route. Especially considering her current situation with Ty sitting next to her.

"Do you have enough room?" His face was too close to hers.

"I'm fine." Not the truth. The pressure of his body next to hers created tension. She pulled a fraction of an inch away, while a traitorous part of her leaned in a tad closer.

* * * *

Sliding his arm across the back of the seat crossed Ty's mind. But resting his arm over Winter's shoulder would be pushing things. He'd settle for being glad David didn't ask her out again. Although, he was clueless about her feelings toward the pastor. He noticed the way she held his hand in that final handshake—too long.

How could Ty convince her that he'd changed? What would it take for her to admit she needed him on this ministry team? And in her life?

Lord, would You help me out? You and I both know I messed up ten years ago. I hurt this woman more than I care to think about. I ruined our chance of being together as husband and wife. But You, in Your mercy, have brought us within sitting range of each other. I believe You want us back together, for better or for worse, with all the blessings of marriage. Tomorrow she's leaving. Unless You do something, Winter is walking straight out of my life. Please, give me the chance to make it up to her. To love her all the days of my life.

A belch of smoke puffed out of the car's engine. The station wagon rattled and groaned.

Ty sat up straighter. Was God answering his prayer already?

"What's going on?" Randi questioned loudly.

"I don't know." Neil shook his head.

"You'd better pull over." Ty pointed to a small parking lot. "I'll take a look."

Winter met his gaze with a puzzled expression. No doubt she wondered how he knew anything about the engine of a car.

As soon as he and Neil stepped out of the vehicle, he popped the hood. "How long since her last tune-up?"

"Too long. Something stops working before we get her checked. I'm not mechanically minded. I wish we had someone like that with us."

Ty's heart beat faster. Was this his miracle? *Thank You, Lord!*

"I'd be honored to be such a person." He searched the engine with a professional hand. He met Neil's surprised gaze. "I've been a mechanic for five years. I can fix things up with Old—what name did I hear?"

Neil grinned. "Old Clunker. You can see why."

"Well then, Old Clunker needs new spark plugs. See the corrosion? The oil is filthy. That knocking could be serious. Something is loose back here." With his arm deep in the engine, he tightened a bolt by hand. He pulled a Kleenex out of his pocket and wiped grease from his fingers. "I noticed the tires look worn too." He shut the hood with a loud clang.

"She's destined for the junk heap." Neil groaned.

Ty chuckled. Would Winter allow him to travel to Salem as their mechanic? Had God opened the door for him to help with Passion's Prayer? To spend time with the woman he loved? Maybe, to prove himself?

He and Neil climbed back into the front seat of the car.

"We need another vehicle, Winter." Neil faced her without turning the key.

"She'll get us to the next stop. I'm sure of it. Let's pray."

"I'm serious. Even Ty agrees, and he's a mechanic."

"Mechanic?" Her gaze swiveled to his. "Since when?"

"For the last five years."

Her face said it all. How could he be a mechanic? He had a master's degree. The last time she saw him, scrambling up the corporate ladder outweighed every priority, including her.

She frowned. "You think we need a new car to go four hundred miles?"

"No."

"No?" Neil and Winter both questioned at once.

"No, but your car needs some serious repair. Old Clunker, as you call her, should make it to your next engagement if I work on a few things before we leave in the morning."

"We?"

He ignored her question and her squinting eyes. "Then I can do a major overhaul while your conference is in progress."

She shook her head, her glare intense.

Neil clapped his hands. "You're a godsend, brother. Of course, you can be our mechanic!"

"But, Neil—" Winter protested.

"God sent us someone who knows how to fix cars." Neil started the engine. "Can you believe it? Praise God!"

Ty read barely contained fury in Winter's expression.

"I must warn you this isn't a high-paying position." Neil sounded worried, like Ty might not be willing to take the job under those conditions.

"You won't owe me a cent." He focused his attention on Neil, avoiding eye contact with Winter. He could afford this. As co-owner of TK Automotive, he could take time away from the business. And with how well things were going, Kyle wouldn't mind. Ty would even chip in for some of the parts. "I'd consider it a privilege to serve your team."

Winter groaned.

"Then it's settled." Neil put the car in gear. "Everyone be ready at seven in the morning. We'll get an early start for Salem, Oregon."

* * * *

Nothing is settled! Winter silently protested. This could never work. Ty couldn't travel with them. He simply could not! Sitting this close to him for four hundred miles would be pure torment. How did he get his way?

What argument could she give Neil for her opposition to Ty joining them without revealing the whole rotten story to the rest of the group? They heard Neil proclaim Ty their mechanic, and that his presence was nothing short of a miracle. How would she carry on as normal with her married-for-six-months ex seated next to her?

I can't do this. I don't want to do this.

She had to tell Neil about Ty. That's all there was to it. Then her adviser wouldn't think so cheerily about this mechanic joining them.

There was one thing she refused to put up with on tomorrow's trip. If Ty tagged along with them to Salem—a huge *if*—she would not sit next to him. Rearranging the seating would be the first task of the journey.

* * * *

Stealing a glance at Winter, Ty saw how steamed she looked. But, even so, he praised God that the car's breakdown had gone in his favor. He wanted to laugh or shout. Instead, his thoughts turned prayerful. *Father, please bring Winter and me back together. Help us work toward reconciliation. I want to love her like You love the church and to be the man of God she needs. Change her heart, Lord. And change me.*

Winter had told him the team wasn't aware of who he was, so the scenario could get downright embarrassing if the past came rolling out at some unexpected moment. But he'd willingly take the risk. For her love, and for their possible future together, he'd endure embarrassment, rejection, and delving into a painful, sinful past—whatever it took. He only hoped one day she'd be open to marrying him again. Then, together, they'd serve God all the days of their lives.

By the look on her face, the task before him would be the most challenging thing he'd ever done. But with God anything was possible.

Seventeen

By the time the team showed up at the motel parking lot early the next morning, Ty had already checked over the Old Clunker. He replaced spark plugs, changed the oil, put in new filters, and adjusted the timing. Still under the hood cleaning gunk off the battery terminals, he noticed Winter standing behind him. He glanced over his shoulder, taking in her pale features. Was she still upset with him?

Neil and Jeremy loaded suitcases at the rear end of the vehicle, and it sounded, by the thumps and bangs, like they were having trouble getting everything to fit into the station wagon. He'd made things tighter with the addition of his bag, plus a toolbox. Fortunately, they had one of those luggage carriers on top of the car too.

"Is it fixed?"

Ty stepped out from under the hood and wiped his hands on a greasy cloth before facing her. "Preliminary work is done. I still need to fix more parts in the engine throughout the week." He winked at her. "Can't get rid of me that easily."

Seeing the way she avoided looking at him, he imagined her thoughts—she didn't want him traveling with them. Period. No doubt she'd fight his presence every inch of the way. Even knowing that about her, he was surprised when she climbed into the backseat between Deb and Randi.

* * * *

"You sit in the front, Jer," Winter told her nephew, who was still standing outside.

"Okay." He cast Deborah a woebegone look.

When he sat down on the front seat, Deborah patted his shoulder, her hand lingering for several moments. Then their gazes met.

Seeing those first stirrings of love between them caused an ache in Winter's heart. Ty had been her first love. Her only love. She stared out the window. *Why did I have to run into him again?*

Neil started up the car. "Sounds good this morning, Tyler. Quieter. That gasping noise is gone."

"Thanks." Ty cleared his throat. "A few bugs still need my attention."

How long would it take for him to fix the car and leave? One day? Two?

"Glad you're along." Neil drove out of the motel parking lot whistling a cheery tune.

She wanted to scream. How could she act normally with Ty sitting two feet away? Maybe she'd sleep all the way to Salem.

Two hours later, Neil pulled into a rest stop. "I need to stretch."

Deborah and Jeremy jumped out of the car and walked toward the parked semitrucks, their linked hands swinging between them.

"Would you look at that." Randi plopped her hands on her hips.

"Let it go." Winter groaned and exited the car.

"Let it go?" Her assistant looked like she'd rather chase after them and yank their hands apart. "Fine." She spun toward Ty, her eyes bright. "Want to take a walk?" His glance zinged between Winter and Randi. A *guilty* glance. "Sure. Care to join us, Sa—Winter?"

She glared a warning at him. "No thanks. You go ahead." Then she took off in the opposite direction. Compared to Neil's sprint around the perimeter of the parking lot, she crept at a snail's pace. But she didn't care as long as she was far from Ty.

Even so, she couldn't stop herself from glancing at him and Randi standing by the picnic tables at the other side of the rest stop. Their laughter irked her. Irrational jealousy clawed at her throat, and she gulped against the odd sensation.

Randi grinning at him like he was the most fascinating man in the world sucked Winter back in time, again.

* * * *

"Who's that girl in the lobby?" She questioned Ty when she picked him up after work one day. They shared the Jeep but hoped to upgrade to two vehicles soon. Ty's business major had paid off, and he was working as a manager at Clayborne's, a resort east of town. The owners were thrilled with his work ethic and promised him a milestone promotion. "The blond?"

"What blond?"

"Gorgeous blond, miniskirt-and-tight-sweater blond, batting-her-eyes-at-you blond. Take your pick."

"Oh, her." He chuckled. "Cindy Meyers. The boss's niece. Just moved here from Colorado. Boy, is she going to sprint up the ladder. Lucky me. She's going to be my assistant." Admiration purred in his tone.

"Trouble." She didn't think he heard.

"Don't start."

"Start?"

"Being a jealous brat."

She drove to their apartment without saying another word. They ate dinner in silence. Afterward, Ty said he had work to do. Like usual, he disappeared for the remainder of the evening.

On Tuesday, Winter picked up roast beef sandwiches from the deli and planned to surprise him with lunch. Forgoing her usual "Shave and a Haircut" knock at his office door, located on the third floor of Clayborne's, she burst into the room. "I brought y-you—" Her words stuttered to a halt.

Dressed in a shimmery-peach sleeveless dress, Cindy sat thigh to thigh next to Ty on the settee. No passable air space lingered between them. Official-looking papers rested on their laps, however, the cozy scene lacked any sense of business interpretation.

Cindy met Winter's gaze. A knowing passed between them.

The woman's dainty shoe tangled in Ty's pant leg. As he stood, he fell back, almost landing in her lap. He laughed oddly. Cindy's manicured fingers moved to his chest, steadying him. Possessively, it seemed.

Winter stared into Ty's flushed face. "What's going on?"

"Nothing." His cheeks said otherwise. "We're finishing up some proposals. What are you doing here?"

"I brought lunch." She held up the deli bag that felt like it weighed fifty pounds.

"Oh, Cindy and I already ate."

Of course, they did.

* * * *

"Winter?"

At Ty's unexpected voice, she jumped.

"Neil's ready to pull out." He stared at her. "You okay? You look kind of pale." His hand lifted as if he were going to touch her, but he jammed his fingers into the pocket of his jeans.

She inhaled, then exhaled. Why did she keep wandering

back to days she'd rather forget? Tears pooled in her eyes, and she scrubbed them away with her sleeve.

"My being here must be causing you all kinds of grief." His voice came softly. "I'm sorry."

A tear escaped down her cheek. The gentleness of his finger whisking it away surprised her. "I was just thinking. Memories and stuff."

"Any chance we could face those together?"

"No."

"You said you forgave me."

"I know." She thought she had.

With the back of his knuckles, he brushed her cheek. He paused, his fingers stilled near her face, then he drew a butterfly-soft circle around her dimple, seemingly lost in the moment.

She gulped. Took two steps back.

"What were you thinking about when I walked up to you?"

She shook her head. "I don't want to talk about it. You're here to fix the car. That's it."

"I understand. But, Sas, if you change—"

"Don't call me that! Don't even think it." She whirled around and stomped toward the car. He had no right stirring up their past by calling her that name.

She climbed into the car and pressed her face into her pillow.

How could she endure his presence? To survive with her heart intact, she had to come up with a plan to keep him as far from her as possible. And she knew just the person who could take care of that for her. She closed her eyes, picturing her assistant giving Ty the boot.

But what if Randi objected to sending him away, now that she might have feelings for him? Ugh.

* * * *

Ty didn't plan to stop calling Winter *Sassy*. For him the name equaled saying she's the *woman of my dreams* or the *love of my life*. It reminded him of their good times. And there had been moments of unbelievable happiness, especially in the first months of their marriage. Warmth spread through his chest. How he missed the closeness he'd been privileged to share with her. The intimacy for sure, but the camaraderie he knew in this life only with her made him long for more. All these years they were apart, and he still dreamed of what they enjoyed for such a brief time.

Until he messed up everything. He shuddered with a sudden chill of regret.

Unfortunately, when Winter heard his special name for her, she probably recalled the bad memories. If they were ever to reunite as man and wife, they had to face their past together, however awful those discussions might be.

With that thought in mind, he closed his eyes and spent some time praying.

An hour later, Winter mumbled something.

"What's that?" Randi asked.

"How could you do that to m-me?" Winter slurred.

"What?" Randi questioned. "I didn't do anything."

"I trusted you."

Wait. Was she dreaming about him? Ty swiveled to see her sleeping. Her head leaned against Randi's shoulder.

"Hey, you guys," Randi whispered loud enough for everyone in the car to hear. "Winter's talking in her sleep. Listen."

"You don't understand. I loved you."

Oh, man. "Wake her up." He glared at Randi.

"Let's not." She grinned as if they were indulging in a joke.

"I didn't know my aunt talked in her sleep." Jeremy snickered.

"Sometimes she does when she's tired or stressed." At least, Deborah had a sympathetic tone.

Winter mumbled some more words.

"She's talking about a guy." Randi cackled.

"I said to wake her up." Ty reached back to nudge Winter's knee.

Randi slapped his hand away. "It's not hurting her. We'll get a kick out of ribbing her later. She can take a joke."

That she wasn't taking this seriously irked him.

"Not the blond!" Winter cried out.

Ty winced. He glanced at Neil and saw his concern.

Not waiting for Randi's intervention, he released his seatbelt and turned around. With his stomach stretched over the front seat, he grabbed both of Winter's shoulders, then shook her gently. "Wake up."

"Let go of her." Randi shoved against his shoulder. "I look out for her. Not you."

He wanted to tell her to get lost. Instead, he ignored her.

"Don't do this. Ty—" Winter pleaded.

A simultaneous gasp rang out in the car. He took in Randi's and Deborah's disbelieving stares. But nothing could be done about that now.

"Winter, wake up." He stretched farther over the seat. The car swayed, ramming him into Jeremy's shoulder. "Sorry, man." He shook Winter again. "Come on, sweetheart, open your eyes." The endearment slipped easily from his lips but might be difficult to explain. Did anyone else notice?

* * * *

Winter came alert slowly. What was going on?

Ty? Above her, his beautiful brown eyes filled with concern. His kissable lips hovered such a short distance from hers, transporting her back in time to when they were first married and so in love. She smiled at her adoring husband.

"Hey, Ty." She tilted her lips, inviting him to bridge the gap between them.

* * * *

A wild cacophony beat in his chest. His heart felt like it could race out of his body. Nothing would please him more than to meet her lips, to taste the sweetness he knew she offered. The need to take her in his arms pulsed through him.

One kiss.

He inched closer. She looked so sweet. So welcoming. But, wait. How could he answer the invitation of her sleep-laden stupor without causing her untold embarrassment? Without exposing their past? Explaining their marriage would fall under her jurisdiction. Not his.

He gulped. And drew back.

* * * *

Why wouldn't he kiss her?

Disorientated, the dream of Cindy flirting with Ty lingered in Winter's mind. She stared into his moist brown eyes until, finally, the mental fog lifted. She saw his hands gripping her arms and noticed how everyone in the car stared at her.

"What's wrong?"

"You had a bad dream, that's all." His fingers slid down her arms, paused at her wrists, stroking them. He met her gaze and smiled, then he turned and resumed his seating position. The cool withdrawal of his touch sent a shiver up her spine.

"What was I doing?"

"Moaning gibberish. Calling out *Ty's* name." Randi glared at her.

Winter gulped. Had she betrayed their past herself? Her face burned with embarrassment. Ty glanced in her direction, and she silently begged him for answers she knew he couldn't give.

Eighteen

"You have a thing for him, don't you?" Randi strode across the motel room decorated in deep greens.

"Who?" Winter dropped on the bed.

Randi flopped on the opposite queen-sized bed. "Mr. Mechanic with the luscious brown eyes." She smacked her pillow. "Until I saw his gaze trailing you everywhere you went, I thought I might like him myself." She punched the pillow again and dropped her head into the dent.

Inwardly, Winter groaned. She slipped out of her shoes and leaned against the headboard. "I thought you didn't want any of us getting involved with guys. You know—*no* dating?"

"We're going to notice the opposite sex occasionally. Especially the great-looking ones." Randi turned on her side and stared at her. "I want to get married someday."

Winter rolled her eyes. "Does this mean you're going to let up on Deborah and Jeremy?"

"With a five-year age difference? Are you kidding?"

"What's so terrible about five years?"

Randi huffed. "Deb deserves a real man, not some kid."

"Watch it. That 'kid' happens to be my nephew." Winter snatched her brush from her travel bag, then tugged it through her hair.

"Sorry." Randi sat up, scrounged in her bag, then withdrew a nail file. Perched cross-legged, she sanded the small metal tool across the ends of her fingernails. The grating sound put Winter more on edge.

"Back to my question. Do you have feelings for Ty?" Randi's eyebrows lifted.

How could she answer that? "May I take the fifth?"

"No. You called out his name in your sleep." Randi snorted. "A woman can't bellow a man's name as if he were her lover, and then profess to care nothing for him."

Lover? Far from that.

But how could she answer truthfully? In some ways, she'd like nothing better than to rid herself of her secret. But the conditions for such a confession had to at least be harmonious. Which they weren't. And besides, she needed time to seek God's will about Ty's presence with the team. If Neil found out Ty was her ex-husband, he'd send him back to Coeur d'Alene on the next bus. She sighed. "Could we talk about this some other time?"

"No. I want to know what's going on." Randi obviously wouldn't be satisfied until she collected some information.

"All right." Winter set her brush on the dresser and it clunked in the otherwise quiet room. "I knew Ty many years ago."

"What?" Randi's eyes bugged.

"Remember in Coeur d'Alene? An old friend called and wanted me to go out for coffee? I told you to tell him no?"

"Yeah."

"Ty."

"Ty Williams?" Randi's jaw dropped. "I'm such an idiot!" Her hands pulsed through her hair in a show of frustration. "I never connected the two. So that's why he came along with us?" She socked the bed with her fist. "To pursue you? The rat! I thought he—" She groaned. But then a curious look crossed her face. "An old flame?"

"You might say that."

"How old?"

Winter swallowed hard, debating how much to tell. "The team's been together five years. I knew him before that."

Randi shrugged. "So, you wouldn't mind if I were interested?"

Ugh. Her feelings toward Ty were jumbled. Would she mind Randi chasing after him? Of course. She still recalled her jealous feelings from earlier today. But did she want him for herself? Another matter entirely.

"Shall I, at least, keep him away from you?" A safer topic.

"Yes, I'd appreciate that." But even saying that made something inside hurt. Did she want Ty kept away? To go without his affection, and his smile, for the rest of her life?

Probably for the best.

And yet, what was God's will in all of this? What if He led Ty to that meeting in Coeur d'Alene? And if so, just to fix the Old Clunker, right?

She slid under the covers and turned out the light.

"Don't worry. I'll take care of everything." Randi's cryptic words made Winter wonder if she had thoughts of karate-kicking Ty. "Good night, Captain."

"Night."

Hours later, after suffering a nightmare about Ty, she awoke tossing and turning around 1:00 a.m. The sheets were tangled around her ankles. She felt sweaty and sick. Her thoughts drifted toward another sleepless night … a long time ago.

* * * *

"Please, come to the Philippines with me?" She stared at her husband, willing him to want to be with her.

"For the tenth time, I can't." Ty raked his fingers through his hair. "I have a mountain of work. School loans to repay. We need another car. You're still in school. No income there. Two round trip tickets to the Philippines are too expensive. One is questionable."

His words stung. Guilt crashed over her. "I have to go to my parents' fiftieth anniversary. Even Judson is flying in from Alaska."

"I'm not saying you shouldn't attend. Just don't harass me about going."

"I'm not harassing you." Hurt scratched at her resolve to get along with him. "What's wrong with you lately? Where's the nice guy I married five months ago?"

"Buried under a sea of work." He growled.

"Yeah?" Her gaze raked over him, challenging his excuses and lack of devotion, especially considering how much time he spent with Cindy. "When you come up for air, let me know. Maybe I'll still be around." She turned away, caring little if she hurt him.

He reached out and clasped her hand. "Is that a threat?"

"Could be." She pulled away from him and left the room.

Why wouldn't he attend her parents' fiftieth anniversary? A momentous occasion like that warranted cooperation. Wasn't that what marriage was about? Compromising? She gave up enough of their personal time while he pursued his career—or whatever it was he was pursuing.

The next Tuesday, she arrived at Clayborne's for the lunch she prearranged with him, only to discover he and Cindy had eaten and left the building together.

A business outing? Or something else entirely?

* * * *

As the hours passed, a headache drummed behind Winter's eyes. A queasy feeling gnawed in the pit of her stomach. She covered her face with her pillow and groaned.

"What's up, Captain? Aren't you joining us for breakfast?" Randi questioned in a chipper voice around eight o'clock.

"No, I feel rotten." Her voice sounded odd, even to her own ears. "I couldn't sleep. I think I might be sick. Give me a couple of hours, okay?" She turned over, hoping she'd feel better later. She had so much to do. But, even with a five-day conference to prepare for, speaking publicly was the last thing in the world she wanted to think about right now.

Nineteen

"Where's Winter?" Ty stood and asked the ladies as soon as they entered the restaurant adjoining the motel.

"She's not feeling well. Poor thing," Deborah answered.

"Is she all right?"

"Nothing for you to worry about, *Mr.* Williams." Randi's curt tone set him on edge.

He dropped into his chair. He really needed to apologize. The way he befriended her the other night was nothing less than deceitful. He felt terrible about that. At the time, nurturing a friendship with her seemed like a good idea. Now, he wondered if there might have been another solution. He should've come clean by now.

Lord, I'm sorry. My hair-brained idea wasn't so smart. I can see I've hurt Randi, and who knows what Winter thinks. But how can I apologize without revealing our past relationship?

"Randi, all of us are concerned about Winter's well-being," Neil spoke reprovingly. "Tell us what's going on."

"Her stomach is upset, and she didn't sleep well, that's all." Randi rattled off the information, but she seemed to be avoiding Neil's censoring look.

Ty could relate to not sleeping well. Last night, he rested

on an uncomfortable rollaway bed in a motel room where two men seemed to be vying for the blue ribbon in a snoring contest. The past was there to haunt him too. As much as he'd given it to the Lord, he knew he was such a fool during his youth.

If he and Winter were still married, they might have children by now. What would their kids look like? Would a little girl have long red hair like her mother? With an adorable single dimple? He shook his head, feeling a pressing weight on his chest. If he'd been more honorable, they could be a real family now, instead of torn apart. His wrong was bad enough, but the final blow came when he watched Winter walk out the door, out of his life, without trying to stop her. Ten years and he still lived with that bad decision.

Was she avoiding him now? Or had she come down with the flu? Could he do anything to help? What if he brought some soda to her room and checked on her himself? He chewed on the idea for a few minutes.

Why not? He stood suddenly, and the chair legs screeched against the floor. "Excuse me." Without discussing his plan, he strode from the table. If the group watched his exit, he didn't care. His mission loomed foremost in his mind. Either he'd find Winter sick or address the reason she was avoiding him.

At the first-floor lobby, he located a soda dispenser. He put in enough money for two cans of Seven Up, then he went in search of an ice machine. Once he found it at the end of the second-floor hallway, he scooped up a bucket of ice and jogged up the stairs toward Winter's third-floor room.

If she was ill, maybe this would show her how much he still cared. He could only hope.

At her door, he knocked several times without a response. "It's me, Ty." He leaned his mouth close to the door. Was she even in there?

"Go away." He heard her faint, muffled response.

She sounded sick, which made him feel like a louse for doubting her. Maybe, she hadn't been avoiding him, after all.

"I brought Seven Up for you."

Several minutes later, the door slid open a smidge. Her hand squeezed through the narrow opening, grasping at air, but he held the can just out of reach. He could barely see into the darkened room beyond her face peeking through the crack. Her hair had that just-waking-up look. She wore red flannel pajamas. *Cute.* He grinned. Then, reminding himself why he was here, he pushed his foot through the opening and easily stepped past her. "I'll just put this soda on ice for you, okay?" He marched into the room.

"Ty, don't. I feel awful."

"Please, let me help."

"Ty—"

Despite her protests, he went in search of a glass. Behind him, he recognized her whimper as she crawled back under the thin motel blanket.

"Randi's going to be furious."

He didn't care about that. Winter was all that mattered.

With the Seven Up and ice in the glass, he approached her bed. A blue pillow covered her face, but he could still see red flannels peeking out from under the top sheet. The scene brought to mind memories of lingerie she used to wear when they were married—lacy, frilly things. His heart thudded in his ears. Time to subdue those thoughts.

"Hey, beautiful," he spoke softly. "Sorry you're not feeling well."

She pushed the pillow aside. "Go away. Don't be witty. I feel like death warmed over."

"Try this." He held out the glass. "It'll make you feel better."

She groaned, but then she grabbed the glass and took a few sips. She made a face and tried to hand it back.

"Try some more."

"I don't want any more. Now, go. Okay?" She met his gaze, and her determination seemed to ebb. "Thanks for the soda, Ty, but I'm sick. I don't want visitors." She turned toward the wall. Her fingers raked through her long hair, then she slung her arm over her head as if to hide from him.

"Sassy"—he knew he was taking a risk in calling her that— "you are the most beautiful woman in the world to me."

She groaned.

"I'm sorry you're sick." He dared to stroke her hair, not knowing how she'd react. "I love you." Her arm lowered, and she met his gaze. Seeing her tender expression, he leaned toward her cheek and kissed her right in the center of her dimple.

Her eyes closed.

Yes! She didn't push him away. Neither did she protest when he called her Sassy. Hmm. He looked closely at her pale face. "You really don't feel well, do you?"

She shook her head. "Thanks for the drink. I'll see you in a couple of days." She waved him away.

He wouldn't leave that easily. He swept strands of damp hair from her face. On the nightstand, he spotted a hairbrush. Not certain whether she'd allow him the small ministration, he picked up the brush and sat on the edge of the bed.

"What are you doing?"

"Helping you feel better. Just relax." Gingerly, he brushed her hair with long, careful strokes, being especially gentle on her scalp. He kept brushing her hair until it lay smooth and soft against the pillow.

* * * *

"Mmm. That feels wonderful." *A little too good maybe.* She shouldn't allow him to sit this close to her. Or to touch her. She pushed herself into a sitting position and grabbed the brush from his hand.

His eyes widened, and he stood.

His words from a few minutes ago echoed in her ears. *I love you.*

Then a horrible feeling came over her. *Oh, no.* She sucked in a breath. "Ty? Uh." She cupped her hand to her mouth. "I'm going to be—" Stumbling off the bed, she had only enough time to reach the garbage can beside the dresser before she got sick.

"I'm so sorry." He followed her and pulled her hair back. "It's okay, sweetheart. You'll feel better now." After a few moments, he hurried to the bathroom and returned with a wet washcloth. The cool fabric soothed her as he wiped her face. Then he helped ease her back into bed.

She couldn't believe that happened in front of him. "I'm so embarrassed."

"Don't be." He offered her another drink.

She took a sip of the cool liquid. "Thanks for being here. But you should leave before Randi returns." She closed her eyes, relaxing.

"Can I get you anything else before I go?"

* * * *

It seemed she hadn't heard his question. Almost immediately she was snoring. Then, much to his surprise, her eyes opened. She looked straight at him.

"Do you need anything?"

She smiled warmly.

He grinned back, feeling like a lovestruck teenager. But then he noticed her glassy eyes. Was she even awake?

"Maybe, another *kissth*?"

What? Was she serious? Sleep-talking? He swallowed back a chuckle. She had to be ninety-five percent asleep, but could he resist her sweet, although sleep-induced, question?

Certainly not!

Leaning over her, until his lips contacted her soft cheek, he kissed her. She didn't respond. Didn't even seem aware of him. The kiss was brief and gentlemanly, but he longed for her to know what he did. To know he loved her and wanted to kiss her for real.

Would she even remember her request tomorrow?

Her eyes were closed now. And she was snoring again.

He chuckled, then he moved to the garbage can and knotted the plastic liner, placing it by the door where the maid could find it. He slid the straight-backed chair over to Winter's bedside, and sitting down, watched her sleep. He was just thankful to be near her.

What if he hadn't come to her room? She'd have been sick all alone.

He shut his eyes and spent a few minutes praying for her healing. When he opened his eyes again, the burgundy Bible on the nightstand caught his attention. He picked it up and fingered the worn leather. This was the book Winter held hundreds, maybe thousands, of times. He flipped open the cover and the name written in cursive leaped out at him. *Winter Cowan.* Not *Winter Williams.* Something squeezed tight in his chest.

Tears stung his eyes. He took a stilted breath. Then he reined in his emotions. He needed to stop dwelling on the past. Focusing on the future was healthier. A future with Winter and him serving the Lord together. Contemplating God's plan for their lives inspired hope. He needed that today.

The Bible fell open between his hands. He thumbed to the book of Proverbs, the third chapter, and located a favorite verse.

Trust in the Lord with all your heart and lean not on your own understanding.

"Lord, I trust You," he whispered.

A small card fluttered from the book to the floor. He bent to retrieve the yellow-edged rectangle. Before placing it back in the Bible, he turned the card over.

Tyler D. Williams.

He stared unbelievingly at the engraving of his high school graduation name card. Had Winter carried his name in her Bible all these years? Had she been praying for him all along? Perhaps, loving him? Dare he hope?

Leaning his elbows on his knees, he cupped his head in his hands and prayed for their marriage and for God's will.

The door squeaked open.

"What are you doing here?" Randi rushed into the room with a crazed look in her eyes.

He stood to face her.

"Get out this instant or I'm calling Security." Anger steamed from her pores. "Who do you think you are?"

"I'm her"—he gulped back "husband"—"friend."

"I said get out!"

The ruckus awakened Winter. She clamped her hands over her head. "Randi, stop shouting. It hurts."

Ty squatted beside the bed and stroked her brow. He smiled at her, disregarding the tension boiling in the room. "Feel any better?"

"I think so."

"I told you to leave." Randi jabbed his shoulder.

He sighed, barely holding back his irritation with the woman.

* * * *

"It's okay, Randi." Seeing her assistant's crossed arms, her legs braced like a guard defending a castle, Winter wondered if she planned to practice her martial arts on Ty. She motioned for her to back off, to relax, but Randi ignored her ineffective sign language.

She met Ty's warm gaze. But then, she remembered how he helped her while she was sick. Embarrassment burned up her cheeks.

"Leave now, or else." Randi's face was pinched like a snarling dog.

Ty stood. "I didn't do any harm. I brought some soda for Winter. She was sick and alone."

"I don't care why you did it. Just get out." Randi rocked her thumb toward the door. "And while you're at it, take the next bus back to Coeur d'Alene."

"Randi." Winter groaned.

"I'll see you later. Get well soon." Ty brushed his fingers over her hand resting on the covers, and then he left the room.

"Good riddance." Randi snorted. "I don't know what I ever saw in him. I'm sorry he bothered you."

"He was kind." Winter's fingers moved to her cheek as familiar words rushed into her mind. Was that her voice imploring him for a kiss?

No. Not after she threw up and sickness reeked from her skin. Ugh. How could she face him again?

But then she remembered something else. Did he call her *beautiful*? Say he loved her?

Or was that only a dream?

Twenty

"Who speaks when Winter's sick?" Ty asked the group gathered for lunch. Avoiding Randi's glare, he glanced at Neil. Fortunately, the team leader stood up for him earlier when Randi tried getting him booted off the team for entering Winter's room alone. While Ty's intentions were honorable, her assistant went ballistic. "Do we cancel or what?" He swallowed a spoonful of clam chowder and wiped his lips with a napkin.

"We won't cancel." Neil shook his head. "God will show us who should speak."

"Winter's gotten sick only twice in the last five years." Deborah shrugged. "Once, she got the flu. Last year, she caught strep throat, as did Randi and Neil. Yours truly spoke for two days." She pointed at herself. "Call me a singer, piano player, and a speaker." Her grin made Ty think she enjoyed the challenge.

"How about you? Ever speak publicly?" Neil asked Ty.

"Shared in a j-jail ministry." He didn't mean to stumble over the phrase, but it came as a response to an anticipated adverse reaction.

"Would you have been the one in, or out, of jail?" Randi's question caused a lurch in his chest.

"Randi, Ty is the newest member of our team." Neil stared hard at her. "I'd appreciate everyone's kindness."

She didn't argue with the team leader, but she dished Ty an icy glare. "Let's get this over with. I need to check on Winter."

"How's she doing?"

"That's none of your concern."

She seemed to emanate hatred toward him. Somehow, he needed to clear the air with her. Between him waking up Winter in the car yesterday against Randi's wishes, and her finding him in the room with Winter today, he'd dug a trench for her angst.

"Winter's feeling better." Deborah smiled. "Thanks for asking. I know she'd appreciate it."

Knowing Winter was improving made him feel better too.

"Any word on bus prices?" Randi drummed the table with her fingers.

"I'm here to do a job." He spooned another bite of soup into his mouth. He wasn't going anywhere without the team.

"Then I suggest you do your job and stay clear of Winter."

The faces of the other team members showed that while they knew of Randi's protective ways where Winter was concerned, her blistering tone took even them by surprise. To Ty, her hostile behavior seemed unbefitting of someone on a Christian ministry team.

"Randi—"

"I'll do that when *she* asks me to."

Neil and Ty spoke at the same time.

"Consider it done." Randi smirked. "Winter instructed me to keep you away from her. That's what I intend to do."

Her threat obliterated Ty's dreams. After helping Winter through her sickness, after she nearly begged him to kiss her, he thought, well, what did he think? That their relationship would instantly change? That she'd run to him with open arms?

As if she were as eager and waiting to renew their romance as he was?

Sigh.

"Let's begin with those who are willing to speak tonight." Neil looked at each of them. "Randi?"

"No." She stood and left the restaurant.

Ty could only wonder why Passion's Prayer kept such a rattlesnake on their team. *Lord, I'm sorry for my judgmental attitude. But I don't get it.*

Neil cleared his throat. "Sorry about that, Tyler. Randi is Winter's man-protector. She goes overboard with her role sometimes."

How could Ty explain the real problem?

"Deborah?"

"I'd love to speak if that's God's will."

"Jeremy?"

"Absolutely."

"Tyler?"

"I'm willing." Although, the idea of speaking in front of a large group twisted uneasiness in the pit of his stomach.

"I'm open to that, too." Neil bowed his head and quietly asked for God's will to be done and for Winter's good health to return.

"Let's spend the next hour in prayer." The team leader glanced at each of them. "If any of you feel God leading you to speak tonight, stop by and talk with me."

Everyone departed in separate directions.

Ty wanted to run upstairs and assure himself of Winter's well-being. However, if he showed up at the ladies' motel room after Randi's scathing remarks, he feared another bad scene.

Did Winter tell her assistant to keep him at arm's length? To send him packing? Or did Randi invent that?

Leaving the restaurant, he strolled along the back streets of Salem. With each step, his mind played over the ways God had worked in his life, transforming him from the selfish man he was ten years ago into a believer and follower of Jesus Christ. In a million ways, his life changed. And because of his faith, he had a different outlook on his purpose for being alive. He wanted to help people. Encourage them. Even more so since he met up with Winter and Passion's Prayer.

Several times in the past, he shared his testimony. Could he speak tonight without revealing Winter's involvement in his younger days? Blabbing their shared history would doom their relationship, for sure. At some point, Winter would tell her team everything. Until then, even though he didn't understand her silence, he wouldn't say a word.

It seemed he hiked a couple of miles when he came upon the Willamette University campus. He scanned the stunning architecture of the educational buildings, the wide, natural-looking stream flowing through the grounds, the students flooding the sidewalks, all heading toward a myriad of classes. The scene reminded him of his college days, back when life was easier and more carefree.

Before he met Winter. Before he got into trouble. And before the Lord changed everything. *Thank You, God.* He didn't give up on Ty. Even at his lowest point, God was with him. Ty contemplated his journey over the past years, and he figured he'd go through everything again—though it had been rough—if it meant bringing him to the place he was in now. A place of peace and hope.

Considering what he'd been pondering for the last hour, was God possibly directing him to share his testimony tonight? What would Winter say about that?

Just then, he gazed up at a street sign and read "Winter Street."

"You've got to be kidding!" His chuckle turned into a hearty laugh.

The people who lived in Salem saw this street sign all the time. But for him? Winter's name on a sign, on this day, right when he was thinking of her, was a blessing.

God directed his path all the time. But? *Wow!*

Thank You, Lord. Bless Winter. Touch her and heal her. And, please, heal our marriage. Help us reconcile according to Your Word. I'm willing to do whatever You ask. I'm Yours. If You want me to speak tonight, I will. Make me into the man You want me to be. And while You're moving in hearts, could You speak to Winter? Show her I love her? Thank You.

Unable to get that sign out of his mind, or the idea of sharing his life story, he jogged back to the motel. At the lobby window, he glimpsed his reflection in the glass. Doubt scratched at his confidence. Would anyone benefit from hearing about his past? His words had impacted the guys in prison, but that didn't compare to the gathering at Faith Community Chapel. Not even Winter knew what happened to him ten years ago. What would she say if she heard? *When* she heard? He had some explaining to do himself. Coming clean, being honest, was the only foundation for a lasting trust between them.

When he reached the men's motel room, Ty told Neil he felt impressed to share about his journey. Neil clapped him on the back and praised him for being open to God's leading. He felt the exact impression about Ty—and himself. They would both share their testimonies.

Exhilarated, and humbled, Ty spent the next hour praying and preparing for the evening ahead.

Twenty-one

Propped cozily against the headboard, sipping tea, Winter already felt better. "Who's speaking tonight?" Her voice sounded raspy, but the lemon and honey tea soothed her throat.

Randi stepped from the bathroom, dressed in a periwinkle skirt and matching blouse. "Neil *and* Ty are giving their testimonies, or so I've heard." She rolled her eyes.

"What?" Ty was speaking? What if he said something about their past? "I should go and listen." She stood too fast, and the room swayed. Closing her eyes, she waited for the dizziness to pass. Could she go and sit in the back of the church without anyone noticing her? She didn't want someone getting sick because of her, but she wanted to, had to, hear Ty speak.

Randi helped her sit down. "No way. You've been sick all day." She handed Winter a package of crackers she brought from the restaurant. "We've heard Neil's testimony. Do you care to hear Ty's? How interesting could that be?"

How interesting, indeed. Winter munched on the cracker. The way he came to her rescue this morning, and the tender way he took care of her, made her curious to hear how he came to believe in Jesus. The old Ty would never have remained in a chair by her bed watching her sleep as if staying by her side was the most important thing in the world. What brought about such a change?

What if he spoke about their past in front of a crowd? In front of Randi?

Winter gulped.

If she tried standing again, her assistant would probably restrain her. Still, her curiosity churned. Did Ty have a charismatic public-speaking voice? Or was he unsure of himself?

"I won't enjoy a word." Randi, seemingly satisfied Winter would stay put, hurried to the vanity and lathered her hands with vanilla-scented lotion.

"Why is that?"

"Just something about him." Randi had a hard glint in her eye. "He's crazy over you, though."

She met her assistant's gaze in the mirror. "Ty?"

"Yes, Ty."

"He'll get over it. They always do." She yawned like it didn't matter. But speaking the words hurt.

"You're probably right." Randi crossed the room and touched the back of her hand against Winter's forehead. "You feel cooler. Rest tonight. Tomorrow you'll be good as new." She turned toward the door. "I'm heading out."

"See you later." As soon as the door clicked shut, Winter threw back the covers. "If Ty's speaking, I'm going to be there." She stood slowly this time. She'd shower, then arrive at the gathering unnoticed. A taxi ride to the church, a scarf draped around her head, and no one would be the wiser. Tonight, she'd find out what Ty was up to, and whether he was sincere about his faith and had an honest change in his life.

* * * *

Ty sat in the front row and listened as Neil shared how he came to Christ as a young adult, and how he met Molly at a church in Tennessee. In a tender voice, the team leader spoke of the great love he shared with his wife for fifteen years. He told about Molly's courageous battle with cancer that eroded her vitality and their chance at happiness. How he felt forsaken and lost after her death.

His heart-wrenching story pierced Ty to the core. It made him contemplate that while Neil's wife was snatched from him due to illness, Ty betrayed his wife and broke her heart. And because of his wrongdoing, he lost her. He lived with the result of his bad choices every day. But he'd give anything, and everything, to have her back in his life. If it took until the day he died, he'd prove it to her.

As Neil brought his testimony to a close, Ty wondered if there was a dry eye in the house. He shed his share of tears too.

As the time approached for him to speak, he felt relieved that Winter wasn't here tonight. Otherwise, he'd be even more nervous. Not that he wanted her to be sick. Just not here right now. He didn't plan to divulge any secrets. But knowing she could hear him skipping personal details of their lives would have upped the ante on his emotions. Plus, he'd rather tell her his personal story himself. And boy, did he have plenty to share.

When he heard his name announced, a cold sweat crept over him. But he forced himself to stand and acknowledge Neil's call. He wouldn't let the team down. Plus, God had shown him His will about speaking tonight. He wanted to follow the Lord's leading in every part of his life.

Behind the pulpit, he cleared his throat. "Hello." He adjusted the microphone.

Voices in the audience returned his greeting.

"After that moving testimony, I barely know where to start." He heard the raspy sound in his voice and cleared his throat again. "I wasn't raised in a Christian home. Growing up, I heard very little about Jesus other than in Christmas carols."

He perused the audience, noticed Neil watching him, saw Deborah's reassuring smile, Randi's glare.

He swallowed, then continued. "As a young adult, I met a lady who tried to live by the Bible's principles." He wished he could speak the entire truth. *Lord, help me. And be with Winter back at the motel.* "Though I thought I loved her, I found shameful pleasure in mocking her faith, her morals, and in making life miserable for her. She invited me to church, but I refused every time. Pigheaded, she used to call me."

A pang of sadness filled him. But, inwardly, he thanked God he wasn't that man any longer.

"You see, a person can be consumed with themselves. That was me. Too busy for church. Egotistical. Full of myself. Out for a laugh and a good time. But then, like a child's block tower, my character self-destructed."

His voice grew stronger. "Hot out of college with a business degree, I planned to chisel out my share of the big time. But my big time brought me to my knees. I found myself lost in a world of foolish living and ungodly habits. Before I knew it, I betrayed the woman I loved."

He drew in a sharp breath. "Eventually, I lost her."

He exhaled with the force of his regret. He'd better redirect his thoughts before he said something about him and Winter that he shouldn't. Even though she wasn't here, Randi would surely tell her everything he said before the night was over.

"My life went downhill from there. A female acquaintance in my company lured me into doing something illegal. I'd always thought of myself as an intelligent person. I knew what we were doing was wrong, but the drive to get rich and experience its power overcame me." He paused. "I won't go into the details of how we used a fictitious name and established a line of credit linked to the company account. Just know our goal originated with the same mental justifying that gets a lot of people into trouble—an unhealthy lust for money and too much self-importance."

He swallowed hard. "When the dust settled, I was the one in prison. I'd been the manager in charge, the one with the big ideas. My accomplice—a relative of the boss with wealth and connections—got off with a hand slap and community service. I stayed in prison for five years, paying my debt for embezzlement."

What would Neil and the others think of his revelation? He couldn't worry about that now. He hoped they'd thank God for the change in his life.

"The picture was ugly." He sighed. "I still feel ashamed that I stooped so low. But the good news is God turned everything around.

"Some guys from a church held services at the prison. Week after week, they came back. Through their sharing, I learned what it meant to turn my life over to God. I remembered what that woman tried convincing me of years before. And I finally gave Jesus my heart, my life, my broken dreams, my guilt, my everything. I didn't have many positive things to lay at His feet. But the day I accepted the amazing love and forgiveness of Jesus, a peace beyond description filled my heart.

"My life changed. The same guys continued visiting and discipling me. God's Word became my food. Like a starving man, I gobbled it up. I memorized verses and grew in Christ. And finally, I served my time."

He drew in a long breath. "Ladies and gentlemen, when I took my first steps outside those prison walls, I walked away a free man, inside and out."

He gazed across the congregation. "I can't tell you every single part of my life fell perfectly into place. However, I can say God is good. He turned my life around, and I would never revert to my previous way of living. That man is gone forever. Praise God!"

He paused, knowing he was almost finished. "A couple of months ago, I became discouraged. I prayed for God to begin a new work in me, and not long afterward, a personal situation led me to Passion's Prayer. Here I am with the team, although I'm only a mechanic."

The audience chuckled.

"Sometimes life feels desperate. We hit rock bottom as I did. Tonight, if you're hurting, or need a friend, welcome Jesus into your life. He'll be your hope, comfort, your all. No matter where you are in life, He is the only way to peace and joy."

At his nod, Neil returned to the pulpit and led the congregation in a time of prayer. Ty stepped off the platform and sat down on the front pew. Had he said enough? Too much?

Lord, have Your way.

* * * *

Embezzlement?

Winter drew her scarf close around her face. She couldn't believe Ty had ended up in jail. How long was he with Cindy before that happened? She slid lower in the pew, mulling over his words. The two of them did need to talk. But could she face the part that would hurt the most?

Forgive as I have forgiven you. Unconditionally.

She gulped.

Without second thoughts.

That kind of forgiveness and walking in grace was the way to true peace—she knew that. So what held her back? What clogged her throat at the mere thought of forgiving Ty his wrongs? To do so didn't mean she had to accept him back into her life as a husband or a romantic interest. Goodness, no. But accepting him as a person who had changed? A man who humbly asked her forgiveness. Couldn't she do that? Shouldn't she?

Before anyone noticed her, she slipped from the pew and left the chapel. She had a lot of thinking and praying to do.

Twenty-two

They were just leaving the restaurant parking lot when a burst of thick blue steam spewed out from beneath the Old Clunker's hood. The engine rattled and coughed.

"What's happening?" Neil called out.

"You'd better pull over while you can and let me check." Ty pointed to the right side of the street. "There's a parking lot with overhead lights."

Neil steered the car until it lurched into a grocery store parking space, then died a noisy, shuddering death under a garish fluorescent glow. Ty hopped out and yanked the hood up. After checking the engine, he hated to break the bad news. He stepped over to Neil's window, wiping green gunk from his hands onto a Kleenex. "It's not good. We'd better leave her here. I'll come back in the morning and verify the damage."

"What's your professional opinion?" Neil frowned.

"Professional, my foot," Randi muttered.

Ty ignored her comment. "My guess would be the head's blown. That rattling sound makes me think the pistons are going too. Looks like a major overhaul."

Air whistled through Neil's teeth. "What kind of costs?" He appeared to be bracing for the worst.

Ty shrugged. "With my free labor, I'd estimate the cost for parts at five hundred dollars. Possibly six."

Neil groaned.

"Maybe now would be a good time to get that new vehicle?" Jeremy inserted.

"Winter won't go along with such an idea, and you know it." Randi's voice rose. "If we can't afford to fix this old tank, we can't afford car payments. Shouldn't we get a second opinion? Mr. Williams may be wrong." She leaned forward and glared at him. "We heard about his motives tonight. His joining our team was a mistake."

"Randi!" Deborah sounded like she couldn't believe someone on their team could be so vindictive.

Ty couldn't believe it either.

"Well, it's true. He's a thief and a liar!"

A gasp snagged in Ty's throat.

"Randi, that's enough." Neil clutched the steering wheel. "Ty's done nothing but helped us. Right now, we need a mechanic."

Randi harrumphed. "Wait until the other churches on our schedule hear we have a swindler on our team."

"Randi!" Neil looked exasperated.

Swindler? Did the others think that? This conversation was becoming a nightmare.

"Where's your spirit of charity?" Deborah asked softly.

Randi glared at Ty. "I bet we'll have more cancellations than we can deal with."

Surely that wasn't true. He shuffled back and forth in the awkward silence. "Let's lock up the car. We can walk to the motel."

"Walk?" Randi's question pierced the air. Everyone stepped out of the vehicle but her. "It's cold, and I'm in heels."

"The motel isn't far." With a weary sigh, Ty opened her door, then swayed his hand in the direction of the motel. "I can see the sign from here. Leaving the car behind is the best solution."

"For you, maybe." She vaulted from the station wagon. "How about calling a cab?"

"The motel is only a few blocks." Neil pointed down the street.

She extended her open-toed high heels. "What if I break my ankle?"

Neil shrugged, then shook his head.

She groaned and charged ahead of everyone, her heels clicking an irritated, staccato beat in the cool night.

What would she tell Winter now?

* * * *

The sound of the door opening and closing awakened Winter. She watched Randi tiptoe across the room. "You're finally back."

Her assistant jumped. "You're awake. How are you?"

"Tired, but almost normal."

"Wonderful. I didn't mean to make so much noise. Sorry."

Winter glanced at the clock on the nightstand. "Two a.m.?"

"Car trouble." Randi stepped out of her dress shoes near the closet. "My feet are killing me. That so-called mechanic made us walk." She tromped into the bathroom with her pajamas in hand. "We had a meeting in the lobby too," her voice called from behind the closed door.

A meeting without her? Winter pushed herself into a sitting position. "At this hour? What happened?"

Randi shuffled back into the room. "Something came up. We didn't want to disturb you."

Neil should have talked to her first. He could have called. "What's this about?"

Randi fixed two glasses of ice water and passed one to Winter. "The meeting was about Ty." She said his name like a dirty word.

Winter's heart sank. Was her team already sending him away? "What about him?"

"We found out tonight he's an ex-con. Some of us don't think he should be associated with Passion's Prayer."

"Not associated—? Who doesn't want him on the team?" Two days ago, she didn't want him involved with Passion's Prayer either. Now, she'd seen and heard the difference in him for herself. After her prayer time this evening, she wouldn't mind the chance to talk things over with him.

"I don't want him on the team. He should leave immediately." A determined look streaked across Randi's face. "I think Neil agrees."

Neil felt that way too? Something didn't make sense. Her co-leader believed in second chances. Third chances, even. He wouldn't kick Ty off the team that quickly. In fact, he seemed to almost treat Ty like a son. What was Randi up to? "So, you conducted a meeting in the middle of the night without me, to oust someone from our team?" Heat burned in her voice. "Since when does this ministry make decisions without its whole leadership? I don't care for the sound of this secret meeting."

"I'd hardly call it secret." Randi scoffed. "We're looking out for your best interests. In a few days, you'll be well, and these decisions will make sense."

Decisions? She couldn't wait to hear Neil's side of the story. "How is it in my best interest for Ty to leave?" Was she defending him now? She could hardly believe her own flip-flopping. But she wasn't about to sit by while Randi kicked him off the team. Not after the way he took care of her. Not after the way he said … he loved her.

"I thought you didn't want him here, either."

She swallowed back a harsh response. Like that was none of Randi's business. Or that she needed a change of heart. Winter certainly experienced one while listening to Ty tonight.

"You told me to keep him away from you. That's my job."

Her words stole some of Winter's thunder. "That was before."

"Before what?"

She didn't have to answer. This behavior from an assistant—even one she vowed to always be friends with—bordered on disrespect. Something she'd address when she felt more like herself. Right now, she was caught up in too many emotions and the aftermath of sickness. "I trust him now, that's all."

Randi chortled. "You wouldn't if you'd heard him speak tonight."

"Why?" Not for one minute did Winter wish to explain why she wrapped her head in a scarf and took a cab to the church. Or how proud she felt hearing about Ty's conversion. But she would speak up if Randi persisted in trying to get rid of him for nothing more than sharing a bit of his past.

Didn't God forgive all their pasts?

"If you must know"—Randi lowered her voice as if confessing the biggest national secret—"he embezzled money and spent five years in the slammer." She dropped onto the opposite bed and bunched pillows behind her. "How will that look if word gets out? Our team holds high standards—standards you've demanded." She pierced Winter with a stern look. "Embezzlement doesn't sit well with those ideals. Of course, it's not like the five of us have money. But what if he steals from a church? Passion's Prayer would be ruined!"

Of all the convoluted ideas. "Randi Simmons, where do you get off taking over like this?"

"Neil is concerned too. We would've talked everything over with you, but you're sick." Her voice changed to sugar and spice.

Winter bit her lip, not wanting to say something explosive that would destroy their friendship. "Why does Ty perturb you so much?"

Randi rolled under the covers. "He was in jail. This scenario doesn't bode well for any of us. Plus, there's his obvious attraction to you."

"Men have shown interest before. Look at David Michaels."

"Yeah, but something's different about this guy." She looked like she was analyzing Winter. "Maybe it's because the two of you knew each other before." She yanked the sheet over her head and turned to the wall, ending their conversation.

Winter slid beneath the covers, stewing. If she hadn't been sick, none of this would have happened. Ty wouldn't have come to her room alone. Wouldn't have told her he loved her. Speaking tonight wouldn't have been on his agenda. But all those things did happen. And she wasn't sorry about any of it, er, except for vomiting in front of him. She grimaced.

Earlier, when she heard him speak, not one ounce of concern entered her mind about Passion's Prayer's reputation. Ty gave his life to Jesus, and the change in him was irrefutable. As he said, he was a different man because of God's forgiveness. Why he chose to steal or what led to that demise was beyond her understanding. She was certain of one thing—his devotion to Christ was sincere. The day he wept and asked for her forgiveness, she recognized his spiritual metamorphosis. Tonight, she witnessed that change in him again.

Although, knowing that didn't mean she planned to waltz back into his arms. But neither could she condemn him. She'd stick up for him, if necessary. She believed in second chances too. And something about seeing Ty as a man of faith touched her heart. He had a humility and sweetness about him that was endearing.

If she came clean now and told her team he was her ex-husband, he would get the boot. Nothing she could say would convince them otherwise. Could she put off telling them for a few more days? She could use a little more time to think and pray.

She'd almost drifted to sleep when the door creaked open. "Getting in kind of late?"

"Did I wake you?" Deborah slipped into the room. "I'm sorry. How are you?" She tiptoed to the closet and hung up her coat.

"Better."

"Praise the Lord. I feel terrible you might have caught this from me."

"No worries. How are things between you and Jeremy?"

"We're getting closer. Does it bother you?" Deborah pulled a drawer open and took out her pajamas. "He's your nephew. And like Randi keeps telling me, there's the five-year age difference."

Winter leaned up on her elbow. "Your friendship with Jeremy doesn't bother me. I trust both of you."

"Thank you." Deborah rushed over and gave her a hug. "Did Randi mention anything?" she whispered.

"About Ty? Yes."

"She wants him gone with a vengeance. I can't figure out why. He's so nice." Deborah hesitated like she didn't want to say anything more. "I even thought she might have a thing for him, but then she went ice cold. Did she explain about the Old Clunker?"

"Not really. What happened?"

Deborah mimed steam billowing out of the engine. "We need Ty now more than ever. I think he's a godsend. A miracle. God provided a mechanic right when the Old Clunker needs surgery." She smiled, then rushed into the bathroom.

Ty a miracle?

The car's breakdown weighed heavily on Winter's mind. God always supplied the ministry's needs, but sometimes finances were tight. For them to travel across the country, sharing God's love, debt free, the Old Clunker had to be fixed.

That meant, for the time being, they were dependent on Ty's mechanical knowledge.

Who would have thought she'd be in this predicament? Needing her ex-husband?

Unbelievable.

Deborah reentered the room and slipped into the rollaway bed. "Lord, please touch our old car," she prayed softly, "and supply the money we need to fix her. Thank You for Your provision." A silence. "And thanks for sending Ty right when we needed him."

Right when we needed him.

"Amen." Winter knew she'd have to vouch for him the following morning. Randi would, no doubt, be determined to send him back to Coeur d'Alene. Maybe Neil felt the same way. But it seemed Jesus might have another plan.

She fell asleep praying for her team.

And for Ty.

Twenty-three

Ty was back for his second cup of coffee, and he didn't see anyone from the team at the motel restaurant. He could use a few minutes to think. Ever since Randi's spiteful words last night, he'd barely thought of anything else. Would Neil send him home? Would Winter concur?

Things weren't working out like he hoped, that was for sure.

When Randi strode into the restaurant at half-past seven, he wanted to bolt out the fire exit. The moment she noticed him, her eyes narrowed into Cruella DeVille's intense glare. She pivoted on her heel and rushed for the exit.

Fine by him. He didn't want to talk to the vixen anyhow. He slurped his coffee and set the cup down harder than he should have. Then he groaned. His attitude stunk. Somehow, he had to make things right.

He sucked in a big breath, and his pride. "Uh, Randi! Wait a sec." When she glanced back, he stood and extended his hand toward the seat across from him. "Join me?" He cracked a smile but felt far from gallant. *Lord, please help me with this.*

Randi's reluctance—and her hate, for whatever reason—was obvious.

"We should talk." He gulped.

Her gaze assessed him, head to foot, and she grimaced.

He glanced down at his work clothes. Grease streaks criss-crossed his sleeves. Clean, yet dirty. Certainly not smelling the way her gaze accused. He wore clothes like this to work every day back home. He couldn't take a car apart in a three-piece suit.

Warily, Randi trudged to his table and dropped into the chair across from him. "I'm surprised to see you here this early." She flipped over an off-white mug and waved at a waitress toting a carafe of coffee from table to table.

"You know what they say about the early bird." He eased himself back into his chair. What could he say to make peace with her?

The waitress paused at their table and filled both cups with the steaming brew.

"Thank you." He took a sip.

"Yes, and I wonder which worm you're after." Randi lifted the cup to her lips. Her gaze fastened on his like a prosecuting attorney staring down a witness.

"I've already checked the car. Now I'm back for my second cup of coffee." He lifted his mug. "Nothing sinister about that." He smiled, but it was obvious nothing could disarm her irritation.

She took another sip of her coffee and stared out the window.

He cleared his throat. "I owe you an apology."

She tensed. Her eyes narrowed.

Not knowing how to express his thoughts without divulging information better left unsaid, he had to say something to diffuse the tension. "I'm sorry for any false pretense on my part the night we met."

She set her coffee cup down with a clunk.

He swallowed hard. "I wanted to be friends with you. But I must admit I was hoping for an invitation to Pastor Michaels' house for another reason. I went about it in the wrong way. I'm sorry for that. And for hurting you."

Her fingernails drummed on her mug. "What was your act about that night?" She leaned her elbows on the table, as if to draw closer, and glared at him. "I know about your crush on Winter."

Crush? That made him want to laugh. But he supposed he did have a crush on her—a lifelong sort of crush. And so much more.

But back to that regrettable night. How could he explain?

Randi stood, her knuckles pressing against the tabletop. "Tell me one thing, *Mr.* Williams." She tipped her head, her gaze drilling his. "What exactly are you here for?"

He didn't look away. "To fix the car." He'd been in tough boardroom warfare before. It wasn't like he was going to cower before Winter's PA.

"I don't believe that." She maintained her intensity. "You're after something. I'd like to know what that something is."

His lips compressed. He would not rise to her baiting.

"You think Winter would fall for you?" She snickered. "Oh, Ty, you are so misled."

His cheeks burned.

She straightened, fists clenched at her sides. "She won't have you."

A kick in the gut would have been less painful, but he kept his silence.

A look of satisfaction crossed her face. "Winter could have her pick of a dozen men." She smiled like she won a game-winning point. "Every one of them a million times better than you—pastors, best-selling Christian authors, famous recording artists, missionaries."

He wished she'd just walk away. Or maybe he should.

"Everywhere we go, men are drawn to her charisma." She

pointed to herself. "It's my job to keep them away. Just like I'm going to make you leave." Her smile turned sinister. "And I will make you go away."

He swallowed a cotton ball of dryness.

"I thought it might be different this time." Her voice softened, surprising him with its gentleness. "That you and I—" She cleared her throat. "But what does it matter?"

He saw he'd hurt her feelings. And that she was still holding a grudge. "I'm sorry."

"For letting me see your true colors? Don't worry. Soon, everyone will know who the real Ty Williams is."

What did she mean by that?

"You're not Winter's type. On a scale of one to ten, you are a zero."

Zero?

She stalked out of the restaurant, her head held high.

His heart plummeted.

Lord, I blew it when I first tried to get into Passion's Prayer. I was desperate to see Winter. My solution was wrong. I'm sorry for making a mess of everything. He leaned his face into his hands and groaned.

Standing, he dropped enough money on the table to pay for the cups of coffee and a generous tip, then trudged toward the stairway. Neil wouldn't be pleased with the car's damage report. But the sooner he found out about it, the sooner they could get the project finished.

Where would the team find an extra six hundred dollars? And where would he locate an empty garage? He could cover the expenses himself, but finding a dry place to work on the car on short notice would be a greater challenge.

* * * *

Later that afternoon, Neil secured a small garage a mile from the motel for Ty to work in. Ty paid for the tow truck expenses, and immediately began dismantling the engine. Although they were uncertain about repair funds, by faith he jumped into the detailed procedure of removing one bolt at a time. There were a zillion parts. And he didn't have all the proper tools with him. Yet he praised God for the opportunity to serve Winter's ministry team.

As he worked, his thoughts were never far from the woman whose love he hoped to win. He prayed for God to open a way for him to talk with her soon, despite Randi's negative opinion and threat to send him away.

Twenty-four

Two days later, the dissected engine lay scattered on the garage floor like toys flung across a nursery. Ty stared numbly at the grease-laden parts on the cement, and relief washed over him that the removal phase was done. He had the garage for a week, the exact amount of time Passion's Prayer would be in this city. At the pace he was going, he should be finished in time.

At Saul's Engine Repair, he'd wheedled the cost of the head rebuild down from what the owner originally quoted him on the phone. It seemed Saul had a soft spot in his heart for people in ministry. When Ty told him about Winter and Passion's Prayer traveling around sharing about God's love, not expecting much in the way of offerings, the man sniffed back tears. Then he talked for a half hour about his son who went on a six-week missionary trip to Africa, and how his life was changed because of the experience.

Saul said he had a part-time employee who'd re-bore the piston block the next day for a portion of the usual fee. There were also new parts to be purchased—bearings, pistons, piston rings, a head gasket—but Saul said he'd give them a deal on those too.

Ty figured he might be able to keep the expenses under five hundred. Neil would be glad about that. And if Ty visited another local vendor, Jerry's Wrecking Yard, he hoped to locate a similar car with usable secondhand parts. But considering how archaic the Old Clunker was, maybe Winter and Neil should consider putting this one to rest and purchasing a more reliable vehicle.

Exhausted, and hungry enough to demolish five cheeseburgers, Ty trudged back to the motel. With each footfall, he longed for two things—an hour-long hot shower and a buffet of food. Well, that, and spending time with Winter.

Walking along the sidewalk, he rubbed his fists against his lower back. The tight muscles ached from the strain of bending and twisting himself into the engine compartment and lying under the car on the cold cement floor for two days. He massaged his eyes, forcing himself awake.

He'd missed the hydraulic jack and floor dolly back at the shop in Coeur d'Alene, machinery that made working on cars a whole lot simpler. Some of the bolts needed an air-powered wrench, but he removed everything by hand. However, any pride he felt in his accomplishment was overridden by fatigue.

By the time he arrived at the motel room, everyone was gone. He hated missing the conference, but he was too beat to show his unshaven face in any civilized gathering. Straight into the bathroom he trudged, almost too tired to undress. He couldn't wait to experience his first shower in days. A shower. Food. Then sleep.

While he was under the pelting stream of hot water, the muffled sound of someone entering the motel room reached him. "Hello!" he hollered over the spray. "Hello?"

No one answered.

Did Neil or Jeremy run back into the room for something?

The water massaging his back felt marvelous, but fatigue overwhelmed him. He'd have to forego the hour-long shower.

Concerned someone might still be in the motel room, he

pulled on a pair of clean boxers and wrapped a towel around his middle. Entering the main part of the room, he saw that no one was there.

He shuffled toward the bed, and his toe skimmed a piece of paper beneath his foot. He bent over and picked it up. He groaned when a sharp pain pinched his back. Gingerly, he eased down on the bed and focused his eyes on the discarded paper.

"Passion's Prayer Conference at Faith Community Chapel." Winter's smiling face stared back at him from the flyer. He grinned, despite his fatigue. With his finger, he outlined her face. He imagined touching the dimple in her cheek. Through tired eyes, he stared at the scenery behind her. Was that Lake Coeur d'Alene? Or was he only imagining the landscape looked like his hometown?

A familiar scent drew the flyer closer to his nose. Vanilla? Why would the paper smell like that?

The delicate aroma tickled his senses. Winter wore this scent the night he prayed for her. Vanilla. The aroma of dreams and hopes and possibilities for their future together. He slipped under the sheets and fell asleep holding her picture close to his heart.

* * * *

Disoriented, Ty awoke to whispered voices and the sound of drawers opening and closing. He crawled from under the pillow and found the room filled with Winter's team members. *What in the world?* His hazy glance strained to see his wristwatch. "Sorry, I overslept."

Through a fog, he watched as Neil and Randi scrounged through drawers, tossing clothes and books aside, searching for something. What were they after? Deborah and Jeremy stood in the far corner of the room whispering. And Winter, well, she looked amazing. Just watching her stole his breath away. Did she realize what she did to him every time she was this close? How he longed to touch her cheek and tell her how much he loved her? Too many days had passed since he sat with her while she was sick. Did she remember her sleepy request for a kiss? Why wouldn't she meet his gaze now? Was that a flush of crimson staining her cheeks? Winter embarrassed?

"Hey, Sassy."

Every movement in the room froze.

Uh-oh. Did he speak too loudly?

Neil's eyebrow rose high on his forehead. Deborah and Jeremy stared at him, then turned away. Winter's cheeks hued even redder, if that were possible.

Randi stomped to his bedside, a snarl parting her lips. "Where is it?" Her hands parked on her hips, she blocked his vision of Winter with her domineering stance. "What did you do with it?"

"With what?"

"Like you don't know."

"Randi, don't be hasty." Neil closed a drawer. "It's probably misplaced."

What were they after?

"Misplaced by the only thief in this room." She leaned over Ty, glaring.

Thief?

Fully awake, he sat up. Was the team leader searching through Ty's suitcase? "What are you doing?" He couldn't fathom why this gathering was taking place in his room. His long sleep after two days of no rest had dulled his thinking. He felt drugged like he needed another eight hours to feel human.

"I'm sorry, Tyler." Neil's face turned ruddy. "We're searching everyone's bags, not just yours."

"But mainly yours," Randi said snidely.

No one disagreed with her.

The burn of accusation, the guilty rush, Neil fingering through his belongings, were all reminders of a time he never wanted to experience again. He considered these people followers of God, Christians not given to judgment. Was Winter condemning him too? The way she averted her face made him think she was.

"What do you think I've taken?" His voice squeaked.

Winter's gaze locked on his. Did she sense his fear?

"Don't play innocent," Randi mocked. "You know exactly what we're looking for."

"Randi." Winter shook her head. "That's enough."

Randi stalked over to the other side of the room.

Ty remained under the covers, although he wanted to hop up and help them find whatever was missing. He'd tear the place apart himself, but knowing he was only wearing boxers kept him in his bed.

Neil sighed. "It's not here."

"What's not here?" Ty thrust his hands through his hair. The darts of blame in these friends' gazes pierced his heart. The experience had been gruesome enough when he was accused by a jury for a crime he had committed.

Neil sighed. "You've been gone for the last couple of days."

"Taking your car apart." Too late, Ty realized how sharp his voice sounded. "Making arrangements for parts to be fixed and replaced," he continued in a less hostile tone. "Without sleep until now. Or food." A loud growl rumbled in his stomach.

"We appreciate your hard work, really we do." Neil glanced at the others.

Randi let out a snort. Winter shot her a curt glance.

"Cut to the heart of it." Ty was resigned that whatever it was had to be bad.

"During the meeting the night before last, someone gave us money for car repairs." Neil shrugged. "We were ecstatic, as you can imagine."

"Great." The project could move forward. The car wouldn't

do them any good torn in pieces. But Neil's expression said something was still amiss. "So what's the problem?" He scrubbed his hands over his three-day whiskers.

Neil shook his head. "The money has disappeared."

"All of it?" Ty realized where this conversation was headed.

Randi grunted. "Nice act, Mr. Mechanic."

"Randi, please," Deborah spoke.

"You think *I* took the money?" He searched each face in the room and witnessed their judgment.

"We don't want to think that." Neil maintained a gentle tone.

"I'm the one who spent the last forty-eight hours fighting with nuts and bolts that should have come off with power tools. To save you money, I did the work by hand. I paid for all the parts. My arms ache so badly, I can hardly lift them, and you accuse me of this?" In his tirade, he pushed off the bed and stood, hands on hips.

"Ty!" Winter yelped.

His gaze followed her downward glance. Immediately, he realized what everyone in the room was seeing—him in nothing but navy boxers. Grabbing the top sheet, he scrambled to wrap the thin fabric about himself. Winter's eyes avoided his imploring her to understand.

"We're not accusing you."

Sure sounds like it to me.

"But we don't know what happened to the money." Were her eyes tearing up?

"I hid the funds in my briefcase, then stashed the bag in the closet before we left last night." Neil spread out his hands. "You were here when we got back."

"I took a shower and went straight to bed."

"Besides, Ty didn't even know about the money," Deb defended him.

It felt good to hear someone stick up for him.

"What does that matter?" Randi's face darkened. "He's been in this room alone where the money was."

"Yeah, sound asleep."

"Obviously you must have found it first."

Ty gritted his teeth. "I should have known better than to think I was welcome here." He tucked the corners of the sheet at his waist, forming a skirt. "I thought it would be different with Christians in a ministry promoting God's ability to change people." He glanced at each one of them. "If I hadn't shared my testimony the other night, none of you would know I spent time in prison. You would have nothing to hold against me." But his gaze snared with Winter's, and he figured her thoughts matched his—she had something to hold against him. Something deeply personal.

He crossed his arms and watched her, willing her to believe in him. To trust he would do *nothing* to jeopardize his chances of reconciling with her. Then he recalled a blue piece of paper, a Passion's Prayer flyer, he saw on the floor when he got out of the shower last night. The one with Winter's picture and Lake Coeur d'Alene. And it smelled of—?

Vanilla. Of her.

Did his ex-wife sabotage him? Hide the money so it looked like he ripped off the ministry. When he called out, did she run, accidentally dropping the flyer? What if she desired him out of her life so badly that she stooped to such a lowdown trick? Didn't Randi warn him Winter wanted nothing more to do with him?

Whoa. His thoughts were more jumbled than he realized. Winter wouldn't go that far.

Would she?

"What shall we do now?" Deborah asked.

"Pray." Neil folded his hands.

"I have room on a credit card," Jeremy offered.

"No." Winter glanced around the room, apparently avoiding looking at Ty. "We won't purchase a thing until the money has been found. This week's food allowance will be rationed, if necessary, so we can purchase car parts."

"What?" Randi stomped to the center of the room. "Why should we suffer? We're smart enough to figure out the perpetrator." Her glare homed in on Ty. "Did anyone check his wallet?"

Everyone's gaze riveted toward him, even Winter's.

They can't seriously think I did this. He groaned. "My wallet's in the right-hand drawer." Disgusted with the whole affair, he flung his arm in the vanity's general direction. Let them search through his suitcase, and his wallet, for all he cared. He wanted this bizarre trial to end.

Lord, why did it have to come to this? Why can't my past be just that—my past? I'm a new man. You changed me completely.

Randi reached into the drawer and pulled out his brown leather wallet. He would've chosen anyone in the room but her to handle his personal things. She opened his trifold wallet, and something about her expression, almost wicked, foretold of trouble. In shocked amazement, he watched her riffle through his wallet and extract bills, large ones that hadn't been there yesterday.

What?

"Aha! One, two, three, four, five hundred dollars." She waved the money in the air like a victory flag.

His heart thudded to the floor.

"The exact denominations." Neil's jaw dropped.

"What did I tell you?" Randi handed Neil the bills.

Ty held out his hands, pleading for these people to believe him incapable of such a crime. "I don't know how that money got in my wallet. I did not put it there. I don't even need your money. I have my own resources. Somebody, call the police!"

"Let's do." Randi's eyes glinted. "Then they'll haul you to the slammer—right where you belong."

"Randi!" Winter and Deborah both protested at once.

"They'll fingerprint this room, that's what. Someone came in here last night while I was in the shower." He pointed toward the bathroom. "I called out, and whoever it was left without acknowledging me. I thought Neil or Jeremy returned to get something. Why would anyone stash money in my wallet? Who would want to frame me?" His gaze collided with Winter's.

She looked uncomfortable. Guilty?

Randi picked up the phone. "Shall I report this illegal activity?"

"No!" Winter grabbed the receiver and dropped it in its cradle.

Neil, Deborah, and Jeremy faced her, their eyes showing trust in her judgment.

Ty censored her through different glasses, dark lenses of injustice. To what extreme would she go to make him pay for his wrongdoing ten years ago? To humiliate him. His blood pressure rose at the thought.

"Our fingerprints are plastered across this room." Winter swayed out her hands. "The money has been found. There's no point in calling the police."

Neil nodded and a fraction of Ty's tension eased.

"What? You can't be serious." Randi seemed bent on seeing him put in jail.

"We'll hold a team meeting later and decide where to go from here." Winter strode toward the door. Deborah and Randi followed her.

A second before the door closed, Randi paused and glanced back at him with a menacing look that made his skin crawl.

Twenty-five

Winter hated tension, and her assistant's pores practically oozed it. With her face pinched and her shoulders curled, Randi paced across the small space in the motel room. Her foul mood, combined with her recent attitude toward Ty, made Winter want to have it out with her right now. But this thing about the money weighed on her mind, robbing her of her normal leadership abilities. After the meeting, she'd find out what was going on with her assistant. Above all, their ministry team was committed to following Christ and living in peace.

Honesty too.

She gulped. Yes, there were still some things she needed to confess to the group.

Randi tromped past her chair for the sixth time.

"Won't you sit down?"

"I can't."

Lord, help me.

On the floor with her back against the heater, her legs crossed, and her Bible open in her lap, Deb looked up and smiled.

Just seeing her peaceful demeanor, Winter couldn't help but compare the opposing characteristics of these two roommates. Randi's edginess versus Deb's calm was a contrast as defined as night and day. She longed for Deborah's peace, while she could do without Randi's agitation and discord.

In the vanity mirror, she noticed frown lines forming a "V" between her eyes. She tried to relax her face. Great. Wrinkles at thirty. What she needed was rest. Oh, to sleep for ten uninterrupted hours, escaping the upcoming meeting and its long-term results.

Help us make the right decision, Lord. Give us wisdom and peace.

Did Ty steal the money? She couldn't imagine him doing such a thing. Yet, ever since she heard Randi's burning accusation about the funds being stolen, her thoughts had been churning.

Ugly words. Heated arguments. Each word conjured up cryptic pictures from the past.

* * * *

The thirty-minute commute to the Spokane Airport was dismal for more reasons than the falling rain and the cloudy sky.

"I don't understand why you didn't stay home last night."

"Stop harping, would you?" Ty gripped the steering wheel. "Let me concentrate on driving."

Obviously, he didn't want to talk. Too bad. "I'm not harping. But we aren't going to be together for two weeks." Frustration altered her tone. "I had our five-month anniversary candle burning, romantic music playing, and you never came back until after midnight. Where were you?"

"I had to work." His typical excuse.

"Our last night, and you'd think my husband of five-and-a-half months would want to come home to me. You used to be interested in *us*."

"I told you, I was working late on an important project. I have deadlines." With his jaw clenched, he stared forward.

The way he wouldn't even glance in her direction heightened her anger. "No doubt your Girl Friday was with you." Her words dripped with accusation, but she wouldn't take them back.

"Cindy is my assistant. Of course, she was there!" He thrust his hand through his hair. "We're swamped until this renovation project is finished. You should be glad since it will mean a hefty raise. Not to mention a promotion and a new office for me."

As if she cared about those things. "How many times do I have to tell you money doesn't mean much to me? I was raised to believe family is more important than financial success."

"Don't give me that poor little missionary line. I'm sick of it!" He smacked the steering wheel, and she jumped. "I see how much you like the diamond necklace I bought. How you keep touching it. You didn't hawk the jewel to buy food for the needy, did you? Don't tell me money means nothing. You want a car. You plan to finish your degree. Those things cost big bucks. This job opportunity will make way for greater things, especially if Clayborne's gives me the bonus I deserve. A vacation to Hawaii. A speed boat for cruising Lake Coeur d'Alene." He glanced at her with an odd gleam in his eye. "A little fun might be nice for a change."

"At what expense?" She was close to tears. "Our marriage?"

He glowered at her.

Her hand moved to stroke the diamond-encrusted heart necklace at her throat. She knew it was an expensive piece of jewelry. But she loved it because Ty gave it to her as a belated wedding gift. A tear trickled down her cheek. She faced the window to keep him from seeing and knowing how much he hurt her.

She hated spending their last minutes together fighting, but that's all they were doing lately. Fighting before he left for work. Arguing when he returned home. Silence during dinner.

"I wish you'd change your mind and come with me to Manila." She tried to keep her tone soft. "We could afford it.

I'll get a job to help pay for the tickets when we get back. Please?"

For a heartbeat, she thought he might relent. His eyes looked warm and caring, kindnesses she hadn't seen in him for weeks.

"Are you crazy?" he suddenly yelled. He shook his head like he was talking to the daftest person in the world. "In the middle of the most important project of my life, you ask me this? You don't get it, do you?"

"I guess I don't."

He stopped the Jeep in front of the airport terminal. "I've got to hightail it to work." His pager buzzed. "That'll be Cindy at Clayborne's."

She accepted his brief kiss. Then she watched him accelerate down the road. The flood of tears she'd held back poured from her once she dropped into her window seat on the jet. For a moment, she wondered if maybe she shouldn't go to the Philippines at all.

* * * *

The knock they'd been waiting for brought her back to the present.

Randi rushed to answer it, but her words of welcome died. "What are you doing here?"

Alarmed at her assistant's hard tone, she glanced up to see Ty entering the room behind Neil and Jeremy. She gulped.

"This meeting's about me, isn't it?" Ty frowned.

"You're not welcome. It's a closed meeting." Randi blocked him from moving forward.

"In my opinion, he is allowed. Winter?" Neil's question hung stale in the air.

She met Ty's stony appraisal. His demeanor mirrored the man she was thinking about from ten years ago. His eyes were narrow slits, his lips taut, his arms crossed warrior style, and anger radiated from him.

She took in her assistant's glare aimed at Ty, and his aimed at her.

Resignedly, she nodded at Neil. But the group's decision would have been easier without Ty Williams present.

* * * *

Reading Winter's hesitancy, Ty's heart hardened a notch. Of course, she wouldn't want him to be present. Not if she planned to condemn him for an act she committed. What he wouldn't give for a few minutes alone with her before the meeting began. Then he'd discover the truth. Why was she staring at him with that wounded look in her eyes? Or was that fear?

Did she think he was cruel enough to reveal the depth of their previous relationship? To blab he'd been her husband and knew her personally? No, he pledged not to embarrass her in such a way, and he wouldn't.

He'd envisioned their relationship progressing toward reconciliation, but it seemed that was not to be the case. Since the day he nursed Winter through her sickness, she never sought him out. He'd been too preoccupied with fixing the car to do so. He ached to speak with her now, to remind her of his hope for them to get back together. To find out why she put the money in his wallet, if she did.

Jeremy dropped down on the floor beside Deborah, and like magnets their gazes and hands sought each other's. Ty watched Winter's eyes fill with tears as she looked at them, and he couldn't drag his gaze away from her face. He read her sadness, recognized the longing, the remembering. His chest constricted. And something softened within him.

Sas.

If it were in the realm of possibility to go back in time and fix something, he knew the exact time and place he'd relive.

A decade ago, when she urged him to go with her to the Philippines for her parents' anniversary party, he'd jump at the chance. The money and job promotion would mean nothing. Spending those two weeks with his wife would be the most important time in his life. Then, maybe, she'd still be looking at him like Deborah was gazing into Jeremy's eyes.

He grabbed a hard-backed chair, dragged it near the door, straddled it. And waited.

* * * *

Turning from Jeremy and Deborah, Winter met Ty's shadowed gaze for a second. Long enough to wonder what he was thinking.

"Are we having a meeting or what?" Randi's hands clenched and unclenched. "We've got things to do before tonight's session."

Winter groaned. She'd almost forgotten about the conference.

Thankfully, Neil took control of the meeting. "Let's pray." He prayed for each person on the team. Then he asked for God to shine a light on their hearts, and for honesty to be spoken.

"As is our tradition, each person will have the opportunity to express concerns." He glanced at each of them. "Share what's on your mind in a spirit of love. Then we'll yield it all to our Lord. We may not reach a decision during this meeting, but we'll rid our hearts of frustration and sin. Who'd like to begin?"

Silently, Winter thanked him for his leadership.

"I'd like to read a verse from Ephesians." Deborah lifted the Bible from her lap. "'Be kind and compassionate to one another, forgiving each other, just as in Christ God forgave you.' Whoever took the money from that envelope in Neil's briefcase and put it in Ty's wallet did something wrong. Whether it was him or one of us." Her peaceful smile removed any sting from her words. "We need to forgive each other and go on from here. Bitterness is an evil we must avoid, especially if we want to be open to God's leading.

"Love is what matters. Our love for each other and for God. I forgive whoever did this." Her kindness lightened the oppressive feeling blanketing the room.

"That's right." Jeremy nudged Deborah's arm. "The money's found. The Old Clunker can be fixed—even though I'd rather dump the deathtrap."

No one else spoke for a minute, even though his comment was delivered with some humor.

Neil cleared his throat. "I don't believe Ty stole the money."

Winter exhaled the breath she'd been holding. If he didn't suspect Ty, neither would she. But who hid the money in his wallet? Who wanted him off the team that badly? Randi? Surely her assistant wasn't capable of such meanness.

"He seems like an honest person," Neil continued. "I've felt nothing but Christ's love and fellowship with him. However, the evidence points in his direction. His past. The money was found in his wallet."

Ty grimaced.

"God is the leader of this ministry." Neil spread out his hands. "He sent us a mechanic right when we needed one. That's you, Tyler. We need the car running in a couple of days, or our schedule will be ruined. I agree with Deb. Let's forgive and forget this unfortunate situation happened."

Randi snorted. "Easier said than done." She stomped to the center of the room. "How can we forget this intruder"—she jabbed a finger toward Ty—"was in prison for embezzlement? The last I heard that was stealing money. How do we know funds won't go missing again?"

Ty groaned, but Winter didn't risk meeting his gaze.

"Forgiveness is fine." Randi crossed her arms. "But forgetting? I think we should learn from our mistakes. I vote for Mr. Williams to fix the car, and then we'll buy him a bus ticket back to Coeur d'Alene."

An awkward silence filled the room.

Ty locked gazes with Winter. She nodded at him, hoping he'd say whatever he wanted to say first. As one of the team leaders, she felt her words should conclude the meeting. His stubborn expression said he was waiting for her and he'd wait as long as it took.

She inhaled slowly, gathering her thoughts. "I had a different reaction as each of you shared. When Deborah challenged us to forgive as Jesus forgave us, I felt moved by her words. Jeremy's point that the money has been found is true. Neil gave an accurate assessment—the bills were discovered in Ty's wallet. All of us are witnesses to that fact."

Ty flinched.

"We know he gave his testimony about embezzling money before God saved him." She bit her lip. Was this the time for her to tell them everything? Share what's on your mind in a spirit of love, Neil said. But she wanted to give Ty a chance on their team. And something inside of her didn't believe he took the funds.

"Randi, you're ready to rid us of Ty like he's the plague." She gazed at him. "But my gut feeling is he needs a second chance. Like we all do."

* * * *

Did she say second chance? Ty had stopped staring at her, but now he faced her. Was she sending him a message? Did she mean that they, as a couple, needed a second chance? Or was he reading more into her statement than she intended?

Everyone turned toward him. He saw them waiting for, expecting, an admission of guilt.

He cleared his throat. "I don't have the words you wish to hear. I'm innocent. Honestly, I have no idea how five hundred dollars landed in my wallet. Like I told you, I don't need your money. I have a good job."

Randi made a rude sound.

"That you consider me a thief is devastating. The man who stole and went to prison for it no longer exists. He's dead and buried. I'll fix your car like I said I would, then leave if that's what you want." He stood. "However, I hope you'll let me stay and prove my innocence. Maybe then you'll see your own error in all of this."

He held Winter's gaze, then left the room.

No one stopped him.

Twenty-six

In her front-row seat, Winter tapped her foot to the chorus. In a few minutes, she needed to speak from a heart filled with God's grace and love, despite the day's events, and regardless of how tired she felt.

Or her regrets.

Lord, I feel like a failure. I've struggled with forgiving Ty, even when I thought I had. Now this thing with the stolen money has me confused. The turmoil in our team isn't right. It's not honoring to You. It's not walking in love or peace. I need Your strength and wisdom.

The congregation sang two more worship songs. The time had come for Deborah to sing their theme song.

Winter skimmed the outline resting on her Bible. Why did she feel like she hadn't even prepared?

Is it because of how we treated Ty today? How I treated him?

Her heartbeat quickened. The remembrance of his dark gaze drilling hers with something akin to accusation flashed through her mind. Why had he looked at her with such disappointment? She scanned the congregation, seeking his face, but he wasn't present. Was he working on the car? On a walk? She hoped not. Rain from the coast had been falling incessantly all day.

She did want to see him. For the two of them to talk things over. But how weird would that be, now?

Deborah sang the lyrics to "Only You."

"Change my heart," Winter whispered. "I surrender all I am to You. I love you, Jesus. Open my eyes so I can know You better. Make me into the woman You want me to be. I need Your words. Your love." After a few minutes, a peace she hadn't experienced all day seeped into her spirit, enveloping her like a giant hug. God was working in her, healing her, and changing her, she could tell. She wasn't perfect. Far from it. But she was relying on His grace and strength.

"You are faithful and true," she joined her voice quietly with Deborah's. "Only you … by Your grace and Your mercy, change my life so all can see … only You." On the second time through the song, she stood and sang with the rest of the congregation, praising God with her whole heart.

The look she last saw on Ty's face tiptoed through her mind. *I'm sorry I didn't seek him out earlier. I'll do my best to make things right with him. Tonight, if possible.*

Deborah's song came to a vibrant conclusion, and Winter walked to the lectern.

* * * *

On the floor under the Old Clunker, Ty was tightening a bolt when he heard someone enter the garage. The place had been quiet all evening. At the door's screech, a chill skirted up his spine. He craned his head out from under the car until he had a clear view of the doorway. What he saw caused a tug in his chest. Was she a mirage?

"Ty? It's me." Winter closed a black umbrella, which appeared to have been useless in the stormy weather.

He scooted away from the car until his body cleared the bumper. Slowly, he stood, wincing from the strain in his back.

He wiped his hands on a rag he retrieved from his back pocket. All the while, his gaze was trained on this unexpected visitor. The uncertainty on her face as she stood there looking ready to flee tugged on his heart and compelled him to move closer.

"How was the meeting?"

"Amazing." She smiled. "A husband and wife and three children accepted Jesus. Then, a dozen or so young people stayed afterward to talk with the team about ways to reach out to their community."

"That's wonderful."

"I know." She glanced around the small space as if avoiding his gaze.

Here, looking wary, was the woman he desired more than anything in this world—more than food or sleep or rest. He longed for the chance to hold her like he once had the liberty of doing. To be with her like a man desires to be with the wife he adores, to kiss her passionately, until she knew beyond all doubt and reason that he loved her, would die for her if need be.

She looked so beautiful with her wind-tossed hair and her luscious green eyes gazing everywhere but at him. Why did she come here?

* * * *

Feeling out of place in the tool-laden garage, Winter licked her lips and smoothed wet hair out of her face. Her gaze skimmed over wrenches and car parts spread across the floor, and at a winch-like contraption with *Saul's* painted in black parked near the front of the Old Clunker. She looked everywhere but into those brown eyes drawing closer to her. He seemed so caring. So in love?

Could it be?

She bit her lip.

Why did she walk over this late at night? Randi would be furious. She should have waited until daytime. Sure, she realized she might still harbor feelings for Ty. But she wasn't trying to stir something up with him romantically, was she?

Gulp.

He didn't stop moving until he stood directly in front of her. "Why are you here?" His words came out whisper soft. His breath fanning across her cheeks smelled of wintergreen candy.

"I-I was worried." She felt shy standing next to him. "You weren't at the church. I wanted to make sure you were all right."

Now I'm going to turn around and leave.

Except she hadn't dealt with the issue she promised God she'd settle tonight.

* * * *

Ty smiled at her, hoping she could tell how good her words made him feel. *I was worried* translated in his mind to *I love you.*

He reached out and stroked away a wet strand of hair resting on her cheek and tucked it behind her ear. His palm skittered across her skin. He saw her gulp.

He gazed at her lovely face, taking in each detail he missed over the years. Jade-green eyes, irresistible dimple, sweet lips. Unable to resist touching her again, he slid his finger down her cheek. Her soft, rain-kissed skin sent warmth rushing through him. The fact she wasn't pulling away made him think she was enjoying the contact as much as he was.

Did she want to be with him like he wanted to be with her? Was it possible she still cared for him? A longing to hold her and kiss her took over his thoughts. He wanted to remind her he really did love her.

"Oh, Sassy." Leaning in closer, his cheek came to rest against her hair. He felt her stiffen, but she didn't push him away. He held her like that, gently, but close, allowing her the chance to move if she wanted. Damp locks brushed against his eyes, tickled his skin. Smelling the apple scent of her shampoo, he inhaled deeply. The alluring aroma brought back scenes from another time and place. "I've missed holding you so much."

"Ty—" Her voice cautioned him to go slowly, maybe to step back. But even as she said it, he felt her relax against him.

He tipped up her chin and gazed deeply into her eyes. She stared back at him, watching him. Seeing the welcoming look he remembered cross her face, ever so softly, he leaned in and touched his lips against hers.

Her eyes widened just before he closed his own.

The kiss was ultimately gentle as if they weren't touching at all. But when he felt the slightest quiver beneath his mouth, it sent his senses reeling. "I love you, sweetheart." He deepened the kiss.

He'd daydreamed this moment to exhaustion, but dreams fell short of the real thing. She fit perfectly in his arms like she always belonged, had never been away. She was his and—

* * * *

"Ty, no. I can't!" She nearly tripped over the car parts in her effort to get away from him.

"But—"

She braced out her hands toward him, her eyes beseeching him to understand, to stay back.

What had she done? What had she allowed?

After all these years of not permitting romance in her life, in one moment she blew it all and let Ty kiss her. Why did she let him? Or, heaven forbid, did she kiss him? She trembled at the possibility. Then, as she stared into warm brown eyes that said he'd like to kiss her again, she found herself inching forward. Traitorous emotions. But what could it hurt if her fingers roamed through his tousled hair? Or if she gently wiped the grease smear from beneath his eye?

His lips looked so kissable. And now that the kiss had happened …

She leaned in. But then, a dark chill rushed through her. She pushed her hands against his chest.

His shadowed eyes showed confusion. "I just want to hold you. That's all." He opened his arms, but she scurried to the far side of the car.

Fighting back tears, an almost-forgotten picture crept like a snake into her thoughts, hissing that this man could not be trusted.

* * * *

The two weeks she spent in the Philippines had dragged on forever, as if everyone was on normal time while her life moved in slow motion. She was anxious to get home to her husband. They spoke only once on the telephone. Ty was distracted, not focused on what she told him about her parents' anniversary celebration. Her whispered "I love you" wasn't returned, but she excused it. He was tired and overworked.

Now, on her way home from the Spokane airport in a taxi a day early, she couldn't wait to surprise him. Her heart raced as romantic homecoming scenarios waltzed through her thoughts. She imagined their kiss. The way his arms would wrap around her in welcome. The loving words she'd whisper in his ear.

He'd probably be cleaning the apartment in anticipation of her arrival tomorrow, even though it was late at night. Most likely he hadn't tidied up once during the entire two-week period. But that didn't matter. Nothing mattered tonight except for reuniting with her husband.

Misunderstandings, like they had before she left, mustn't come between them again. She missed him too much to allow petty arguments to control their marriage. Everything was going to be different now. She'd see to it.

At their apartment building, she tipped the taxi driver. Then, seeing their Jeep in its parking spot, she nearly skipped up the stairs. What would Ty say when he saw her? What would he do? Maybe he'd pick her up in his arms and carry her across the threshold like he did six months ago. Or, maybe, he'd dance with her and tell her how much he missed her. She'd like that.

Eagerly, she dug through her purse for her keys. Then remembering she left them on the dresser before leaving on her trip, she knocked on the door. Not wanting to give herself away, she didn't tap out her usual "Shave and a Haircut" knock. Instead, she rapped three solid knocks, then waited.

Again, she knocked, louder this time.

Was that laughter coming from inside the apartment? Was the TV on?

The door suddenly opened.

"How much do I—?" Ty stood staring at her, his mouth wide open.

"Ty!" She threw herself into his arms. "I missed you so much I came home a day early. Surprised?"

"Oh, yes."

She kissed him on the mouth but was disappointed by his lack of enthusiasm. Why wasn't he holding her close like she held him?

"Who is it, Tyler?" a female voice cut through the room bathed in shadows.

Their kiss broke. Winter's arms slid from his neck. In disbelief, her gaze plowed past her husband's troubled eyes, beyond his bare chest, into the living room she decorated with garage-sale treasures and her precious souvenirs from the Philippines. Her five-month anniversary candle glowed on the coffee table. Empty wine bottles littering the table and couch seemed out of place considering neither she nor Ty drank.

Apparently, he'd changed.

"Tyler." The word whistled through the air like an incoming arrow aimed right for Winter's heart. Her gaze clashed with Ty's. *Guilty*.

The woman stepped from the shadows into the candlelight. She had flowing blond hair and a towel wrapped around her with a "W" monogram.

Winter knew the worst thing she could have imagined happening in her marriage had happened.

"No!" The shock and heartbreak threatened to suffocate her. Then she fled into the night.

* * * *

"Sassy?" Where had he lost her? She stood there as if frozen, her face pasty white. "Are you all right? Do you want to sit down?" He pointed toward the corner. "There's a chair over there."

"No, I can't stay. I wanted to check on you. That's all. I didn't mean for any of this to happen." She stepped over tools and parts, creating more space between them. "I told you not to call me Sassy."

"That's who you are to me."

"I'm not that person. Not anymore."

"To me you are." He smiled at her, but her glare subdued his grin. What changed between them in the last thirty seconds? A weary sigh rumbled through his chest. "Where's the bloodhound? I'm surprised Randi would let you out of her sight this late." He heard the edge of bitterness in his tone—maybe because of hurt pride over Winter's rejection, or maybe because Randi annoyed him so much—but he didn't try to hide his feelings as he faced her from the opposite side of the car.

Her cheeks hued pink. "I'm playing hooky from sleeping."

"She thinks you're asleep?"

She nodded with a hint of embarrassment, and he caught

a glimpse of her mischievous side he loved and sometimes dreaded when they were married.

"The whole pillows-under-the-sheet-in-the-shape-of-a-body thing?"

"Sort of. She'll be mad when she finds out I'm gone."

"No doubt." He followed her around the car until he was standing close, but not too close. The measures she took to walk over in the pouring rain and check on him touched him. Kissing her again flitted through his mind. But the way she dodged away every time he stepped toward her kept him from doing so. While part of him ached to pursue her, he could see something had altered between them since their kiss.

"Why were you worried about me?"

She drew a line along the car's navy pinstripe with her fingertip. "Things were unsettled today. You left angry. I was concerned."

"Concerned for me? That's nice." He took another step closer.

"Yes, as a team member."

Inwardly, he bristled. "You're saying as the leader you wouldn't want discord among the ranks?"

"Of course not."

Yet she walked over here alone to see him. "You weren't concerned about me … as a man you once loved?" He held his breath, waiting.

She huffed and glared at him. "Ty Williams, until last week, I barely thought of you."

Another zinger.

The hurt landed somewhere in his gut. "I couldn't let you go as easily." He lowered his voice. "You've been on my mind since the day you left me."

"I told you—oh, never mind." She nearly ran to the exit, then stopped. "Did you do it?"

Huh? Where was she in their timeline? Did she want to talk about *that* now?

Following her, but keeping his hands stuffed in his coverall pockets, he wondered if this was the right time for such a discussion. She said she forgave him, but her pain remained a solid wall between them. If they could communicate about the past, and he assured her of his love, maybe her guard would come down a little and she'd allow him some space in her life. "You mean about Cindy?"

"No! Let's not dredge that up."

"We have to sometime." He wanted to wrap his arms around her and comfort her, but he didn't. "I love you. And I want you to be my wife again."

She drew in a sharp breath.

Maybe that was too much too soon. But he didn't back down from what he said. "You and I need to face what happened between us, and then we can bury it. Not that I expect you to forget everything instantly. But with God's grace, we can let go of the bad memories. Maybe you could learn to love me again?" He smiled, hoping she could see the invitation in his gaze.

"I meant, the money." Her tone turned gritty. "Did you take the money?"

A lightning bolt of anger slashed through him. Since the moment she entered the garage, not once did he think about the money found in his wallet today. He was simply overjoyed for her to be with him. That she cared about him. Now, the group's accusations flooded him again. He shuffled several feet away. "I've given you my answer to that." He heard the sharpness in his tone, but he didn't apologize for it. He picked up a wrench off the floor and dropped it into the toolbox. Metal against metal clattered in the still garage.

"This is me, Ty. For my hearing alone." She stepped

beside him and placed her hand on his wrist. "Did you take the money?"

He stared at her hand resting against his skin, the first physical contact between them she initiated. He looked her squarely in the eye. "You would know that better than me."

"What does that mean?"

Reaching for her hand, he drew it close to his nose and inhaled her vanilla fragrance.

"What are you doing?" She jerked her hand away.

"Gathering evidence. I think you did it." Like an interrogator, he circled her. The hot rush of blame he felt earlier in the day rose in him.

"Did what?"

"Took the money. Buried it in my wallet. Left the room when you heard me calling." His voice accelerated as he eyed her from every side. Her face blanched, but he went on fueled by the injustices she and her team had heaped on him. "I guess you felt justified. Did it feel good to watch me squirm before your friends?" He paused and leaned in closer. "Was it worth the effort to get rid of me?" He heard the snide tone in his voice, but the words kept coming as if propelled from some unseen force. "Are you still afraid I'll tell them about us? About our *divorce*? It might sully your reputation, huh?"

Smack!

The slap across his cheek cracked loudly in the small garage. The hit took him by surprise. He touched his stinging face and glared at her. She stared back just as intensely.

"Remember th-this." Her voice broke. "I did not invite you back into my life." She wiped tears from her face. "I decided to give you a chance, because"—she sniffed, and it looked like she was barely holding herself together—"I saw a change in you. I wanted to see what God's will might be for us. I never condemned you in front of my team members, and I didn't hide money in your wallet." A heartrending sob burst from her.

Now he felt like a heel. Was that his voice he heard in his conscience yelling at her? At the woman he was trying to reconcile with? The one he said he loved?

Man, oh, man.

Where was the love of Christ shining in his life now? Where was the tender heart he professed to have for Winter? The one where he said he'd die for her if necessary?

He moved forward, aching with guilt, hoping to hug her, and apologize, but she pushed him away and turned her back toward him.

"Um, Winter, look—"

Not knowing what he could say, he knew he needed to fix this—maybe to mention he was a jerk or a stupid idiot—but his words didn't come fast enough. Before he had a chance to say anything else, she grabbed her umbrella and ran into the night.

His hand moved to his cheek where his skin felt hot from her slap. He shook his head in disbelief. What started as an amazingly tender moment between them turned into a disaster. How he wished he were someone else long enough to kick himself in the seat of the pants.

Grabbing his jacket, and not caring about the raindrops plastering his hair to his head, he followed her into the downpour. Never mind the frustration strumming through him over having kissed her and then arguing with her like a fool, he had to assure himself of her safe return to the motel.

The slap she dealt him bruised his heart. And it made him realize she could defend herself. Even so, he felt protective.

He loved her. Still wanted her for his wife.

If God, and she, would only give him another chance.

Twenty-seven

Shortly before dawn, Ty fell asleep. Putting the engine back together, mixed with his frustration over what transpired between him and Winter, kept him awake until he crashed on the dilapidated green chair in the corner. The lumpy furniture offered little comfort, but after folding his body into the only possible position his frame would fit, he dropped off to sleep.

A few hours later, the screech of the garage door jerked him awake. Did Winter come back to talk? He sat up.

High heels clicked across the cement floor. Not Winter's. Randi strode toward him, her fierce gaze latched on him like a shark after its dinner. Neil, Jeremy, and Deborah trailed behind her.

He wanted to ignore them, but one glance at their troubled faces shot him out of his chair. "What's wrong?" his morning voice croaked. What did they think he did now?

"Where is she?" Randi stopped so close she nearly stomped on his shoes. "What have you done with her?" Her body language screamed she'd like nothing better than to punch him.

Tensing, he wondered why the others didn't hold her back or yell at her for acting this way.

"I demand to know what you've done with her!" Randi's fervor was like a neglected teapot overflowing with steam and boiling water. She grabbed the unzipped portion of his coveralls. He took a step back, but she clung tenaciously. "Where is she?"

Lack of sleep negated his usual quick thinking. "I don't have the foggiest idea what you're screaming about." He raked his hand through his already tousled hair.

Neil clasped Randi's arms and pulled her away, finally. "Winter is missing."

"Missing?" Adrenaline shot through Ty. How could she be missing? He watched her walk back to the motel and had seen to it that she arrived safely. "You've looked everywhere?"

"Yes." Neil nodded. "Everywhere we know to look. When we couldn't find her at the motel or the restaurant, we came over here."

"What about her cell phone? Did she call?"

"That's the problem," Deborah spoke. "We can't find either of our cell phones. We tried both numbers with the motel phone without getting a response."

Randi covered her face with her hands like she was overcome with emotion. "Someone left pillows in her bed to make me think she was there. If you've harmed her, I'll—"

Neil stepped between her and Ty, stopping whatever she planned to do. "Randi! Why don't you head back to the motel and get some coffee?"

She stared back at him, unmoving.

Her words finally registered. "You say there were pillows under her covers this morning?" Ty rubbed his hand over his unshaven chin.

"You should know." Randi squinted at him.

"I know that last night Winter told me she put pillows in her bed before walking over here to talk with me."

Randi lunged toward him. Again, Neil stopped her.

"She came to the garage last night?" Neil's eyebrows arched.

"She walked over late. Said she was concerned after yesterday's meeting."

"What did you do to her?" Randi's voice screeched.

"I didn't *do* anything. We talked. She left. I followed her to the motel to make sure she got back safely." How could she not be there? Had she been kidnapped? Or hurt? *Oh, God, please, no.* He had to find her and tell her how sorry he was for his harsh, judgmental words.

"Was she upset when she left?" Neil tipped his head and stared at Ty.

His hesitation cost him as the team adviser inspected the left side of his face. Ty rubbed his hand over the spot where Winter hit him.

"My second question would be, is that a slap mark?"

Ty swallowed hard. Was there any way around that question, other than refusing to answer?

"I knew it! You came on to her, didn't you?" Randi shouted. Then almost whispered, "Poor Winter."

"Oh, cut it out, will you? Yes, she was agitated." He wished he didn't have to confess the truth. "And, yes, she slapped me." At their gasps, he rushed on. "But not because I pushed myself on her." Their kiss romped through his thoughts, but he buried it under the reminder that the kiss they shared was mutually enjoyed. At first, anyway.

"What was she angry about?" Neil probed.

Ty closed his eyes, hating this interrogation. Winter was missing. They were desperate for answers. He sucked in a shaky breath. "She grilled me about the money found in my wallet. And I, well, I accused her of planting the bills to get rid of me." He couldn't reveal his heated words about her not wanting the team to know of their shared past.

"Are you insane?" Randi cried.

"I know it sounds stupid, but I had my reasons. And she got angry."

A strange look crossed Randi's face, almost like she was pleased. But that didn't make sense. In the next second, she covered the expression with a frown.

"That doesn't sound like Winter." Deborah shook her head.

"No, it doesn't," Jeremy agreed.

"You followed her all the way to the motel? She never left your sight?" Neil pressed.

"She walked in the front entrance. I jogged back in the rain." He stared into four sets of eyes drilling him for more information. "What she may have done after I returned, I don't know. She has a mind of her own."

"You kissed her, didn't you?"

Stunned by Randi's blunt question, he clamped his teeth down. When it came to his and Winter's private lives, he didn't have to answer.

"That's irrelevant, Randi." Neil glared at her.

"Winter's stuff is my business!" She jabbed her finger at Ty. "Did you kiss her?"

The air in the room crackled with tension. He stared at the floor, scraped the rubber edge of his shoe against a black paint blotch on the cement, avoiding eye contact with the team.

A second later, she lunged at him.

"Randi, stop!" Neil tried holding her back.

Ty countered her attack the best he could. He grabbed her wrists and propelled them upward. With her hands above her head, he inhaled a familiar fragrance. Vanilla. Only the aroma wasn't sweet as it was on Winter's skin. On Randi the scent smelled bitter. It stunned him as much as the slap did last night. Nausea roiled through him. What a fool he was to accuse Winter of stashing the money in his wallet. She was as innocent as he was.

Here stood the culprit!

Lightning fast, Randi yanked her foot back and nailed him hard in the shin. He gasped and stumbled backward.

"Randi!" Deborah yelled.

"That'll be quite enough." Neil wrapped his arms around Randi's shoulders and propelled her toward Deborah.

Hobbling in a circle, Ty held his breath to control words that threatened to erupt on the vixen. As if in a distance, he heard Deb and Jeremy trying to calm Randi down, but he was seeing red. "Did you call the police?"

"If we don't find her soon, we will." Neil's face was lined with worry. "Deborah, please take Randi back to the motel."

Good.

"No!" Randi jerked away.

Neil intervened before she attacked Ty again. "You will stay at the motel until you and I have had a discussion about all this." His expression said he'd had enough of her foolishness.

Finally.

"Don't fire me," Randi begged. "I'm worried sick about Winter, that's all."

Neil stared at her for a long moment as if weighing the truth behind her words. "Deb?"

Deborah nodded. "Let's go. It'll be okay."

Randi whimpered as the team musician wrapped her arms around her shoulders and led her out of the garage.

Ty could only hope Neil gave her the boot. He grabbed the rag out of his back pocket and rubbed a grease spot clean from the front passenger door. He had to get his feelings under control so he could think straight. Where would Winter go to get away in Salem, Oregon? To get away from him?

Oh, man.

"Why don't we split up and search the area?" Jeremy suggested. "Maybe she's at the church or a restaurant. How about the pastor's house? She might've stopped there if she needed to talk with someone." He didn't accuse Ty, but his gaze zeroed in on him.

"Good idea." Neil nodded. "Jeremy, go to the church and check every room. She might be praying somewhere in the building. Then stop by the parsonage. See if Pastor Jay and his wife have been in contact with her since last night. I'll hit the cafes and parks in the neighborhood. Let's meet back at the motel lobby in two hours."

"Right." Jeremy left.

"What about me?" Ty faced Neil. "Where should I look?" *She's my wife!* He wanted to shout it.

"Well ..." At Neil's single-word response, Ty's gut clenched. The leader of Passion's Prayer didn't consider him a team member enough to assign him a task. Because of his ex-con status? Because he was the last one to see Winter? Or because she left her handprint on his face?

"Why don't you stay here?"

The words were kindly spoken, but Ty couldn't accept them. "I want to help look for her. Please, let me search with you guys."

"I think she might come back here." Neil put his hand on Ty's shoulder. "Especially if she left angry, slapped you." Looking embarrassed, he glanced away. "If I know her like I think I do, she'll return to apologize. Her temper sometimes gets the best of her, but she'll let you know she's sorry." He clapped Ty's arm. "Stay, and if you want, meet us at the motel in a couple of hours."

"But you don't—" *Understand*, he finished silently. Ty groaned. Neil didn't grasp how well he knew Winter's disposition. She had a good heart, a passionate spirit, but this time she had just cause for striking out at him. Why did he unload on her in such a mean way? If he could turn back the clock and say something reasonable to her instead of ranting like a mad man, he'd do so in a heartbeat. Did something terrible happen to her on her way back to the room? He should have followed her all the way to her floor, ensuring her safety. Unfortunately, they didn't separate on the best of terms.

After Neil left, Ty shuffled over to the chair he slept in and knelt. He moaned Winter's name in prayer. "Protect her from harm, Father. Please, allow me another chance to make things right, to show her I've changed. I'm sorry for my attitude about the missing money. I overreacted and blew it. Heal our hearts, Lord. Show me how to love Winter the way You want me to. The way she needs." He stayed on his knees praying until it was time for him to meet the team at the motel.

When he stepped into the lobby, Deborah, Randi, and Jeremy were seated in cushioned chairs facing the center of the room. Randi crossed her arms and didn't make eye contact, which was fine with him. Deb smiled in welcome.

"Any news?"

At Deborah's and Jeremy's negative head shake, he sat down and waited with them for Neil's arrival.

A short time later, the team leader pushed open the glass door and rushed into the lobby. "Anything?"

The four shook their heads.

"Guess I should make that call to the police." Neil sat down, and his shoulders sagged like he carried a great weight.

Lord, help us.

After two minutes of no one saying anything, the glass door opened again, and Winter breezed into the lobby as if she'd just been on a short walk. Her hair was windblown, her face ruddy, her eyes vibrant. Ty stared at her, gaping. A glance at the others revealed their equally shocked expressions.

Winter had company too. Beside her, David Michaels stood there with a huge grin on his face.

Could the day get any worse?

Her laughter about something David said crashed over Ty like a tidal wave. What happened since he last saw her? And where did Pastor Michaels come from? He lived in Coeur d'Alene, Idaho, a good eight-hour drive away. Did he fly into town to see her? How could he just show up?

Beside Neil, Ty stood, the soreness in his spine twisting his tense nerves.

"Winter, you're safe." Randi lunged across the room, wrapping her in a tight embrace. Deb followed. The three were soon hugging and giggling.

Neil didn't budge from where he stood. His body language mirrored that of an enraged father who spent hours searching for a daughter out too late on a date. Ty didn't feel like her father, but he didn't appreciate how this looked. He remained by Neil, waiting for the bad news.

"Where have you been?" Neil crossed his arms. "Didn't you realize we'd be sick with worry? Since six this morning we've been hunting for you—ever since Randi found pillows in your bed instead of you." His voice rose a few notches. "What's the meaning of this?"

Winter had the decency to look humble. Not that Ty was buying it. "I'm so sorry, Neil, and everyone else. It was a spur-of-the-moment thing. I acted hastily. I apologize for making you worry."

Ty glanced back and forth between her and the pastor. Where did they go? Was she with him *all* night? How could things have gotten this crazy since last night when he kissed her?

"Didn't you get my voicemail messages? I left two."

"No. We couldn't find the cell phone," Neil answered gruffly.

"Oh, no." She stepped away from Randi and Deborah and returned to David's side. "I don't know what to say. I called last night to tell you I was going for a drive with David. Then I phoned again a few hours ago. I didn't want Randi worrying when I went for a walk last night, so I put a couple of pillows in the bed. It was silly, I know." Her gaze locked with Ty's for a split second, then she faced the others. "When I got back to the motel, David was here." She swayed her hand toward him and smiled as if thrilled with the pastor's presence.

Unbelievable.

"His arrival took me by surprise. We went to the restaurant and had coffee. One thing led to another, and we decided to take a drive. We talked and talked, and before we knew it, we were already to the Columbia River."

"I wanted to keep driving all the way back to Coeur d'Alene." Pastor Michaels chuckled.

I bet you did. Ty gritted his teeth.

Winter laughed. "I'm sorry for causing alarm. I thought we'd return before you woke up. But we were hungry and stopped for breakfast in Portland." She shrugged and grinned at David again.

Ty's heart dropped to his shoes.

Wasn't it God's will for him to reunite with Winter? Had he misunderstood the leading of his heart to join up with Passion's Prayer? To do everything within his power to show her how much he still loved her?

Like a spectator, he watched the group exit the lobby. Laughing and joking, they moved toward the restaurant, the six of them complete without him. Even Neil's stance was more relaxed. He walked beside David, engaged in conversation. Apparently, all was forgiven.

Standing alone, reeling with regret, Ty watched Winter walk away from him for what he feared might be the last time. Why did Pastor Michaels show up? Did Winter change her mind about dating him?

Heavyhearted, Ty trudged toward the exit. Glancing back, his gaze snared with Randi's. Outside the restaurant's entrance, she paused. A mocking smile flitted across her lips. Was this whole misadventure part of her scheme to keep Winter away from him? Would she go to such an extreme? That Randi might have the power to sabotage his plans caused a deep ache in his gut.

He hoped Neil didn't forget about her rude actions earlier. Because if he did, things were bound to get a lot worse.

Twenty-eight

Each step he took forced Ty farther from the motel, away from how he hoped things would turn out, and away from the woman he wanted to spend the rest of his life with. How could he bear saying goodbye to her again? He still had bad dreams of last time.

Even after ten years, he remembered that dreadful night, how she asked him if he was surprised to see her. Surprised? Stunned. Gut-punched shocked. And deathly afraid.

He'd answered the door expecting a pizza delivery, not her. When she wrapped her arms around his neck and kissed him like a woman in love with her husband, as if he wasn't about to rip out her heart, he just held her. Overcome with guilt, hot juices rolled up his throat.

He appeased his conscience that his wife wouldn't find out. She wouldn't get hurt over what she didn't know. But that was before he watched their love die a horrific death.

When she left him, his heart splintered, a fault line of despair, as the woman he vowed to be faithful to for his whole life fled, her faith in him crushed beyond repair. He didn't think it possible to hurt so much, so suddenly.

But he had. And he did.

He couldn't give her up now. He wouldn't quit trying. Not without making every possible effort.

Lord, help me. What should I do?

Picturing the way she smiled at David back at the motel churned in his stomach. His throat tightened. He'd like to tell the pastor to take a hike.

Tell her your heart, whispered through him.

He stopped walking.

Is that You, Lord? Did You notice she looked happy with David Michaels? She barely noticed me. I don't think she's ready to handle what's in my heart.

She's strong. Tell her your heart, reverberated within him.

Doubts. Questions. Insecurities. They all hit him at once.

What if she married David? Was Pastor Michaels a better match for her since he was already involved in ministry?

But, no, that couldn't be God's plan. Winter was—or had been—Ty's wife, not David's. That meant he had to do all he could to win her back, to prove they were still supposed to be together.

For better or for worse, till death do us part. What God has joined together, let man not separate.

The desire that smoldered in his chest for ten long years rose within him. Somehow, he had to finish what he set out to do when he joined up with Passion's Prayer. To show Winter he loved her and that he was sorry—

No! He wouldn't keep treading the ancient ground. Instead of sorrow, he prayed she'd see the new man, the one who wanted a God-blessed future with her, the one who loved her beyond words, the man who cared more about her than he did about himself.

Enough to let her go?

He gulped.

He couldn't think about that right now. He didn't plan on

giving up on hope. Whatever it took, he'd fight for the woman he loved.

He stroked his rough chin, wishing he'd taken time to shower and shave. But that couldn't be helped now. How could he get Winter away from the team and David long enough to talk with her alone? He'd have to ask, and pray she responded favorably.

Making his decision, he took off at a sprint and ran straight for the motel. At the lobby window, he slowed down when he saw how wild his hair looked in the reflection. He smoothed his fingers over loose strands, then he scrubbed at a grease spot on his cheek. A couple of hours of sleep curled up in that chair hadn't improved his look of exhaustion. And the welt on his face stood out like he lost a fistfight. His physical appearance wouldn't make a good impression, but hopefully she'd see past the way he looked, straight into his heart.

He took one more steadying breath, then he strode into the motel restaurant, ready to face her and, if he had to, make a fool of himself in order to declare his love.

A short distance from the team, he paused and watched the group. Winter laughed, her face glowing. Even Randi appeared relaxed. Did he have the right to disrupt their meal? To create conflict? He was the outsider who came along because he begged to be included, even though Winter didn't approve of him joining them in the first place.

Deborah, the first to notice him, waved and smiled. "Have you eaten lunch? Come order some food. You must be starving."

"Uh, not right now." Not until things were settled.

"Why are you here?" Randi glared at him.

Ignoring her question, he forced himself to use Winter's proper name. He knew she wouldn't like it if he slipped up and called her "Sas" in front of the others. "Winter, may I speak with you privately?"

Surprised glances turned his way, including Winter's.

"No way." Randi dropped her spoon with a loud clunk. "Whatever you have to say can be shared in front of us, her *friends.*"

"Randi." Neil's voice carried a gruff warning. "After we're finished here, you, Winter, and I are going to have a meeting."

Randi didn't say another word, but her barb hit a sore spot in Ty. Unexpected tears blurred his eyes. He blinked to absorb them, hoping no one noticed.

By the concerned look in Winter's eyes, she did. "I have a moment."

He didn't want her to feel sorry for him, but he needed to talk with her. "Great."

She set her napkin on the table and stood. "I'm going to talk with Ty. I'll be right back."

Relief pulsed through him.

"Winter, I don't—" Randi started to speak, but Neil interrupted her by loudly clearing his throat.

David stood. "Would you like me to go with you?"

Winter shook her head. "That's not—"

"Yes!" Randi patted David's arm. "She needs someone like you to protect her."

Ty rolled his eyes.

"I'll be fine." Winter's smile seemed to reassure David. "Finish your meal."

Before they left the table, Ty noticed Neil's gaze trained on him. It seemed as if he was offering his blessing for Ty to make amends. He returned the look with a brief nod.

Winter preceded him out the door. The delicate aroma of vanilla mixed with a hint of apple shampoo tickled his senses. He placed his palm lightly at her back and directed her away from the restaurant, toward the lawn at the far side of the building where various topiaries decorated the motel grounds.

Near the farthest edge of the grass, they stopped by a lion-shaped bush in need of a trim and faced each other.

In the bright glare of sunshine, she gasped. "Oh, Ty, I'm so sorry." She touched his cheek.

He gulped. "It's nothing."

"I feel terrible." She withdrew her hand. "What craziness came over me last night? That I lost control like that is embarrassing. Please forgive me?"

"Don't worry about it." He didn't want them using their time talking about that. "I'm sorry for provoking you."

She glanced away. "Last night when we were talking, I felt pretty mixed up." Her face brightened. "Today, I'm more focused."

"Because of Pastor Michaels?" His tone came out more accusing than he intended.

"Not in the way you're implying. But the man's timing was impeccable. The way he showed up when I needed a friend, when I felt so confused, was perfect." She shook her head like she was still amazed. "We talked about a lot of things. And the drive helped me relax."

Could they not talk about David Michaels? Ty reined in his thoughts. "Did you tell him?"

"About the money? Yes."

"No, I don't care about the money!"

Her eyes widened.

Now that he knew who was behind that shenanigan, the subject disgusted him. He'd like to tell Winter his suspicions, but first he wanted to talk to Randi and get her to confess to the wrongdoing. "I meant"—he softened his tone—"did you tell Pastor Michaels about us? About our past?" This conversation was turning out all wrong, not the romantic interaction he wanted. Why couldn't he say what he meant?

Tell her your heart.

I'm trying. Really, I am.

"No, I didn't." She sighed. "Now, what did you want to talk with me about? I shouldn't keep the others waiting. You know how protective Randi can get."

This hardly seemed like the right place. And yet, he needed to broach the subject. "I wanted to talk to you about us. About our past."

"You mean about ten years ago?"

"Yes. Let's say what needs to be said. Then bury the past, as much as we can. I love you. I need you in my life. Don't you miss me at all?" He smiled in a way he hoped would remind her of the love they once shared. Or maybe of the sweet kiss they shared last night.

"I can't have this conversation right now." She stepped away.

He moved in front of her. "Sweetheart, you're the wife of my youth. In Corinthians, it says if we're separated, we should either remain unmarried or be reconciled to—"

"Yes"—she cut into his words—"I know the verses. But I can quote others justifying us never being together. You know that's true."

"Agreed. And those are some of the things we need to talk about." He tucked a strand of hair behind her ear. "You hold my heart, even now when you're toying with the idea of accepting David Michaels into your life."

"Whoa." She thrust out her hands. "I didn't say I felt that way about him. We took a drive and talked. We're friends. That's it."

Relief washed over him. "Oh, well, I'm sorry. I guess I jumped the gun."

"I guess you did."

"But the way you took off with him, then came back all giggly and happy, what should I think?" What must David think?

"I needed time away from *our* tension, that's what you can think."

He felt the old kick of guilt.

"And it was nice spending time with someone who gets ministry stuff."

Unlike him.

But, at least, she wasn't thinking about marrying David. That made him want to jump up and down. Then his thoughts sobered. "I want you to know I'm sorry about what I said and how I talked to you last night. It was stupid. The whole blame thing with the money started to get to me, and I took it out on you."

"I'm sorry too."

When she smiled at him, his heart seemed to restart. "About that talk?"

"Sometime, yes. Not now."

"Fair enough." But he longed to say something meaningful before she returned to Pastor Michaels. "I've been thinking a lot about the promise I made to you ten years ago."

She went stalk still, her green eyes watching him.

"I still plan to honor my vows."

"Ty—"

"I know, you aren't ready to talk about it. But please believe me when I say I love you. And I'm thinking, by the way you kissed me last night, you might still love me too."

A soft gasp left her lips.

Had he been too bold?

But then, she stared back at him with an openness, a sweetness in her gaze, that transcended the years they were apart. He couldn't help himself. He leaned in and touched his lips to hers. Once.

It was all he could do not to kiss her again. He pulled back a couple of inches, waiting to see what her reaction might be.

She didn't kiss him back, but she didn't shove him away, either. Did she still love him? She nibbled her bottom lip, a sign she was pondering something. Then her gaze went from staring into his eyes to glancing at his lips.

Oh, sweetheart.

As if the past became entangled with the present, as if no timeline existed between this moment standing on a lawn in Salem, Oregon, and the last kiss they shared as a married couple, she kissed him. Hungrily. Eagerly. With stark amazement, he met her affection, pulling her against him, relishing the feel of her in his arms.

Oh, Sas.

* * * *

Winter's fingers combed through Ty's hair, toying with its silky texture. She kissed his familiar lips and it was like coming home after being gone for a long time. She ran her hand down his scruffy chin. Felt his rapid heartbeat beneath her palm on his chest.

Then she gulped. What was she doing kissing this man? She didn't date, let alone kiss a guy, even if he was her husband ten years ago.

And yet, she didn't walk away from him, either. She stared into his dazed eyes. Eyes that drew her closer. Made her want to touch his mouth with hers again.

All day she'd relived last night's kiss. This one turned out equally as sweet. Maybe better. But what was she going to do now that they kissed twice? She could hardly act aloof, especially since she kissed him this time.

Not that she was ready to say she was in love with him. Attracted to him? Oh, yes.

His grin widened, and she couldn't hold back her own smile. He'd kissed her like a man fully in love, and she returned that kiss for all she was worth. And it felt so right. When he drew her back into his arms, hugged her to him, she rested her face against his chest and sighed, loving the calm she felt in his embrace.

But then the complications of her traveling ministry and her life as a public speaker ran through her thoughts. If Randi found her in Ty's arms, there was going to be an ugly scene. Winter pressed her hands against his chest and backed up, informing him with her gaze that they were all done kissing—had to be, for now.

"I have to go." She had some serious pondering to do about her and Ty before she'd be ready to endure Randi's scrutiny.

He clasped her right hand between both of his. "Can we meet for dinner?"

"I'm not ready for that conversation. And then there's—"

"David."

"He's here for a couple of days."

"Did he ask you to date him?"

Knowing she had no obligation to answer that question, she considered his inquiry. "He did, but I told him no, again. I don't date, you know?" She stared at Ty then laughed. She messed up her no-dating philosophy with those kisses. She certainly had some issues to pray about. "I still have to get ready for tonight's meeting."

"When can I see you again?"

"I need to think about this before I know whether or not—"

His lips gently fell against hers, surprising her, yet silencing her doubts.

"Have a little faith," he whispered against her cheek.

Okay.

"Winter!"

Uh-oh. She turned around. Randi stood by the motel entrance with her hands on her hips, her golf-ball-sized eyes bulging with fury.

"I warned you I had to go." Winter put more space between

her and Ty. "I need a little time before explaining everything to my team. But I will. Promise." She squeezed his hand, then left him standing by the lion-shaped bush.

Did she love him? What of her plans to stay single and focused on the ministry? What would happen to Passion's Prayer if she became romantically involved with him?

She probably shouldn't have let him kiss her, last night or just now. But now that it happened, how could she forget?

"What were you doing kissing that degenerate?" Randi demanded.

"I still like him." She met Randi's befuddled expression with a grin. It was true. She liked Ty Williams. A lot.

But do I love him?

Maybe there was one more thing she should tell him. Ignoring Randi's grumpy expression, she jogged back to Ty. "Okay."

"Okay?"

"We could meet somewhere. I love ice cream."

A smile stretched across his face. "Then ice cream it is."

They stared at each other, grinning like fools. But, strangely, she didn't care how she looked. Even though she knew she'd have to explain her behavior to Randi.

"I noticed an ice cream place back that way." She pointed toward the street behind them. "Finley's Ice Cream Shoppe, I believe."

"Thank you." He leaned in and brushed her cheek with his warm lips.

Remembering her assistant was watching, she turned to leave, but then she thought of one more thing. "No serious talk. Not today. This will be about us spending time together. That's all."

"Us and eating ice cream?" He rocked his eyebrows. "What could be better?"

"Exactly."

"Then, I accept." He reached for her hand, lifted it to his lips, and pressed a kiss against her skin.

Which made her want to kiss his cheeky grin, but instead she scurried back to Randi, who still stood with her hands on her hips.

"I don't believe it."

Winter couldn't believe it, either. Still, she waved at him.

He winked and blew her a kiss she felt all the way to her toes. What had she gotten herself into?

Twenty-nine

The old-fashioned ice cream parlor reminded Winter of a 50's malt shop with its black-and-white floor tiling, oversized red jukebox, and swivel stools at the snack counter. She and Ty sat at a table in a somewhat private nook of the L-shaped room, eating gooey banana splits.

Sitting across from him, she felt as if the air were electrified with what-ifs. What if she still loved him? What if they got married? What if their renewed romantic relationship changed everything?

So far, Ty had adhered to the no-serious-talking rule. In fact, every word he said was lighthearted and sweet. But Winter's thoughts kept wandering into the danger zone, and that needed to stop.

After swallowing a delicious bite of chocolate syrup and vanilla ice cream, she playfully put her hands in front of Ty's face, vertically, then horizontally, forming an imaginary picture frame. "I can see you with slicked-back 50's hair. Maybe a ducktail in the back." She grinned, hoping to let him know she wanted to have some fun.

"Oh, yeah?" He dropped his spoon into the glass dish, then smoothed his hair back with a make-believe comb. "How's that?"

She laughed, picturing Danny Zuko in *Grease* doing the exact thing. "You'd need a black leather jacket."

"Of course." He jumped up and acted like he was putting on a fake coat. He strutted in front of their table, his hips swaying. "How's that, *doll*?"

She giggled. "You'll need dark sunglasses too."

"Can't forget that." Grabbing two straws, he twisted them into a figure eight, then slid the invention over his nose. He squinted and made faces with his nose and mouth, like he was having a hard time keeping the frames from drooping. "Like my style, baby?" He held up two thumbs like The Fonz.

She chortled at his antics. This was the kind of outing she hoped for. Light and playful like when they were young. She'd been curious to find out if ten years changed that. Apparently not.

Ty nodded toward her jeans. "How about one of those circular skirts for you?"

"A poodle skirt?" She stood and sashayed as if yards of fabric swirled around her knees. "My mom made me one in junior high with a poodle sewn right here." She sat down and pointed to a spot on the invisible fabric. Grabbing her hair back with her hands, she tilted her face. "Like Sandra Dee?"

"Even better." His warm gaze peered at her. "Just need one more thing."

"What's that?" She gulped, thinking he meant to kiss her. Instead, he sauntered to the jukebox, and before he dropped a quarter in the slot, he turned and winked at her.

In a moment, the sounds of Elvis blasting "Hound Dog" rocked the small eatery. And Ty, much to her surprise, threw off his faux glasses and danced the hand jive combined with some kooky Elvis gyrations. Watching his moves, she burst out laughing. When he waved her over, what could she do but push her banana-split dish away and join him?

They be-bopped around the small area near their table, and she laughed so hard her stomach hurt. When the song ended, he drew her close in his arms. It felt wonderful when he did that. Like she belonged in his embrace. Always had.

She gazed into his eyes. Gulped. Was he going to kiss her? Did she want him to?

Mmmm. Yes?

"See. We're still good together." His voice sounded husky.

They stared at each other for a few moments. She didn't want to move away, didn't want this special time alone with him to end. The real world of ministry, and a broken-down vehicle, and an uncertain future called, but this little escapade had been delightful.

"Wait a sec." He let her go and hurried back to the jukebox.

What was he up to now?

The man who dished up their ice cream kept peeking at them from the kitchen area, making her nervous. But, except for an older couple at the long counter, she and Ty had the room to themselves. Besides, with a jukebox in the place, the guy was probably used to customers spontaneously dancing.

Ty put more money in the music machine, then twirled over to her and took her hand. "Here's our song."

"We have a song?" She couldn't remember one.

"We do now." His lips touched her cheek.

Oh.

The strains to slow dance music came on, and he took her in his arms. Just like old times, his hands found her waist, and her arms followed a familiar path over his shoulders and around his neck. She heard him sigh, then he pulled her close. Dancing with him like this was so familiar, and yet kind of strange. Like a dream she had a long time ago.

At first, she didn't recognize what song he chose as *their* song. But soon he was whispering the words to Simon and

Garfunkel's "Homeward Bound" in her ear, and the lyrics came back to her. She let him lead her across their miniature dance floor between the table by the window and the opposite wall where the jukebox sat. Each time the chorus started, his hushed words blew warm breath against her hair, her neck. "Home is wherever you are, Sas."

Nice thought.

When the song finished, she held onto his shoulders, didn't want to let go. But she couldn't keep standing here in the middle of the eatery holding onto him for dear life, could she? He must have sensed her reluctance to end their time together. Gently, he tilted her chin until they were staring into each other's eyes. Chocolate orbs glistened with near-tears. His tender sensitivity touched her heart.

Was her gaze inviting him closer, like he appeared to be doing? Maybe so. Because he lowered his lips until they hovered just above hers. "I love you, sweetheart."

His words caressed her like a silken scarf dancing against her face. Then his kiss fell gently, undemanding and sweet, leaving her happy, but longing for more.

She leaned her cheek against his shirt, smelling the familiar spicy scent of him. She had missed him, this, so much. But what would happen when they went back and joined the others? When everything returned to normal, would she forget this endearing moment with him?

A crazy thought raced through her to forget her responsibilities. To jump on a bus, or a train, and run away with him. Maybe to Nevada, where they could get married tonight. To find somewhere they could call "home" again. Away from her team. Away from—

What did she nearly say? Her calling?

No, of course not.

A twinge of guilt twisted inside her. Passion's Prayer was

her life. She loved serving God and telling others about Him across the country.

But what about Ty? Their future?

Oh, boy. She'd jumped way ahead of things. This was supposed to be a lighthearted outing. No serious talking included no thinking about marriage, either.

She met his gaze. He was so handsome. Strong in character and spirit. She wanted to get to know him again. To hear everything about his life from the last ten years.

He took her hand and led her back to the table. Their magical hour away from the team was coming to an end.

"Maybe next time we can go to the lake and skip rocks." He grinned, challenging her with his gaze.

"Next time, huh?"

"Maybe I've gotten better at skipping rocks." His grin widened.

"Somehow, I doubt that."

They both laughed

When they were seated, he dropped two fresh straws in his cherry soda. Placing the frosty glass in the center of the table, he leaned forward until his lips touched one straw. With his gaze, he beckoned her closer to the other one. "Our date in a malt shop wouldn't be complete without doing this."

A date, huh? It seemed she broke her rule. Still, she leaned forward until they were both drinking from the same glass, their gazes lost in each other.

But the weight of responsibility tugged on her. She needed to get ready for tonight's gathering. People were expecting her. Concerns for the team were pulling her away from him.

Yet all she wanted to do was stay.

Thirty

Ty worked nonstop putting the engine together. All the while he labored on the car, he shuffled through the emotions and possibilities playing through his mind about Winter and him getting back together. Exciting thoughts threatened to distract him from his work. Hope tempted him to daydream all day long, especially after the date they had the other day. But persevere on the car project he did, and tonight the team would ride to church in the Old Clunker again. He was eager for Winter to see for herself that it had been a good idea for him to join Passion's Prayer.

After all his hours alone in the garage, his head was chock full of romantic notions he hoped to carry out soon. Their date at Finley's Ice Cream Shoppe was only the beginning. He'd seen that sweetness back in her eyes that told him she wanted to be with him as much as he wanted her at his side. The thought energized him, quickened his heart and his footsteps.

Now, he waited in front of her motel room door, gathering the nerve to knock. With his palms sweaty, and the drum in his chest beating out a frantic tempo, his fingers clutched her old engagement ring in one hand and a long-stemmed red rose in the other hand.

Was he jumping the gun? After she asked him out for ice cream, and all the fun they had, he'd thought of little else. What would Winter think of his proposal? Would she say yes?

He dropped the ring in his pocket, adjusted the black-and-gray striped tie for the third time, tugged on the sleeve of the dark gray tux he rented, and scrubbed one black shoe across his slacks. He checked his fingernails again. Removing the grease was nearly impossible, but he got rid of most of it with motel soap and his toothbrush. He'd have to remember to pick up a new one later.

Many years had passed since he dressed up for a woman. Doing so now felt strange, but he was willing to do anything he could to show Winter how much she meant to him. He remembered how she liked him to dress up. Hopefully, when she saw him, she'd recall that too.

He sucked in a big breath and rapped "Shave and a Haircut," their special code from long ago.

When Randi answered the door, instead of Winter, disappointment flooded him. He tried to shake it off.

Randi's smile vanished. She nearly shut the door on him, but he inserted his shoe into the opening.

"May I see Winter?" He tried to act as if his rented black shoe wasn't wedged between the door and the metal frame.

Her glare raked over him from his hair right down to his polished shoe stuck in the door. By the look on her face, she was disgusted with every inch she saw. Because of his appearance? Or because she despised him so much?

"Is she here?"

"She's busy." Apparently, nothing had changed with her attitude.

"Tell her I'm waiting, will you?" He tried to be polite.

"We'll be downstairs in a minute." She kicked at his foot.

The way she kept attempting to shut the door on him was wearing on his patience. "Please, Randi? Tell her I'm here."

"Why do you bother? She's already engaged to Pastor Dave."

He shook his head in denial. "That's not possible."

Her eyes glinted. "Wait and see."

She's lying. But doubts crept in. What if Winter cared for David Michaels?

* * * *

"Who is it, Randi?" Winter exited the bathroom.

"Only him." Randi opened the door wide.

As soon as Winter spotted Ty standing in the doorway, she froze. Fascinated by seeing him here, dressed up like a magazine model, her gaze traveled over his stylish clothes, his dynamite smile, and she wanted to let out a whistle. While he wore nice clothes for his manager's position ten years ago, she hadn't seen him this decked out since their wedding day. She'd always loved it when he put on a tie before they went out to dinner, but this? *Wow.* His casual stance as he leaned against the frame of the door, the impeccable tux and tie, the extended rose, the manly grin, all made her want to lunge into his arms and … and kiss him again.

But there stood Randi, glaring.

She tried intercepting her assistant's stare with one of her own, but Randi avoided eye contact. Hadn't the discussion between her, Neil, and Winter the other day made any change in her PA's attitude toward Ty? Neil warned Randi she'd better act differently or there'd be repercussions. But Winter knew he'd give her more chances before kicking her off their team. And she agreed with his philosophy.

Controlling her grin and thoughts about kissing, she schooled her features. Hadn't she decided there could be no more kissing until she sorted out her feelings?

However, seeing him after two days' absence, she realized she had missed him. She stepped forward to accept the rose he offered. An image flashed through her mind of him wearing those straw glasses and dancing the hand jive, and she smiled. It seemed he was valiantly attempting to remind her of the romantic suitor he'd been long ago. Boy, was she remembering. Moments like this were enshrined in her heart, even though she'd stuffed them away like winter clothes and mothballs.

"Oh, Ty." She brought the rose to her nose. "How thoughtful."

* * * *

Squeezing the ring in his pocket, he watched her. Surely, Randi made that up about Winter being engaged. She loved him. Didn't she?

"Hey, Randi, could you give us a minute?" He used the most diplomatic voice he could muster. Her glare annoyed him, but he wanted to stay focused on Winter, not his lack of understanding over why she kept such a rude assistant.

"I'm not going anywhere. I'll stand right here and—"

"Randi." Winter cleared her throat. "I'll be fine. You can go."

"But—oh, all right. Let me tell you, I don't like it one bit." She stormed into the bathroom and slammed the door.

He watched Winter's gaze trail her PA's departure, and cringe. Again, he reminded himself not to think about Randi. For a few minutes, he and Sas were alone. *At last.*

Her hand slipped toward him, and she stroked his tie. "Well, well, well, you look handsome, all dressed up like this." He felt himself standing taller. "What's the occasion?" Her eyes sparkled.

"Well …" He coughed at the dryness in his throat. Was this the right timing for a proposal? Should he wait for a more romantic moment? If he chose to ask her now, he'd better do so before his riotous nerves stole the words out of his mouth, or Randi returned. He'd daydreamed this moment so many times. Placing her ring back on her finger—right where it belonged, where it should've always been—had dominated his thoughts forever, it seemed. And here she stood, gorgeous as ever. Here he was, shaking as if he never did this before, anguishing over what her response might be. He hoped tonight he'd have the privilege of proclaiming to the world that she belonged with him. David Michaels could hit the road.

If he asked, would she say yes? Had she figured out she loved him too?

He glanced at her rosy cheeks, her moistened lips. She smiled at the rose, then at him. If he could only speak words from his heart, everything would be fine. He clasped her hand in his, stroked his thumb over her soft skin. Mesmerized by her loveliness and what he was about to do, his gaze locked on hers. He dropped to one knee.

Her eyes widened.

Will you marry me? burned in his mind. He drew her hand to his mouth. His lips touched her skin just below her knuckles. Then, *ow*! A protrusion on her finger bit into his mouth. Startled, he jerked back and stared. A diamond ring? On her left hand! His gaze shot to hers. Dropping her hand like it was poison, he stumbled backward. This couldn't be happening. He had to get away. To think. To escape this horrible outcome.

Randi was right!

* * * *

Lost in the tender moment, concern overrode her warm feelings when Ty dropped to his knee. What was he doing? This was too soon for him to ask her to marry him. She wasn't ready for that. And yet, he looked so sweet. The way he dressed to please her, the way he gave her a long-stemmed rose, and his whispered words were doing startling things to her heart.

But her hand fell free of his. He stood, facing her with something akin to shock. Or anger?

"Ty?" His dreadful look stunned her. "What is it?" *Oh, no.* She remembered that she tried on a ring David gave her as a ruse to dissuade men from thinking she was single. And it was still on her finger!

Before she could explain, Ty sprinted down the hallway.

"Ty! I'm not … engaged." Ugh. Why did she even try on the ridiculous ring? She yanked it off and held it up. When he didn't pause, she knew he hadn't heard. What must he think? That she kissed him two days ago and then accepted someone else's proposal today? That she was as fickle as a junior-high girl? What if he left before they had a chance to talk?

She closed the door and leaned against it. Lifting her palm, she stared at the costume jewelry, wishing she hadn't tried it on. If he'd taken a second to look at it, he'd see it was fake. Not an engagement ring. David was just trying to help her. He said if she wore a simple ring on her left hand, men might assume she was spoken for and wouldn't ask her out. Now, Ty took the whole thing wrong.

Tears filled her eyes. Was he about to propose? Even if that seemed like he was moving too fast, her heart had responded in joy. And hope.

She studied the rose, inhaling its sweet fragrance. She was glad he chose a red rose. What was that poem about a red, red rose? She tried to recall the words. A few tears trickled down her cheeks. She wiped them away. Sentimental tears. No reason to get weepy. Too soon for a proposal anyway.

Although Ty was forthright about his hope for them to get back together ever since their first conversation in Coeur d'Alene.

Remembering how he dropped down on his knee made her recall the other time he asked her to marry him. The romantic picture caused more tears.

Randi reentered the room and rushed over to hug her. "It'll be all right. He's not your type. Imagine him trying to court you." She snorted. "You're better off with Pastor Dave." She grabbed her left hand. "Where's the ring?"

Winter opened her other hand and showed her.

"Why'd you take it off?"

Walking to the nightstand, she yanked the drawer open and tossed in the ring. "It's not real. I never agreed to marry David."

"You didn't?" Randi looked startled.

"He didn't even ask, for goodness' sake."

"But the way you've been so happy, I assumed—"

"I'm happy because of Ty." There, she said it.

"You've got to be kidding."

"I'm not. And, now, thanks to that phony ring, he assumes I'm engaged."

"Good."

"No, not good."

"You've been too distracted with this Ty-thing." Randi's words cut. "You need to stay focused on what's important. Inspirational speaking. The ministry. We've got big things ahead of us."

Big things? What was she talking about?

Winter wanted to chase after Ty and explain. But it was almost time for them to leave for the conference, and she had no idea where he went. She imagined him as she saw him tonight, dressed in a tux, a rose in hand, romantically kissing her fingers. If he proposed, what would she have answered?

A knock sounded at the door, and she jumped. Ty wouldn't give up on her easily. Rushing to the door, she thrust it open.

Neil stood on the other side. Disappointment flooded through her.

Her co-leader entered the room. "The Old Clunker is warmed up. That Tyler is some mechanic."

Just hearing his name made her heartbeat accelerate. She needed to find him and apologize. He had to hear from her that she'd never accept anyone else's ring as long as she cared for him. Even if she wasn't ready to confess to him, or even to herself, how much she cared. "Do you know where Ty is? I need to talk with him."

"He said he was going for a walk. That he'd catch up with us later." Neil stared at her. "What's going on? He rented a tux today and wouldn't tell me why."

She bit her lip, shook her head. This wasn't the time to let her emotions get the better of her. Neil was an understanding friend, and she feared his kindness would draw out the tears she'd been fighting.

"Are you ready to leave?"

"Give me a couple of minutes, okay?" She turned away, hoping to keep him from observing her distress.

"I'll be in the car." At the door, he paused. "Is there, maybe, something you and I need to discuss?"

So he had seen. And he deserved to hear the truth.

"Yes." She nodded. "Tomorrow?"

"Sounds good. See you in a few." He closed the door.

"Let me do something with your hair." Randi waved her over to a chair. "If you'd get your hair cut, my life would be easier."

"Well, I'm not." She dropped into the chair and crossed her arms.

Randi looked surprised by her sharp retort. "Men are not worth this fuss." She braided two small sections of Winter's hair, then clasped them together in the back with a barrette. "Why do you let him bother you? He's only a mechanic."

"There's a misunderstanding, that's all." She stood and picked up her Bible. She needed to focus on what she was going to speak about and forget about Ty and their relationship problems for a few hours.

Lord, I give it to You. Please, touch him, wherever he is. Show us Your will for our lives.

"How involved were you two, anyway?" Randi grabbed her coat.

Winter kept walking toward the door. "Let's not talk about it now. Neil's waiting."

"My advice is to forget about him."

Forget him? She hadn't done that in ten years. And she wouldn't be forgetting the image of him on his knee in front of her for a long time, either.

Thirty-one

Neil's eyes showed curiosity as Winter climbed into the front seat of the car and perused the interior of the vehicle, checking to see if Ty had joined them. He hadn't. She smiled at Neil, hoping to reassure him everything was fine.

He must have questions about Ty, and probably David too. Tomorrow, she'd tell him all about Ty, their accidental meeting in Coeur d'Alene, and why she kept her past relationship with him a secret this week. Then Neil could help her decide what to do from here. The Old Clunker was fixed, so if he felt Ty should head back to Coeur d'Alene, she'd have to try convincing him otherwise. Even though she didn't want to remarry Ty this instant, she liked the idea of possibly reconciling with him. Picturing him down on his knee reinforced her thoughts about keeping him on the team. Of course, there was always the chance they might need him to work on the car again.

"Welcome back, Old Clunker." She ran her hand over the dashboard. Their car was running because of Ty's hard work. God surely sent him their way. But where was their mechanic now?

If he left the team, she'd miss him. She enjoyed hearing him laugh, feeling him touch her cheek, hearing him say he loved her, knowing he could cry and be tender.

She gazed out the window at passing businesses and recalled the first time she saw him cry—the day she packed her bags. She shouldn't reminisce about the past anymore, especially before a gathering, but of its own accord, her thoughts traveled back.

One last time.

* * * *

Five days passed before she felt brave enough to return to their apartment. She needed to pack her belongings, but she dreaded stepping inside that place.

After seeing a lawyer, she collected a couple of moving boxes and made herself enter the home she and Ty had shared for six months. This would be her final time here.

The horrible truth remained—she still loved him. Part of her still wanted to be with him. The idea of leaving, of not being married to Ty, ripped her in a million ragged pieces. And then, the other part of her hated him for what he did and how he hurt her. She stood in the living room, gazing at the familiar furnishings—the chair she found for five bucks at a garage sale, the secondhand couch a friend gave them, the lampshade she decoupaged with old black and white pictures—and she couldn't bear the overwhelming emotions.

Dropping down onto the couch, she clutched the blue afghan resting across the back between her hands and squeezed tightly, her fists shaking. "I trusted you," she spoke to the blanket as if it were him. "We were supposed to grow old together." Then, not wanting to touch the fabric a second longer, she hurled it across the room, almost hoping it broke something. When it didn't, she covered her face with her hands, sobbing for her marriage that *was* broken and crushed beyond repair.

After several minutes, she wiped her cheeks, stood, and glanced around the room again. Where should she start? She needed to do what she came here to do, then leave. But she had no will to pack. No desire to collect random treasures when her life and her dreams had fallen apart. Clamping her eyelids shut, she squeezed out the remainder of tears. For five days, she'd cried. How could more tears keep coming?

She shook herself. "Get the packing done and get out of here before he comes home and finds you in *his* apartment."

She grabbed the boxes she brought and set them on the coffee table. She newspaper-wrapped each delicate piece of her souvenirs from the Philippines—vases, jewelry, and figurines—then carefully placed them in the box. Knowing she was taking too long with the breakables, she rushed the last few pieces, then grabbed her favorite books off the shelf and dropped them into the other box. She ran into the bedroom, scooped up a stack of clothes and topped off both boxes. She was in a hurry to leave now.

She passed the end table with the decoupage lampshade on it. Seeing their wedding picture beside the lamp, something in her heart ripped. Lowering the box to the couch, she picked up the antique-framed picture with shaky fingers. Like a magnet, her gaze was drawn to Ty's smiling wedding-day face, a face she'd kissed and loved. She dropped to the couch, clutching the frame to her chest, her heart breaking all over again.

Then, she felt rather than heard someone enter the room. The picture slipped from her fingers and crashed to the rug.

"What are you doing?" Ty's soft voice was cautious.

She gulped. Her plan of getting in and out of the apartment before he showed up had failed. She swiped at her tears. Didn't want him seeing her fall apart. She'd carry her boxes down the stairs, call a cab, get away from here, and then she could cry all she wanted.

"Packing." She retrieved the frame from the floor, the top right corner now chipped, and stood. "I was wondering what to do with this picture."

"I'd like to k-keep it." His voice sounded choked. "But you can, if you'd rather." He was so polite, so kind, she had the urge to turn and sob in his arms.

Instead, she set the frame on the end table. Turning toward her boxes, she spotted her celebration candle—the one she saw burning the other night—on the coffee table. She despised it. Had to get rid of it. In one swoop, she snatched up the candle, rushed into the kitchen, and dropped it in the garbage can. It clunked loud and defined in the small room.

"Where will you go?" he asked when she reentered the living room. "How can I reach you?" Why did he sound wounded? Wasn't she the one living with a broken heart?

"You'll receive papers in a matter of weeks. I've been to the lawyer." She was surprised her voice held together when her insides felt like a crumbling wall, breaking piece by piece. She needed to run to someone who cared about her brokenness. Her mom would hold her and tell her everything would be okay. Her dad would assure her that she'd live through this agony and become a better person because of it.

She doubted both things.

She might die of heartache before she reached her parents. Unless she hardened herself to Ty and the memory of what she walked in on the other night.

"Please, don't g-go." His voice broke. A ragged sob burst from his lips. He dropped to the couch, rocking back and forth, his cries muffled by his hands.

She forced herself not to look at him. A stone heart couldn't be affected by the death of their marriage, right? She slipped the rings off her finger and set them on the coffee table. Then she picked up her stuff and left.

* * * *

"Winter, come inside." Randi stood outside the car with the door open. "The meeting starts in forty-five minutes."

Jarred from her memories, she got out of the car and followed her assistant inside the church, still a bit dazed. Needing a few minutes alone to collect herself and pray, she walked down the back hallway to one of the Sunday school rooms. Randi tagged along, but Winter closed the door, keeping her from entering. She crossed the room to a small chair and sat down.

Tonight was the last night of the week's conference in Salem, and she wanted to share something meaningful. That she slipped back to thinking of the past wasn't helpful, neither was the fact she felt bad about the misunderstanding between her and Ty. She promised herself the first chance she got, she'd talk to him.

Closing her eyes, she focused on the Lord. She sang "Only You." She opened her Bible to the book of Psalms and read a few chapters, searching for words on faith and encouragement. She thought about the difficult places the psalmist described and how he praised God through his worst trials, singing of victories and thanksgiving. She wanted her life to be like that.

Instead of praying and asking for blessings like she usually did, maybe she should thank God for everything He'd done for her. For giving her missionary parents. For bringing Ty to help with the car. For their past and how both of them were now serving the Lord. For her experiences with Passion's Prayer, and for all the people they ministered to over the last five years. For everything in her journey that led her to where she was now.

She spent some time doing that, then she wondered, should she share her testimony tonight and thank God for His faithfulness in her life? Neil and Ty shared their stories on the first night. Telling hers might be the perfect conclusion to the week.

Is that Your will, Lord? If so, what part would I share?

Everything whispered through her.

Everything? Her heart pounded faster.

She planned to share the whole story of Ty's and her past with Neil and the rest of the team tomorrow. Not tonight. And not in public.

How could she tell everything without saying too much? Some parts of her testimony were private. She wrestled with her thoughts and prayed some more. How much could she say without casting blame on Ty? Or revealing her divorce?

Maybe the Lord was inspiring her to be open to sharing everything. For her to be honest. Broken. Humble. *Is that it, Lord?*

"Search me, oh, God," she sang the lyrics. "Know my heart. I surrender all I am to You."

Was she ready to surrender her will to His? Even where Ty was concerned?

Later, following the singing, she stepped to the lectern but didn't open her Bible. "This week has been unique for our team. During the first meeting, I was sick. Neil and our new team member, Ty Williams, shared their testimonies. Also, our vehicle had a major breakdown, and someone blessed us with funds for repairs. I'm happy to report, our car, which I've dubbed Old Clunker, is running great now." Chuckles erupted across the room. "Heartfelt thanks to the person who financed this project. And I thank God for sending us a mechanic just when we needed one."

The whoosh of the door opening and closing at the back of the auditorium caught her attention. Ty entered and dropped into the back pew, the farthest spot in the building from her. His eyes returned her stare.

She sent a brief smile in his direction, but his face remained stoic.

Lord, guide my words. Help me not to say too much. Or too little. Your will be done.

She began by telling the group about growing up in a missionary's home in the Philippines and her involvement in the ministry as a teenager.

"When it came time for college, I chose a secular university in the States. Far from home and my dad's watchful eye, I tiptoed through my first experience of living in the world. I made friends with young people, who like me, were caught up in trying to find themselves. Between college life and weekend partying, my relationship with God slid to the back burner. Prayer and Bible study seeped away through the guise of busyness, and ultimately sin.

"I'm sad to say, few were aware I was a missionary's kid, or even a Christian. I kept quiet about my upbringing and beliefs." She swallowed hard.

"The summer I completed my Associate's degree, instead of returning to the Philippines and my parents' expectations, I accepted an invitation to vacation at my roommate's home in Idaho."

* * * *

Idaho? Only half-heartedly listening, Ty jerked to attention. Was she going to tell them about meeting him that summer? About their rocky marriage? He wanted to talk with her about their past, and yes, he wanted Neil and Jeremy and Deborah to know everything, or almost everything, that happened between them. But not here, not in this public arena.

Please, Sassy, not here.

* * * *

Winter met Ty's wide-eyed gaze, saw worry etched across his face. *I have to,* she tried explaining with her eyes. *It'll be okay.*

He still wore the tux, but his hair was messy, windblown. From here, she couldn't see the color of his eyes, but her heart had memorized every hue. The way they sparkled like glistening chocolate when he was happy. The way they became shuttered and dark, like shadows in a forest, when he was distraught. And never would she forget that special shine when he wanted her to know just how much he loved her.

He really does love me.

He braced his chin against his knuckles, his elbows on his knees, his posture rigid like he was about to face a court-martial.

Her smile faded.

"That summer changed my life. I met someone who took my breath away with the slightest glance, someone whose smile made the world a better place to live. Someone perfect." She spoke each word, each syllable, with her gaze fastened on him. "But it was a mistake."

Ty winced.

"The man I set my hopes on wasn't a Christian. I should have broken off our relationship, should never have started one. But my heart had turned cold, and because I'd become more familiar with the things of the world than the things of God, it was easy to forget my upbringing, to close my ears to the little voice inside. Instead, I pursued my own desires. And him."

Gulp.

Not wanting to expose certain details, she decided to share most of the story, promising the Lord, and herself, she'd explain the rest to her team tomorrow.

"Later in our relationship, I discovered this perfect man in a compromising situation that broke my heart. I thought his betrayal would kill me. So I ran as far as I could."

She wondered if the remembrance still had the power to inflict pain in Ty's heart as it did with hers. The Lord was at work, doing healing within, but she still felt a little tearing somewhere in her chest. Like salt being rubbed into a wound.

Talking about her trip home to the Philippines and of parents who helped her through the crisis of her life, she gave

God the praise. She told how she turned to Jesus with newfound devotion. He became her all. Her hope. And after a year, she came back to the States to attend Bible school. There, during a special mission's project at the Tennessee school, she received her call from the Lord to work in full-time ministry. She concluded by telling how Passion's Prayer came together.

Then she shared that God had a good plan for their lives. Even when they couldn't see it, He was working things out.

Thankfulness welled up within her again.

Lord, You have stayed with me through the thick and thin places of life, guiding me, being patient. Thank You. I know You have a good plan for my life—and Ty's. You knew he was going to find me, didn't You?

A comforting peace filled her.

"Out of the ashes of loss, God can grow a perfect garden. Don't give up. If you're in a season of heartache, cling to Jesus. Humanity sometimes brings hurts and regrets, yet out of such experiences a treasure can flourish, something that would never have developed in a perfect environment. This is true in my life. God does give 'a crown of beauty instead of ashes, the oil of gladness instead of mourning, and a garment of praise instead of a spirit of despair.'"

Thinking of herself, she added, "He turns winter into spring, and makes our hearts brand new again."

Closing the conference, she prayed.

When she glanced up, Ty was gone.

Thirty-two

"The zoo it is, then." Neil steered the Old Clunker onto the highway.

Winter could think of a dozen places she'd rather go than to the zoo for their day off. Unfortunately, she lost the vote.

Ty's legs bumped into hers, and she pulled away. The chill between them since yesterday had escalated. He sat as close to the door as he could, and she, in the middle of the front seat, inched a little closer to Neil, keeping herself from leaning into Ty's body. Not wanting to bring attention to her ringless finger yet, she kept her hand tucked inside her pocket. She'd wait for the right moment to talk to him about it.

The rest of the group remained silent for the duration of the ride to the Oregon Zoo, as if each of them felt the tension between the two of them. No doubt they figured out who the mystery man was in her testimony last night. No one asked, but she bet they knew.

Neil had planned a team meeting for this evening. Then everyone would find out the truth anyway.

She still hoped to speak with Ty alone first.

"There's exit 72," Randi announced, and Neil drove down the off-ramp.

Lord, could You prepare these friends to forgive and accept Ty after they hear the whole story? Help me to be honest. Change us as a ministry and make us more like You. And, could You show me how to make things right with Ty?

The image of him bending down on his knee when she had that silly ring on gnawed at her. How angry he looked as he stalked away. Then, after the session, he disappeared without talking to anyone. She wanted to call him, but she didn't follow the impulse. Now, she wished she had.

Neil parked the car, and everyone piled out. Jeremy and Deborah took off at a jog toward the park's entrance, quickly distancing themselves from the rest of the group.

Randi hovered near Winter. "Guess I'm with you."

"Okay." But if she stayed within earshot, how would Winter be able to talk with Ty? She couldn't let the day pass without making things right with him.

"Let's grab Deb and make it a girls' day." Randi grinned.

"I think they"—Winter nodded in the direction Jeremy and Deb had run—"have their own plans." She glanced at Ty, saw him watching her.

Neil must have noticed her woebegone expression. "Randi, how about if you and I are partners for the day?"

Bless you, Neil.

"Huh?" Randi seemed at a loss. "But I thought—"

Neil led her toward the gate. "We need to have a conversation, anyway, don't we?"

Winter almost laughed at the way Neil maneuvered Randi away from her and Ty.

"Winter?" Randi called back over her shoulder.

"I'll be fine."

She stood next to Ty, their silence awkward as they watched Neil and Randi disappear through the gate. "That leaves you and me." He looked so unhappy. Should she blurt out her explanation?

"Yup, looks that way." He strode toward the gate. She had to run to keep up with him. "What would you like to see first?" His voice was polite, but distant. That he wasn't thrilled to spend the day in her company was obvious.

"You don't have to hang out with me." The weirdness between them was his fault, anyway. If he hadn't run off last night, she'd have told him about the ring. "If you'd rather not be with me, I get it. We're old enough to tour the zoo outside the buddy system."

He stopped and faced her. She almost flinched at the anguish in his eyes. "No one in the world I'd rather be with than you." His soft words gave her hope. "Can't promise I'll be good company, though. Not with the way things turned out." He nodded toward the entrance gate and moved briskly ahead of her.

Witnessing his despair, she wanted to yell at him to stop walking and listen to her. But a large group of children and several adults surrounding her on their way to the gate kept her from calling out.

* * * *

Ty wished the day were over, then he could arrange for his flight back to Coeur d'Alene. He hated giving up. But what else could he do? He hadn't seen that wretched engagement ring today. No doubt she took it off so he wouldn't feel bad about it. He sighed, the weight of his grief heavy on his chest.

Once they left the ticketing area, he wanted to grab Winter's hand and pull her toward the penguin house. But he kept his fingers far from hers. Those impulses needed to die. "Come on. I've been here before. They have the funniest penguins."

Thinking of her accepting David's ring made bile rise in his throat. Especially after the way she flirted with him at the ice cream shop the other day. Why didn't she have the decency to tell him about the engagement herself? The fact he heard the news from Randi still soured in his gut. He'd like to demand an explanation but demanding anything of her seemed ridiculous.

In the penguinarium, they faced the large viewing window where penguins flapped their wings and dove like children playing tag. Separated by a foot of space and heartache a mile-wide, neither spoke for several minutes.

"Hilarious, huh?" He said it with a humorless tone. He really wasn't into this.

A brief smile skimmed Winter's lips as she watched the penguins' antics. If only he could make her smile at him. But that was over.

Suddenly, she grabbed his arm. "Ty, I need to say something to you." He looked at her earnest expression and swallowed. "I'm sorry about last night." Her words were spoken fast, like keeping quiet another second might kill her. "You looked amazing, you dressed up special, gave me a perfect rose, and because of me, your feelings were hurt. And you're still upset, I can tell." He met her gaze, saw tears. "I didn't mean for things to end like that. I'm sorry."

Her apology hit the mark. The ice in his chest thawed a little. The wispy sound of her voice and the way her eyes sparkled with unshed tears reminded him of what he lost. His gaze lowered to her lips, rosy and kissable. The way she licked them as if second-guessing his response lured him closer. Would he ever get over his attraction for her? How could he when he hadn't gotten over her in the last ten years?

What on earth possessed her to say yes to David? Now Ty would have to leave the group, because remaining with Passion's Prayer and watching her fall for another guy was a burden too horrific to bear. She was the wife of his youth—and he wanted to remind her of that Scripture again—until he remembered the detestable ring. That thought kept his fingers from touching her dimple or removing the long strand of hair nearly covering her eye. He jammed his fingers in his back pockets.

"Forgive me?" She bit her lip and watched him.

"Yeah, sure." He moved toward the exit. "Shall we get on with the tour?"

"Maybe not."

He turned back. Still standing in the exact spot, her gaze was focused on the penguins. Not him.

"What do you mean?" A spark of irritation skittered up his back. The faster they looked at all the animals and shops, the faster they could get out of here. Then he'd go home to Idaho. Which would make Randi ecstatic. He shuddered at all the problems Winter's assistant had caused. Oh, he was in a foul mood. He shouldn't have come with the team today. But he wanted one more day with Winter. One more day to … what? Torture himself?

"Maybe I'd rather do something else." Her voice had that playful lilt to it. The one he usually responded to immediately. When he was smart.

Subduing his reaction to the soft look on her face, he calmly, and with a good dose of self-control, walked back to her. "Don't tease me, okay? Accepting you're engaged to someone else is hard enough." He studied her. "Will you stop staring at me like that?"

"Like what?" She had the nerve to giggle.

"Like you want to be kissed as much as I want to kiss you." He glared at her, daring her to deny her actions.

"What if I do?"

What if—? She wanted him to kiss her? Well, then, he leaned in a little closer, drowning in her jade gaze pulling him to her with an invisible rope. Then, as if the earth quaked beneath his feet, consequences crashed through his thoughts. What about David?

He stilled.

If he kissed her now, how could he turn off his desire to do so tomorrow? And the next day? He jerked back and glared at her. "Your fiancé might not approve of me sneaking such liberties." He took a deep breath and forced himself to face the penguins, instead of her.

Lord, I could use some help here.

Somewhere between his eyes and the glass observation window, she pulsed her left, ringless hand, wiggling her fingers like dancers on a stage. Was she showing him she took off her ring for his benefit? Or did it mean something else? His heart pounded faster at the possibility.

"Did you take it off to make me feel better?"

"You're a funny guy." Her grin unnerved him. "Haven't you noticed David's absence?"

"Yes."

She kissed his cheek. "I'm not engaged, Ty. He never even asked me."

Relief fought with disbelief. "You're not engaged to David?"

"No."

"What about the ring?"

"That was his scheme to dissuade single men from thinking I'm available. You know, since I don't date?" She frowned at him.

She wasn't engaged. He could barely fathom that outcome.

"David left for Coeur d'Alene this morning. Like I told you, he and I are only friends."

"And he knows this?"

"Absolutely." She laughed.

But something still bothered him. "Why didn't you say something last night?"

"I did." She looked exasperated. "I called out to you, but you thought the worst of me before I had a chance to explain."

Guilty. "I did, didn't I?"

"Yes, you did." A wide grin crossed her mouth. Her very sweet, inviting mouth.

He smiled back, momentarily disoriented from the ascent of his emotions from despair to rapture. But he wasn't about to waste another second in a befuddled haze. He pulled her against him, giving her a solid hug. She giggled and snuggled into his embrace.

"I was so worried." He stroked her hair.

"I know."

When she glanced up at him with that twinkle in her eye again, he kissed her. The gentle peck he envisioned turned into a much deeper, passionate kiss. He'd stay like this, with the love of his life in his arms, forever, if he could.

But whispers, snickering, and the shuffling of feet of other zoo visitors caused him to pull back. Knowing he now had the liberty, he swept loose hair from her face and touched her dimple, unable to believe what just occurred. How could things have gone from the worst thing imaginable—his leaving Winter for good—to this amazing euphoria of having her in his arms again?

It had to be God. *Thank You for performing a miracle on my behalf.*

With his arm wrapped around her, he kissed her cheek, then led her out of the penguinarium. An irksome thought crept into his mind. "You know what led me astray? Randi told me you were engaged."

"She seemed to think I was."

He didn't doubt Winter. But was it possible that Randi was up to her pranks, causing trouble? "When I saw the ring, I lost hope."

She turned in his arms, resting her hands on his chest. "I'm sorry."

"Me too."

Was their misunderstanding a dreadful mistake? Or did Randi lie to force him to back off? Either way, he couldn't dwell on it. Today he was going to enjoy being alone with Winter. He hugged her again.

"Ty." He detected a warning in her voice. "While I'm not involved with David romantically, I'm not one-hundred-percent sure about my feelings for you, either. About our future."

"I understand." But he had the whole day to convince her otherwise. Her kisses said she loved him, even if she couldn't see that for herself. Grabbing her hand, he trotted down the path, eager to show her all the animals. Later, he'd buy her a stuffed bear or something to remember this day by. Suddenly, he had an idea. He stopped and faced her. "Will you be my date?"

Her eyes grew big. "When?"

"Right now. Will you be my date for the day?"

"I don't date." She looked serious.

Kissing and no dating? Should he remind her of their ice cream outing? "I know." He tried not to chuckle. "I respect that, but while we're here at the zoo, will you break your rule and be my date? Please?" He stared into her eyes, willing her to want to be with him as more than just friends.

He could tell she was considering his invitation. "Okay. I'll be your date—for today."

"Thank you." He kissed her cheek.

He felt like letting out a victory shout, but one thought kept him subdued. While he wanted to spend the day with her more than anything else, he needed to have an honest discussion with her, too. One that could end badly.

If Neil kept Randi busy for a few hours, Ty could enjoy his date with Winter. And, hopefully, at the right moment, the two of them could face the issues of their past. It was a conversation he dreaded.

But it was one that also gave him hope for a happily-ever-after kind of future.

Thirty-three

Hand in hand, they strolled through animal habitats, laughing, talking, and enjoying each other's company. Outside the elephant yard, Winter paused for a long while to watch the baby elephant. She laughed when he tossed a pile of hay into the air. Ty observed her every expression, knowing he'd never tire of the pleasure.

"Look, Ty, it's so cute."

As she laughed at the baby elephant and its mom, he wrapped his arms around her and drew her against his chest, so grateful to get to stand close to her. "Do you ever think about those three kids you used to dream about? Do you still want children?"

She shrugged. "I think about them sometimes. My life has changed so much. Now, I'm on the road. Living out of a suitcase isn't a good lifestyle for a child."

"You'd make an amazing mom."

Turning partway in his arms, she met his gaze. "Why do you say that?"

He stroked her hair back from her face. "Remember how you were going to be a teacher? You loved kids. All this time, I imagined you working in a school somewhere."

"I went to Bible College. Then started Passion's Prayer." Her gaze trailed back to the baby elephant, and she stepped from his embrace. "You're right though. I did want to have children."

He linked his fingers with hers. "I love you."

She glanced at him. "I know." She looked like she was debating whether to say anything else. "I think I love you too."

The words touched him deeply. "I'm so glad."

"Maybe you were right. Perhaps, I never stopped loving you, not even, when, well, when—" Her wide gaze met his. "I'm sorry, Ty. I never meant to bring that up."

And right then, he knew the time he'd dreaded, yet wished for, had come. How could they face their future until they faced their past?

"Maybe now's a good time for us to talk." He watched her closely. "How do you feel about a serious discussion today?"

She shrugged, then nodded, but she looked about as happy as if she'd been given a death sentence.

He took her hand again. "Let's find somewhere semi-private where we can talk, okay?"

Again, she nodded.

Silently, they continued down the path until he found a bench set back among a bower of leafy foliage and fall flowers. They both sat down and neither spoke for several minutes. The conversation ahead would probably be tough. But as painful as it might be, they needed to walk over the ground of their past before they could move on with their lives.

He longed to fix things between them, but where could he begin? He slid his arm over her shoulder, offering her his strength and love. In her ministerial role, she had to be a strong person, able to handle enormous responsibilities. Yet, at other times, he caught a glimpse of her vulnerability when she cried or became overwhelmed. The memories they were about to resurrect could kindle either of those traits.

Her tension crept over him, and he felt a ripple of tightness across his chest. He forced himself to breathe out and relax. Maybe if he breathed calmly, she would too.

"Remember that day in Coeur d'Alene, when I told you I was sorry and asked for your forgiveness?"

"Uh-huh." The pallor of her skin and the wariness of her gaze reminded him she'd been avoiding this discussion longer than he had.

"God, in His mercy, has brought us this close despite what I did ten years ago. Despite our divorce." He tucked her hair behind her ear. "I think you and I need to face what happened, and then as much as is humanly possible, try to forget it, believing God has a good purpose in our lives. You have my permission to ask me any question you want, delve into embarrassing issues, whatever. I promise to be honest."

She remained silent.

He cleared his throat, needing something to do. "When we're done, I'd like us to pray together. Then I have something to ask you."

She looked so solemn he didn't know what to think. Would she talk with him? Maybe she wasn't ready for this conversation, after all.

Lord, help us.

She stared into the thick foliage alongside the path. He followed her gaze and saw a bushy-tailed squirrel scamper under the leafy protection and then dodge down the path.

Just when he thought the silence too much of a strain, she spoke. "I've asked Neil for a team meeting this evening. I'm going to tell them about us. Waiting this long was wrong. I'm rectifying my mistake today."

"That sounds good. I'm glad we're having this discussion first." He smoothed his hand over her shoulder. "If you'll let me join you, we can face the others together."

"Okay." She sat quietly again.

"What would you like to ask me about our past?" He took her hand in his and toyed with her ring finger.

"Actually, I have no desire to discuss our past."

"This is your chance to ask me anything. Or tell me anything."

He could see her front teeth worrying her bottom lip.

"What are you most afraid of?"

"Probably how I'll deal with whatever you have to say. I may be tempted to slap you again." She grimaced as if embarrassed to admit that.

He remembered the last slap and how weird they felt around each other afterward. "Should that happen, I'm okay with it. This once." He smiled, trying to reassure her of his sincerity. "My desire is that we can be open and share from our hearts without worrying about the outcome. All right?"

She stared off in the distance.

He waited, aware she wasn't focused. "Winter?"

"You hardly ever call me that."

"I know." He leaned his head against hers and sighed. "Sassy, sweetheart, my love, what is it? What's eating you? You can tell me."

She trembled, then she pulled away and glared at him. "How could you do that to me? How could you … betray me?" Her voice became small and vulnerable like a child's.

He closed his eyes, his chest tightening with bands of guilt. Thoughts bounced in his head until a jumbled mess of words were stacked in a pile, and each excuse fell short of justifiable. He took a deep breath and exhaled slowly. "I was a self-centered fool. Arrogant. Egotistical. I became lost in trying to gain ground in my career. And, well, things had been deteriorating between you and me."

"You blamed me?"

"At first." He hated saying the words, wished to whitewash his offense.

"I loved you. I wanted our marriage to work. Anything you asked, I would have done to improve our relationship."

"I know." He touched her cheek, and she flinched. Tears welled in his eyes at the extent of pain he caused. But not only to her. In his betrayal, he lost everything.

Her expression darkened. "When I saw … her … in our apartment, I thought I'd die." The hurt in her gaze tore at him. "Was it worth the loss of our marriage?"

"No." He squeezed his eyes shut. "Never." A shudder coursed through him. Then he opened his eyes and watched her. Staring into her wounded spirit, he felt himself suffocating in grief. "If I could go back, I'd never, ever, have her in our apartment—or in my life. In fact, I'd resign the day they put her on as my assistant."

How could he explain? "For me, Cindy represented prestige. She was the boss's niece, had access to executive suites, and was full of big ideas rivaling my own. We were going to the top. Well, she made it, at my expense."

"You mean, it was a business deal?" Winter stared at him incredulously. "You have an affair, and she leads you up the corporate ladder? That doesn't make sense. You and I pledged our lives to each other. To forsake all others." Tears edged at her voice.

How strange to look back on a grave mistake and try explaining it without making excuses. What made sense then, now seemed like a fool's notion. "What I did was wrong. I sinned against you and God. I take full responsibility for every foolish decision. It was idiotic. But I can't take back what happened, as much as I would if I could." A long sigh released from somewhere at the bottom of his ribs. "After you moved out, I never once had a relationship with anyone. Not in these ten years."

Disbelief shadowed her eyes.

"As God is my witness, I've been celibate since the day you left me. I want only you, Sas."

Whisking a tear away, she nodded. "I've maintained a strict no-dating rule."

"I know." He stroked back her hair that had fallen forward, brushed away her tears. "I'm glad. And I want you to remember as we talk that I love you. I don't want to delve into this pit any more than you do. But I long for us to be free from the past so we can have a chance at a future together." He kissed her cheek. Then he sat back, watching. Waiting.

* * * *

A bitter taste crept up her throat. Minutes ago, she felt at home in Ty's arms, comforted by his strength, knowing he loved her. But this conversation chilled her insides. She didn't want to rehash those troubling days with him, ever.

Maybe she could change the subject. "Why did you go to prison? Embezzlement, right?"

His eyebrows rose.

"I have a confession to make too. When I learned you were giving your testimony at the conference, I wrapped a scarf around my head and took a taxi to the church. I sat in the back pew and heard every word you said. No one knew I was there."

A smile crinkled his face. "You were curious about me?"

"Sort of."

He nodded. "Cindy had a long-range plan of how to siphon funds from Clayborne's without being detected. You might recall she and I had been spending a lot of time together before you left for the Philippines."

She remembered their newlywed status hadn't been enough to keep him home.

"I'd steadily been changing, hungering after money and recognition. I was ripe for a downfall. I thought we'd get away with it. I know, pretty stupid, huh?"

She couldn't judge him. "We've all been stupid at some time. God was good to speak to your heart right where you were. I praise Him for that."

"Me too, every day."

She didn't know what else to say. Having him on the team hadn't turned out as awful as she first imagined. In fact, she kind of liked having him near. He always acted helpful and kind, whether with her or Passion's Prayer. She knew what she said about still loving him was true too, but she'd been single for so many years. She entertained no expectations of marriage or a relationship. Then again, Ty had been her husband once, could he fill that missing part of her life? Was the death-till-us-part thing still in effect?

"When you left, it hit me hard." He shuffled on the bench.

She met his gaze. Gulped.

"Even though I messed up, I still loved you. I jumped every time I heard a footfall on the stairs, certain you'd come back to me." He looked off in the distance like he was trying hard to remember. "Someone in the upstairs apartment started using our knock, and the beat drove me crazy. I did try finding you."

"You did?"

"Your parents and brother wouldn't give me any information."

Oh.

"Eventually, I figured you must've returned to the Philippines. So many times, I kicked myself for not following you and begging you to come back, but my time ran out." He rubbed his hands over his face. "When I told Cindy we were finished, she went into a psycho rage. She stabbed me in the back. Before I knew it, the authorities were placing full blame for the embezzlement on me. She had the money, the lawyers, the family connections. You heard the rest."

Leaning over, with his elbows on his knees, he stared at the ground. "Starting that night, I lost you, my job, and my life as I knew it."

She felt the urge to pat his shoulder, to comfort him. But she didn't move.

He sighed, then faced her again. "In prison, God touched me and came into my life. I started praying that one day I'd find you and be able to express how sorry I was for hurting you, for wrecking the beautiful thing we shared for such a short time." He touched her shoulder. "I need to say it one more time, Sas. From the depths of my heart, I'm sorry for sinning against you and our wedding vows, and for hurting you so deeply. From this day forward, I promise to spend the rest of my life loving you and showing you I'm sincere about my commitment."

Peace. Sweet, soothing peace.

She felt it oozing through her, stilling the storm that smoldered within her secret places for too long. And even though this conversation pierced her comfort level, it felt good to finally speak the past into the open.

Ty's trespass had been wrong, they both knew that, but sin was sin. She too walked away from the Lord and sinned. "I forgive you." Deep inside, she knew it was true. *Without second thoughts.* "I'm sorry I never gave you the chance to make things right. All my life I told myself if my husband ever did *that*, it was over. So I left. Maybe if I—"

"Hey, don't do that to yourself. What-ifs will drive you crazy."

She knew that too.

"Is there anything else you'd like to ask? I'm an open book." He smoothed his palm over her knuckles, over the back of her hand.

She knew of only one other thing she needed to hear but even thinking the words hurt. "Did you … did you love her?"

"No." There wasn't the tiniest pause.

Relief spread through her. "The betrayal was the hardest. A wedge of jealousy kept popping up, even after all this time."

"I can empathize." He linked his fingers with hers. "I couldn't stand the sight of you talking with David, and your actions were innocent with him."

"I could tell you weren't too fond of him."

"He's a minister, and here I wanted to deck the guy. Then, when I saw the ring and thought you accepted his proposal, I lost it."

They sat in silence for a couple of minutes.

"Does this conversation make you feel any better?" He gazed at her.

She shrugged. "I thought I forgave you years ago. But thinking of that night still tore at me even when I didn't want it to anymore."

"I understand."

"Friends?" She remembered that day long ago when they were dating and she suggested they be friends.

He shook his head slowly. "Sweet lady, I want way more than friendship with you."

* * * *

Ty saw the way she nervously chewed on her bottom lip, and he ached to kiss her. Instead, he reined in his thoughts. "Will you pray with me?"

"Yes, of course."

Clasping her hands, he whispered a prayer of gratitude for forgiveness and for this beautiful opportunity they were experiencing to talk things through.

When he finished, she prayed, thanking God for bringing him to fix the car and for giving them this second chance to make things right.

Following their shared "amen," with love bursting in his heart, and not wanting to stifle his request another second, he grinned. "I love you so much. Will you—"

"There you two are!" Randi ran right up to them.

Oh, no. He couldn't believe her bad timing.

"I've been hunting all over the zoo for you." Randi's eyes glared at their clasped hands, then she grabbed Winter's arm and tugged her to her feet. "Are you ready to have lunch? The rest of us are starving!"

Randi pulled her along, and Winter glanced back at him with a shrug. What else could they do? she seemed to be asking.

He knew what he'd like to do—scoop her up in his arms and run for the nearest exit. Get as far from her assistant as possible.

Another millisecond and he would have asked Winter to marry him again. Would he get another opportunity today?

Thirty-four

With the team staying in a motel, and Winter accompanied by Randi most of the time, Ty didn't know where he could find a place to talk with her alone this evening. He figured she wouldn't go out with him again today, so he asked her to meet him in the lobby at six o'clock.

Sitting on a loveseat in the motel's reception area, he glanced around and decided this room was a good choice, after all. The location gave him the feeling of semi-privacy with its five-foot-high artificial shrubbery along one side, a giant fish tank against the opposite wall, a large window dominating the outer wall, and two computer stations in the corner.

He hoped Randi wouldn't take it upon herself to follow Winter down here. That's all he needed. But, if she did, he'd figure out some way to talk with Winter alone.

He knew she still had reservations about them being together. But he longed to ask her to be his wife, and for them to start moving toward the next step in their relationship. Excited, but nervous, he thumbed through an outdoors magazine.

"Ty, I was hoping to find you here."

He froze. Why hadn't he heard Randi enter the room?

"How's it going?" Her pleasant tone, all sugar and honey,

put him on edge. She sounded like they were close friends, which they weren't. What was she doing here? And where was Winter?

"I had so much fun today, didn't you?" She plopped down on the cushion next to him, too close for his comfort.

"Yes, I had a great day." He repositioned himself near the edge of the couch.

"I've been thinking we should rechristen the Old Clunker. I mean, she sounds amazing now, so why should we keep calling her that?" She giggled, and something about it worried him. "You're a great mechanic, Ty."

"Uh, well, thanks." Did she experience a change of heart? Did Winter confide their past and how they were going to get back together? He'd feel better when they had the team meeting at seven o'clock.

"I've decided I'm glad you're traveling with us after all. We wondered what would happen if the car had a major breakdown. Neil's mechanical abilities amount to changing a tire. I can do that. Your presence has been sorely needed." She laid her hand across his arm.

Flabbergasted, he didn't know what to think, but he removed his arm from under her hand.

"I'm sorry for how I treated you when you first joined up with Passion's Prayer."

Was she serious?

"It's j-just"—her voice broke—"Winter and I are close. I didn't want her getting hurt, you know? She's like a sister to me." A tear trickled down her cheek.

Ty stared, his reaction to her unsettled.

"I was a lonely kid." She sniffed. "Mom died when I was twelve. Dad and I moved every couple of years because he was in the military. I attended six high schools, can you believe it?"

"No." He couldn't believe she was acting nice to him, either.

"As you can imagine, friends were hard to make and harder to keep. Winter was my one true friend. We looked out for each other then, and we still do. I don't know what I'd do without her." She covered her face with her hands and bent her upper body toward her knees like she was sobbing.

Uncertain as to how he should respond, but open to an apology, he patted her shoulder. "It's okay."

In a lightning-fast move that stunned him and set off hurricane-warning bells in his head, Randi lunged toward him, wrapping her arms around him like an octopus. "Thanks for understanding, Ty." She burrowed her face into his neck.

Wait. Was she kissing him? Shock and disgust raced through him. He shoved her back, dislodging her arms. Then he saw her smirking.

"That'll be enough, Randi. I don't know what kind of game you're playing, but—"

Her gaze darted between him and something, or someone, else.

Winter? Air whooshed from his lungs.

Under the archway, her gaze burned with accusation. She obviously saw Randi's embrace. Did she believe that he would—? *Oh, no.*

She rushed out the motel door.

"Winter! Wait."

Beside him, Randi laughed, infuriating him. He grabbed her arm and propelled her toward the exit. "Come with me, you little imp! You have some explaining to do, and you'd better tell the truth this time."

"Let me go." She easily disengaged herself.

"You did this on purpose, didn't you?" He stared hard at her. "Here you were acting nice, and stupid me, I fell for your ploy. Just like you knew I would. You're coming with me and telling Winter the truth."

"Tell her that we're crazy about each other?" She giggled again like it was all a big joke.

"No." He tried to hold his anger in check, but he lost ground by the second. "You'll tell her I did not invite your affection. It was some gimmick you concocted to cause trouble, just like when you stashed money in my wallet. Like David showing up when Winter was upset with me. Like you telling me she was engaged when she wasn't."

"I'll tell her no such thing." Randi jabbed his chest. "You have no proof. She'll believe me over you any day. We made a pact long ago that we'd always look out for each other. That's what I'm doing."

He needed to get away from her before his temper erupted. But he also needed her to convince Winter of the truth. What must she be thinking? "All this caring"—he nearly choked on the word—"is somehow for Winter's good?"

"When Passion's Prayer is known all over the world as the most popular ministry team, she'll thank me for keeping her from making the worst mistake of her life."

"Which is?"

"You!"

"You don't know anything."

"I know you two were involved. And you betrayed her." She jabbed her finger against him again.

He wanted to throttle this woman who deliberately wrecked the fragile trust he'd built with Winter. He had to find her and make sure Randi's sabotaging didn't destroy their chance of starting over. He grabbed Randi's arm and pulled her toward the lobby's entrance. "Come with me."

"Let me go!"

"Miss, are you all right?" The slim motel clerk with black-rimmed glasses moved from the desk and dangled a cell phone in the air.

"No, I'm not all right. This man is a lunatic. Call 911."

That stopped Ty. Like his shirt was on fire, he released Randi's arm and sprinted out the motel door.

He had to find Winter. Up and down the street he searched. Where did she go? When he remembered her propensity for driving off her frustrations, he jogged back to the parking lot behind the motel. The station wagon was gone. He sat down on the curb and leaned his head into his hands and moaned. Then he prayed.

* * * *

Aggravated by her tears, Winter pulled into the passing lane on I-5 heading south. Why was she even crying? It wasn't like she and Ty were engaged. But hugging Randi like *that?* How could he?

She swung around a slow-moving RV and pulled back into her lane, picturing what just transpired.

Minutes ago, she felt a rush of excitement to be with Ty again. They shared an amazing day together, and she wanted to talk with him some more. To feel him hold her hand and look softly into her eyes. She hurried toward the lobby with joy pulsing through her. He'd propose tonight, she was certain of it. Earlier, he almost asked her, then Randi came along. *Dear Randi, always keeping men at bay for me. She won't be able to stop this one.*

She still felt the old attraction for Ty. But today, she found herself looking beyond his handsome face to discovering the new man of God he'd become. The change in him was startling and beautiful. The hours they spent at the zoo—the close embraces, their heartfelt discussions, and the kisses—made her giddy to see him.

Although, as she drew near the first floor, a couple of doubts nibbled at her. Her steps slowed. Was getting back together with

Ty God's will? Hadn't she made a commitment to stay single? And if they started a relationship, would the team accept him? Would Ty, the take-charge guy, be content traveling with Passion's Prayer with Neil and her as the leaders? Her questioning made her realize how much her decisions involved more than just the two of them. In good conscience, she couldn't give Ty a hasty answer—even if his kisses had her hearing wedding bells in her dreams already.

At the lobby, she paused. Another couple was already there, embracing. She glanced away. Wasn't this where she was supposed to meet Ty at six o'clock? She looked at the couple again. Blinked in disbelief. Randi? In Ty's arms?

When the two pulled apart, Winter's heart fell ten stories. Not this again. Seeing his guilty flush, she didn't pause to ask questions or rationalize anything. She ran out the door and went straight for the Old Clunker.

Tears trickled down her nose and she scrubbed them away. Wasn't Ty about to propose to her? Didn't he tell her he wanted them to reconcile? She started up the vehicle, drove out of the parking lot, and pondered the things they discussed during the day. Not only about their past, but also their hopes for the future. Their date at the zoo was so much fun, and it seemed like the years they were apart melted away in the fall sunshine.

Something didn't add up back there. Could there be an honest explanation why they were hugging? Was Randi upset about something? Her assistant had been interested in Ty a week ago. She changed her mind, right? What if that wasn't the case?

Did Winter trust him too soon? He fixed the Old Clunker like he volunteered to do. Nothing else bound him to Passion's Prayer. She could let him go. Even if the thought of dismissing him hurt, seeing that hug upset her more. Unless she had it all wrong.

She drove for twenty minutes, then turned back toward the motel. She kept replaying the way Ty and Randi looked when she stepped into the lobby. The expression on his face was one of shock. How did Randi appear? Winter didn't see her assistant's features since her back was to her.

Randi wouldn't hug Ty in a romantic way, right? Not when she kept nagging Winter and Neil to fire him. And Ty wouldn't hug Randi. Not with the way she'd treated him since he joined the team.

And he wouldn't want to hurt me again.

She drew in a long breath.

Oh, Lord, I may have assumed things without finding out who did what—and why. But You know what I walked in on. It was weird, right?

As soon as she got back to the motel, she'd hunt for Ty and ask him why that scene happened. If she was in the wrong, she'd apologize. Hopefully, she'd have time to talk with him and find out the truth before the team meeting.

Thirty-five

At the motel, before Winter could even step out of the car, Randi stood by her door, fuming. "Where have you been? I've been worried sick. You must let me know where you're going. I'm your personal assistant!"

A flirty assistant, it seemed. "I went for a drive." The two of them needed to have a discussion and get a few things straight.

"I have to talk with you."

"Not here. Not now." Winter jumped out of the car and hurried toward the motel entrance. Her priority was talking with Ty. Then the team meeting. Lastly, she'd decide what to do about her assistant.

"Wait." Randi jogged to catch up. Her face showed puzzlement, probably over Winter's aloof interaction with her. "I've been waiting for you because an emergency call came in."

Winter pivoted toward her. "Who?" Her throat went dry.

"Your dad. Your mom says he's been complaining of stomach pains for a month. He refused to see a doctor until now." She glanced away like she didn't want to tell the worst of it. "He's passing blood and is in unbearable pain. She had your brother drive him to the emergency room. He's been admitted to the hospital."

For her whole life, Winter dreaded this day. Since her parents were in their fifties at her birth, and were now in their eighties, she always knew that unless something happened to her first, she'd have to watch them pass away. Until now, her dad had enjoyed relatively good health.

Mentally setting everything else aside, including her need to find Ty, she rushed to her motel room. She grabbed the team cell phone and tapped out the number Randi had written down. A receptionist at the hospital in Ketchikan, Alaska, the island town where her parents retired to live closer to their grandchildren, took the page for Mindy Cowan.

"Hello?" a tentative voice that sounded much too frail answered.

"Mama? It's me, Winter."

"Oh, sweetie, it's good to hear you. I wish you were here." A sob tore at her mother's voice.

"What's wrong with Daddy?" She couldn't hide her panic at the strain in her mom's tone.

"I'm afraid his condition is s-serious." Mom's voice broke. "They found a large tumor in his colon. I can't believe it."

"Is it—?"

"Yes. Cancer. Widespread." She sniffed. "They don't give him m-much time."

"Oh, Mama." She felt her heart breaking.

"I know you're busy, honey, but can you come home? It would make him so happy to see you before he leaves this w-world."

She heard her mother sniffling in between words, and she fought to control her own tears. "Yes, of course. I'll be there as soon as I can. Tonight, if possible."

"Oh, good. What about your schedule?"

"I'll do whatever it takes to get to you."

"Have you finished this week's conference?"

"Yes. We had a day off." If she knew about this earlier in the day, she could already be on a jet heading north. "We were planning on traveling down the coast to Redding tomorrow. But I'll make flight arrangements. Neil will take care of the next event. I want to see Daddy. Is he in a lot of pain?"

"Yes. He's so stubborn. Wouldn't see a doctor. Said when it was his time to go, he would." Mom sighed. "Now they have him medicated so heavily, he hardly knows I'm here."

"How ... how long?" She dreaded the answer but needed to know.

"Nothing is for sure, but they said"—Mom cleared her throat—"a day or two, a week at the most. Pastor Gray is with him now. Judson is here too, of course."

Alaska seemed so far away. She wanted to be with her parents now. She'd always been close to her dad, but even more so since she became involved in ministry. Darren Cowan was her spiritual mentor, her anchor. What would she do without him?

"Remember our heaven talks?" Mom broke into her feeling of loss.

"Yes."

"Daddy's been engrossed in heaven talk every time he's awake. He's anxious, I believe, so hurry."

"I will. I love you. Tell Daddy I love him too."

"I will. Goodbye, dear."

"Goodbye." Winter fell on her pillow and cried.

A little while later, the door opened, and Randi rushed across the room. She patted Winter's shoulder but didn't say anything.

Neil followed and sat down on the bed next to her. "I'm sorry about your dad." When he extended his arms, she sat up and leaned into his chest. Her cries became sobs, and he held her until her tears were spent.

"I have to go to him." She wiped her eyes with the tissue Randi slipped into her fingers. "Randi, will you make flight arrangements and put it on my emergency card?"

"Will do, Captain." Her assistant hurried to the other side of the room with the cell phone in her hand.

"What about Redding?" She couldn't help worrying about their obligations as Passion's Prayer.

"I checked in with the pastor this morning." Neil shrugged. "They're all set for our team to arrive on Monday."

"We'll have to cancel." She felt such a heavy weight on her shoulders. "I don't know what else to do. Unless you and Deborah want to speak at the conference instead of me."

"How bad is he?"

She drew in a breath. "He's … dying. They don't give him much time. I need to see him before—" She bit her lip, couldn't finish. She cleared her clogged throat. "I need to be with my mom."

"Of course, you do. Go." He patted her hand. "I'll handle canceling or do whatever the pastor in Redding would like us to do given the situation. I'm sure he'll understand. Do you want one of us to go with you? Is Jeremy going?"

She sighed. "I don't even know where he is. I think he went out to dinner with Deb. Two tickets would be a huge expense. As it is, I feel like I'm leaving you stranded."

"I have a cousin who lives on the outskirts of Redding." Neil paused as if thinking. "Maybe we could stay with him for a few days to save on motel costs."

Randi set the cell phone down. "Our flight leaves in three hours. I'll have our stuff thrown together in a jiffy. Can you drive us to the Portland airport, Neil?"

"Of course."

"Us?" Winter didn't tell her to buy two tickets.

"Did you think I'd let you face this alone? I'm your assistant.

Let me do my job." Randi opened the closet door, grabbed clothes, and tossed them into their suitcases.

A strong objection crossed her mind, especially considering what happened earlier. But Randi would keep her going for the next twenty-four hours. And she could use the company. They'd figure out the costs later. "I'll take a quick shower, then we can go."

When she came out of the bathroom, she noticed her pale face, devoid of makeup. Foundation and eye shadow might hide the signs of crying, but she had no willpower to make the effort.

Not that it mattered. She wasn't out to impress anyone.

Ty danced through her thoughts. She wouldn't be able to talk with him now, and since the team meeting would be canceled, their past would remain locked for a few more days. Maybe it would be better if he returned to his life in Coeur d'Alene. Neil could see to that.

She and Randi left the motel room in a hurry, anxious to meet their flight. More than anything, Winter wanted to make it to Ketchikan in time to talk with her dad and hear him call her his princess one last time. And she wanted to be there for her mom.

Then she'd return and find Ty, wherever he was, and have that talk with him.

Thirty-six

After jogging to the church, searching for Winter without finding her, and then running back to the motel, discouragement pressed down on Ty. Why did this happen? All he wanted to do was ask her to marry him. But, now, nothing mattered except for getting the chance to explain to her that while the scene she stumbled upon reeked of wrongdoing, the blame wasn't his. How could he make her see her friend was a flake? Or, at least, that he was innocent?

Entering the lobby, he rushed to the stairwell and ran up the stairs two at a time. At Winter's door, he paused to catch his breath. Why did things turn sour just when their relationship was finding stable footing? Would she even speak to him?

He rapped on the door, tentatively at first, then louder. Maybe someone had heard something from her.

"Yes?" a muffled feminine voice called.

"It's me, Ty."

Deborah opened the door. "Hey, Ty."

"Have you heard from Winter?" He shifted on his feet, anxious for good news. "I've looked everywhere for her."

"You haven't heard?" Deborah opened the door wider.

"Heard what?" A tremor of concern rippled through him.

"When I returned a few minutes ago, the room was empty. Winter's and Randi's stuff is gone." She shrugged. "They've already left."

Her words felt like a punch to his gut. "Left? Where?"

"Her dad is … I found this note. Read it for yourself." She grabbed a folded piece of paper from the bed and handed it to him. "Here."

The writing on the motel stationery wasn't Winter's. He unfolded the paper and read. "Winter and I have gone to Alaska." He looked sharply at Deborah. "Alaska?" Was Winter upset enough to need a body of water between them?

"Read the rest."

The paper trembled in his fingers. "Winter's dad has cancer?" He met Deborah's gaze and saw tears in her eyes. "He isn't expected to live more than a few days." *Oh, man.* "We have a flight to Ketchikan tonight. Neil will let you know about Redding." She left? Without even saying goodbye. Without him getting to explain.

He shoved the note back toward Deb. "I have to go to her."

"I wish we could, but finances won't allow it."

"Where's Neil?" He had to talk to the team leader.

"He must've taken them to the airport. But, Ty, listen, everything will be fine." She patted his shoulder. "Winter's dad is pretty old. He was fifty-something when she was born. That both of her parents have lived this long without medical difficulties has been a blessing."

"I'm familiar with the story." He stared at the woman before him, wishing she comprehended his and Winter's past. Tonight was supposed to be the meeting where Winter explained. Now, her confession would be pushed off until who knew when.

"Randi left with Winter. The rest of us will probably run

the conference in Redding. Maybe you'll get another chance to speak." Deborah smiled like she was excited for the opportunity.

"I've got to find Neil." He turned to leave, then pivoted back. "Thanks for letting me read the note." He waved then jogged down the hallway. He had to make plans. A flight from Portland to Ketchikan should get him there by morning, even with a layover in Seattle. But he had to talk to Neil first. Would the team adviser trust Ty to follow Winter to Alaska without demanding a lengthy explanation?

He doubted it.

Lord, show me the right steps to take. Be with Winter. Comfort her through this loss. Be with her family.

Back at the men's motel room, Jeremy was tossing shirts into his suitcase. No sign of Neil.

"My parents made arrangements for a midnight flight." Jeremy grabbed his Bible and laid it on top of his clothes.

"A midnight flight?" *Good to know.* He'd try to catch the same one. "Sorry about your grandpa, Jer. Are you close?"

The younger man nodded. "In the last few years, we have been. Ever since they retired in Ketchikan to be near my family."

Jeremy went into the bathroom, sounding like he was gathering supplies. Ty moved to the desk and made a call to the airlines. There were still seats available on the midnight flight, so he made a reservation. After he ended the call, Neil entered the room, looking exhausted. At the same time, Jeremy hurried from the bathroom and dropped a small carry-on at the end of the bed.

"They're off." Neil heaved a sigh. "The rest of us can divvy up responsibilities for Redding." He stared at Jeremy's packed suitcase. "What's up, Jer?"

"Mom called. They bought a ticket for me. I have to go. Plus, I'd like to see Grandpa again on this side."

"Of course, you do." Neil sat in a chair and untied his shoes. "I wonder who should speak this week."

Ty pulled his suitcase off the luggage rack and threw in the few essentials he'd unpacked. "Uh, Neil, I hate to ask this, but would you mind driving Jeremy and me to the airport? I know you just returned from there, and if you're too beat, I understand. We can buzz a cab." He wanted to pack his bag and hit the road. All he could think about was being there for Winter during this awful time.

If he had the chance, he'd like to clear the air between them too. But that came second. First and foremost, he wanted to comfort her. And he hoped to see her dad too. Even though Darren Cowan hadn't accepted Ty as Winter's husband ten years ago, he'd like a moment to assure her father that this time he'd keep his promises.

"What do you mean, take you to the airport?" Neil walked in his stocking feet to the opposite bed and sat down. "You can't leave. I may need you to speak this coming week."

Ty dropped to the edge of the bed, opposite Neil. "Neil, I have to go to Winter. I can't let her go through this alone. Losing her dad will break her heart."

"She's not alone. Randi's there. Her family's there." Neil shook his head and patted Ty's knee. "I can tell you have a crush on her, but now isn't a good time. Wait until she's had time to mourn. Then be her knight in shining armor." He glanced away as if hiding his chuckle.

That Neil thought Ty had a juvenile infatuation with Winter perturbed him. "You don't understand, I *must* go to her." He stared intently at the team leader, not wanting to say too much, but wishing he knew the whole story. No matter what, Ty was determined not to divulge Winter's secret. He wouldn't let her down again.

Neil's face went ashen. "No. *You* don't understand. You've

just met Winter, while I've worked with her through five years of travel and ministry. I know her ups and downs. In many ways, I've been a fill-in father." He strummed his hand through his graying hair and yawned. "Randi's with her. Jeremy's going. End of subject." He stood and moved toward the bathroom.

Ty's breathing came hard. He had to convince him, somehow. "I have to go. My flight leaves at midnight."

Neil stared at Ty like he couldn't believe he was arguing with him. "You're part of our team now. Deborah, you, and I will run the conference in Redding. That is if the pastor doesn't choose to cancel."

He knew about submission to Christian leadership, but this was his wife they were talking about. Their future together was hanging by a thin thread. Whether or not he went the extra mile in supporting her through this difficult time could make the difference. Wasn't he supposed to be willing to lay down his life for her? She needed his shoulder now more than ever—whether or not she'd admit that.

Standing, he faced Neil. "I'm sorry you disagree with me, but I've made my decision. I'm flying to Ketchikan to be with Wint—"

"Ty—" Jeremy interrupted.

"I think it's in everyone's best interest that you don't." Neil glared at him with a steel firmness Ty hadn't yet seen in him.

The secret about their marriage loomed in his mind. All he had to do was explain everything. Then the team leader would understand his need to go to Winter. *No, I couldn't. I promised myself I wouldn't.* Divulging their past, without her here, would be a betrayal of the worst kind.

"I have to go." He didn't want to appear combative, but he was desperate.

Neil's longsuffering-sounding sigh let Ty know how exasperated he felt. "All right, Tyler, give me one good reason why you should follow her to Alaska." He sounded like a father giving his son one last chance to redeem himself. "I know several reasons why you shouldn't. Besides what I already expressed, Randi is demanding your termination from Passion's Prayer. Winter even mentioned something along those lines on the way to the airport."

Ty knew the cause for her thoughts on dismissal after what she witnessed—or rather, what she thought she witnessed—and for that reason alone he needed to follow her.

"One reason?" He licked his dry lips. He really didn't want to reveal his and Winter's past.

Neil nodded.

She would be hurt if he told. Possibly outraged. But what else could he do? If he kept silent, Neil would stand his ground about him not going to Alaska. And he couldn't let that happen.

He started to speak, then cleared his throat. He couldn't say the words. *Lord, this is Winter's place to explain. Not mine. What should I do?* He rubbed his face, pressed his fingers against his closed eyelids, wishing for an easy way out. Maybe he could grab his suitcase and dash for the door. Neil wouldn't tackle him, would he? But if Ty made a big scene leaving, no doubt, he wouldn't be invited back on the team.

He sighed, still struggling.

"Well?" Neil prodded.

"I need to go be with Winter, and help her through this time, because …" Ty met Neil's gaze. Disappointing him, and Winter, felt like a blow to the stomach. How could he tell him? He stared at the floor. He couldn't, that's all there was to it. *But if I don't tell—* "Uh, Neil"—he sucked in a breath—"I want to, no, I need to be with Winter, because, well, because she's m-my ex-wife." The words tore from his lips. Part of him wanted to gobble them back into his mouth.

"What?" Neil's voice went high.

A second later, Jeremy stood right in front of Ty. "That's a lie! She's my aunt. I'd know whether or not she was married."

Ty glanced at his watch and inched away from Winter's nephew. Moving toward his luggage, he carefully avoided bumping into Jeremy or looking into Neil's shocked face.

Neil's hand came down hard on the suitcase lid. "You'd better explain yourself."

Ty silently counted the eight steps it would take to get to the door. He gulped, hating himself for spoiling Winter's secret. "If I tell you, will you drive me to the airport?"

"Just explain." Neil's tone brooked no argument.

These were Winter's friends. Choosing when to share their past was her prerogative. She planned to inform the team of their marriage during the meeting tonight. Since the emergency kept that from happening, would she understand his reasons for sharing their story?

Jeremy's and Neil's gazes pinioned him, demanding he finish what he started. "Okay, here's the deal." He paused. Inhaled. "Winter and I were married ten years ago."

Neil gasped. "It was you?"

"No way!" Jeremy exploded.

"Yes, it was me. We met through my sister, Lacey, Winter's roommate in college. The one she spoke about the other night."

Neil looked like he might get sick. He stroked his forehead and stared up at the ceiling as if he couldn't believe what he was hearing.

Lord, help him understand. I've got to go to Winter. I want to protect her, comfort her, be there for her during the worst of this.

"Why haven't I heard about this before?" A scowl creased Jeremy's face.

"You should have told me the first day we met." Neil's glare bore down on Ty.

"I know. And I'm sorry." Regret ate at him. "I left that up to Winter."

"She should have told me then." Neil paced across the room, his movements agitated.

"I agree. But there were reasons she didn't."

Jeremy stepped closer to Ty, again, his arms crossed as if demanding more information.

Ty debated what to say. "She and I were married for six months about ten years ago."

"I can't believe it." Jeremy plopped down where Neil had been sitting and shook his head. "Wait until my parents hear. They'll go nuts! It's a good thing Grandpa doesn't know."

"He knew." Ty would never forget the look of anguish, or mistrust, on Mr. Cowan's face the day of their wedding. "He walked your aunt down the aisle. Your folks attended too."

"No way!" Jeremy shook his head in denial.

"I want to leave the rest of the story for Winter to tell." Ty stared into Neil's pale features. "She had her reasons for keeping our marriage private. When I showed up at the conference in Coeur d'Alene and wanted to join the team, she didn't want me tagging along. However, God brought us together for a purpose. I'm hoping we can reconcile according to His Word. I love her. I'll do anything to stick by her side." He moved closer to Neil. "Please, I need to go to her."

The room grew thick with silence as Neil stared hard at Ty, and he returned the other man's observation.

"I can't believe she didn't tell me it was you." The older man sounded hurt. "I knew her story, just not about—"

"Me."

"Why didn't she tell us?"

"She was giving me a chance to prove myself a changed

man." It seemed he blew that big time by blabbing all this stuff to Neil and Jeremy. He sucked in a deep breath. "She probably won't even speak to me now."

He could see Neil wanted more information, but he'd said enough. Too much. "You deserve the whole story, but you should hear it from her. Please believe me when I say my intentions are honorable. I only want to support her and be there for her, like I should have been all these years."

After a weighty pause, Neil sighed in a way that sounded more like a groan. "I can't imagine how you two danced around your past issues since you joined our team. You fit in so well."

"I know." Ty nodded. "Except for Randi's grudge."

"I'm getting to the bottom of that." Neil stared at the wall, in deep thought, it seemed. "Now it makes sense why Winter went to the garage that night to see you. I've wondered about it all week." He shuffled to the window and pulled the paisley curtains aside. The slump of his shoulders and the way his hand massaged the back of his neck told of his frustration.

Ty wished he had something encouraging to tell this man who befriended him, accepted him on the team, and stood up for him during that awful meeting when Randi tried getting him kicked off the team for visiting Winter's room alone. "She planned to tell you about our past during the team meeting tonight."

"I figured as much." Neil sighed. "I'm trusting you to do what's right, Tyler."

"I will."

"You'll treat her with nothing but kindness and respect."

"Absolutely." Ty gulped. These were mandates he'd follow on his own as a servant of Christ, but hearing the admonition from Neil made him feel like he was taking a solemn vow. He could add a few of his own to the list. He promised to love, cherish, and put her above himself till death do us part.

Neil shuffled across the room to where he took off his shoes. "Guess we'd better load up the car. The airport's almost an hour away."

Ty felt like letting out a whoop. But when he thought of this evening's cost, he sobered. Now he had to face Winter with two issues—the episode with Randi and his betrayal of her trust where the team was concerned. These two things could sink him.

Right now, however, the most important thing was helping her through the loss of her father in any way he could. By tomorrow morning he'd be in Alaska.

Hopefully, she wouldn't put him on the first flight back.

Thirty-seven

Under a threatening sky thick with dark clouds, Ty and Jeremy landed at the Ketchikan International Airport early the next day.

"It's socked in." Jeremy stared out the jet's window. "We're lucky to have landed at all considering the weather."

Ty yawned, just barely awake. He had several hours of less-than-satisfactory sleep during the layover in Seattle. All night, he kept trying to stay alert in case Winter happened to walk past him, but he never saw her. She probably grabbed a room and caught one of the first flights out this morning after he fell asleep.

At the rotating carousel inside the terminal, he grabbed his suitcase. "Do we call a cab, or what?"

Jeremy chuckled, and Ty was glad to see he had finally relaxed around him. Ty hated the strain he felt with Winter's nephew ever since he shared about his marriage.

"Didn't you notice where we landed?" Jeremy nodded toward the doors they were approaching.

"Guess not. Until the fasten-seatbelt light turned off, I was sound asleep."

"We're not on the same island as Ketchikan. The airport is on Gravina Island, while Ketchikan is on Revillagigedo." Jeremy almost sounded like a tour guide.

Ty exited the glass doors into the rain. Through the morning haze, he saw turbulent gray water with white caps waving like flags between the place where they stood and the land across the channel. "I see what you mean. How do we get across the water?"

"A ferry will shuttle us over for a small price. It leaves on the hour and half hour." Jeremy checked his watch. "Which means we better hurry or we'll miss the next departure. Come on."

"I'm right behind you."

Beneath a long, covered corridor, the two men trudged toward the ferry ramp. Here they were protected from the downpour. Up ahead, Ty saw the wind and rain whipping around the ship as if enraged they were coming aboard.

"Hold on to your hat!" Jeremy pulled down on his sweatshirt hood.

"Wish I had a hat to hold on to." Ty yanked the collar of his coat tightly around his neck. "This downpour is wild!" His teeth chattered.

"Typical for Southeast Alaska this time of year," Jeremy yelled over the moaning sound of the 100-foot ferry scraping against the pier.

"Low tide. Smell it?" Jeremy moved down the steeply angled ramp toward the *Ken Eichner II*.

Ty nodded, his focus intent on moving forward against the wind. He'd already inhaled the ocean's scent. The pungent aroma reminded him of family vacations along the Pacific coastline and the frolicking waves he and Lacey played in as children. He smiled at the recollection, despite his soaked hair and freezing cheeks.

Once aboard the ferry, the men hurried inside the enclosed deck-level shelter. A green bench lined both sides of the narrow room, and Ty sat down and placed his bag on the floor next to his feet. Other passengers dropped onto the benches across from him.

"Welcome to Alaska." Jeremy brushed raindrops off his jacket.

"Thanks. A hot cup of coffee would be good about now." Ty couldn't stop his teeth from chattering. He rubbed his hands together for warmth.

"No kidding."

The ferry soon pulled away from the docking platform, swaying and bobbing with the wind and waves. Still sleepy, Ty leaned his head back and shut his eyes, trying to relax, despite the chill—and his concern for the impending meeting with Winter's family.

"Hey, Ty, we're here."

He jerked awake at Jeremy's voice. How could he have fallen asleep when he was so cold? Was he ready to meet up with Winter's family? And Judson? Inwardly, he groaned. Did Winter's brother still carry a grudge? Ty was about to find out.

The ferry bumped into its berth at the other side of the channel, and he felt amazed that the ride had been calm considering how rough the water appeared. The whining of the engines bringing the boat to a stop alerted him it was time to disembark.

Here we go. Like a backhoe moving earth, apprehension dug into him.

The small group of early morning travelers exited the ferry, plunging headlong into the heavy rain, but just as quickly they were saved from the downpour by the enclosed walkway alongside the ramp. Ty and Jeremy followed the others. Trudging side by side, Ty didn't say anything, not even when he noticed Judson waiting at the top.

But his gut clenched. Would his former brother-in-law be angry at him for showing up now?

Judson's umbrella suddenly arched upward above his head, flapping in the wind as if it were trying to hurl itself into the sea. He looked like he'd lost his grip, but then he lunged toward the handrail, grabbing the umbrella just in time. At that moment, he glanced up, frustration showing on his face.

The instant Judson recognized it was Ty walking up the ramp beside Jeremy, Ty felt the man's angst as if he punched him. Apparently, his ex-brother-in-law didn't know he was coming.

"Dad." Jeremy and his father embraced.

Judson's face, which had more wrinkles than the last time Ty saw him, creased with unspoken questions. "Tyler."

"Judson." Ty extended his ice-cold hand, unsure whether Judson would reciprocate. He did, if only for a moment. "It's been a while." Ty followed them toward the parking area, even though Judson didn't invite him to do so.

"What? Ten years?" At a green Corsica, he opened the trunk.

"About that."

Ty and Jeremy dropped their wet bags inside.

Ignoring Judson's stern expression, Ty climbed into the backseat of the car, relieved to escape the chilly elements. Rainwater dripped from his hair into his eyes and down his cheeks. The wind off the ocean left his hands and nose freezing. He put his fingers near his mouth and blew warm air over them, brushing away raindrops in the process.

"Is Winter expecting you?" Judson's voice sliced through the silence in the car. "She didn't mention you were coming."

"No, she isn't expecting me."

The older man's thick eyebrows rose.

"It's a long story. I'm with Passion's Prayer now." Ty hoped to keep things amicable.

"Really?" Judson's derisive tone let Ty know just what he thought of him.

"Dad, did you go to Aunt Winter's wedding?" Jeremy rubbed his hands together, warming them. "Why wasn't I told she was married?"

Why did he have to bring that up now?

Judson glanced at Ty in the rearview mirror. An embarrassed hue darkened his unshaven cheeks. "Mom and I flew down to the wedding. You and your sisters stayed with friends. You must've been nine or so. Don't you remember?" Ty watched Judson's eyes glare at him in the rearview mirror as he started the engine.

"No." Jeremy shook his head, splattering the window with water droplets. "Why didn't we ever talk about them splitting up?"

"It was a quiet, um, separation." Judson drove the car through the parking lot. "Winter didn't live near us. Grandma and Grandpa were still in the Philippines." Judson nailed Ty with another glare in the mirror. "I don't mean to put you on the spot, Tyler, but is this the best time for you to be showing up? Winter's preoccupied with our dad's illness."

Ty returned his stare. "I'm just here to support her."

"What about ten years ago?"

He didn't say it, but by his tone, Ty figured he was calling him a jerk, or worse. Frustration rose within him. Would a grilling take place every step of his trek back to Winter? But then, he deserved it, didn't he? Hadn't he inflicted pain on the whole family when he betrayed her?

"Ten years ago, I blew it." He spoke softly, an honest confession he hoped Judson would accept. He saw Jeremy's questioning look, making him suspect he connected Ty with Winter's testimony. "I'm here to help, not interfere." Staring out the window through the rain pouring down the side of the car, his emotions felt as melancholy as the gray skies of Ketchikan.

Several awkward minutes passed.

"I'll only say this once." Again, Judson glared. "Don't cause trouble."

"Don't plan to." But trouble seemed inevitable. What would Winter say about him following her to Alaska? Would the gesture finally prove his undying love? Or was she still mad about that scene with Randi? He needed to talk with her about that. Which reminded him, Randi would be at the hospital. If he was going to be around her, he'd have to beware.

The verses he recently memorized from I Corinthians trickled through his mind. *Love is patient, love is kind … love never fails.*

Father, may these attributes of love be real in my life. Help me to be the strength Winter needs. And show me how to explain what she walked in on last night. We need Your help.

When they arrived at the hospital, Ty and Jeremy used the men's room to change into dry clothing. Ty put on an Eastern Washington University sweatshirt, glad to be free of his damp shirt and coat.

Inside the elevator, he leaned against one wall and didn't make eye contact with the other two guys. On the second floor, they trudged down the quiet corridor, dad and son walking side by side, Ty staying to the rear.

In front of a closed door, Judson stopped and braced his hands toward Ty. "This is as far as you go. Your presence may upset my family. I won't be responsible for that. If Winter wants to see you, she'll come out."

A few arguments came to mind. He could do what he pleased. Whatever Judson might think of himself, he wasn't the law in Ketchikan. Ty traveled all the way from Oregon to Alaska, endured bitter wind and getting soaked to the skin, and put up with Judson's dirty looks and remarks, all to see Winter, to assure her he'd remain by her side. Despite what Judson had to say about the matter, Ty was determined to do just that.

However, in the face of his former brother-in-law's sorrow, Ty nodded. "No problem. I'll wait here."

Judson and Jeremy disappeared behind the door marked 221. Ty stared hard at the number until his eyes blurred and still the door didn't open.

He sighed. This trip was about Winter being with her dad, not about what Ty wanted. He'd give her all the time she needed. But he ached to see her. And for her to know he was here.

Thirsty and in need of something to do to keep his mind off waiting, he went in search of a water fountain. When he returned, he leaned against the wall across from the door Judson had entered and waited some more. He thought over the verses he was memorizing. Over an hour passed. When the door finally swished open, he bolted upright, eager to see Winter.

Instead, Randi stepped into the hall. As soon as she saw him, she jerked the door closed as if he might sneak in behind her. "What're you doing here? Winter doesn't want to see you."

Love is kind.

Ty swallowed back an angry retort. Tired and in need of a full night's sleep, insensitive words would come easily but be difficult to erase later. "I'd like to see her."

Randi's lack of a comeback pricked his curiosity until he noticed an approaching nurse and Randi's gaze focused on the woman. A greeting passed between them, then the nurse entered Darren's room. Randi faced him again. "What do you think you'll prove by showing up in Alaska?"

Love is not rude.

"As I said, I plan to see Winter."

"You have some nerve coming here after what you did." She crossed her arms.

"Me?" He felt a knot forming in his stomach. "You were the one who hugged me."

"As if I would embrace you."

He pointed at her. "You made it appear as if something fishy was going on so Winter would get the wrong impression." He didn't mean for his voice to get so loud, but his emotions were rising.

The nurse reentered the hallway. "Please, keep your voices down. We don't want our patients disturbed. The lobby is located on the first floor for your convenience." She continued toward the nurse's station.

"The gentleman was just leaving." Randi gave his sweatshirt a nudge.

"Not on your life." He moved two steps away and leaned against the wall again. "I traveled here to see Winter. That's exactly what I intend to do." He closed his eyes, wishing she'd take the hint that the conversation was over.

"Your involvement with Passion's Prayer is finished." She seemed to be gloating. "Winter said so."

He gritted his teeth, demanding control of the irrational thought that he'd like to throw her over his shoulder and dump her into the ocean. That would cool both their tempers.

"What do you have against me?" He raked his fingers through his damp hair. "Since day one, you've wanted me gone."

"Not exactly true."

What did she mean by that? He noticed her squinting eyes, her arms crossed over her ribs, the way her foot tapped the floor, and like a slap, the answer came to him.

Love is not self-seeking.

He'd done this, hadn't he? Humbleness crept over his heart. Had his wrongdoing fueled this woman's resentment and finagling? "Is this hate of yours about that first day we met?"

"No."

"Are you still carrying a grudge, all the way to Alaska, even though I told you how sorry I was?"

"Of course not." Was she lying?

How he wished he'd never tagged along with her to Pastor David's parsonage that day.

"Then what?"

"Get this through your thick skull"—she jabbed her finger at him—"we don't want your ex-con status on our team. Winter's ministry has a good reputation. You're not going to ruin it for us!"

"How could I ruin Passion's Prayer? Isn't Winter's mission about inspiring people in their walk with God? What exactly are you saying?"

"Leave. That's what I'm saying." Her glare intensified. "You will *not* see her."

Love. Never. Fails.

Lord, help?

He pointed at the door. "When Winter walks out, I'll be standing right here."

"I'll make you go."

"You don't have that kind of power."

A challenge flamed livid in her eyes. He didn't mean the words as a gauntlet, but Randi may have taken them that way.

Love does not delight in … evil. The admonition was fading into oblivion.

Determined not to say another word to her, especially something he'd regret later, he turned his back toward her. He would stand this way for as long as he had to, but he wouldn't speak to the vixen.

A moment later, she parked herself in front of him, her stance difficult to ignore. "A man is dying in there. Why don't you leave this family in peace?"

His nerves were shot. "Look, if I have to stand by this wall

all night, I will." Even though he told himself he wouldn't speak to her, he seemed unable to hold back his frustration.

"I won't allow it."

"You are not in charge of Winter's future."

"Want to bet? As her assistant, I keep men away from her. I do plan her future. A bright future without you!" Her gaze burned into him. "You are nothing to her. *Nothing*."

A growl wrenched from somewhere beneath his ribs. "That's where you're wrong." He leaned forward, glaring back at her, daring her not to believe him. "Because *I* am her husband!"

Thirty-eight

Ty's blood pumped hot in his ears.

Randi sputtered and gasped. "Th-that's not true." The fire in her gaze declared she'd like to karate kick him—or something equally as painful.

He clenched his fists at his side, anticipating the worst.

Judson exited his father's room, a snarl on his face. "I told you not to cause trouble."

Ty bristled. "I'm not the one causing trouble." His glare forked Randi's with accusation.

"I was going for coffee when I overheard you." Judson's voice lowered. "Don't you care that our father's ill? He's … dying … just beyond that door."

The rage in Ty's chest deflated. "I'm sorry."

"Sorry?" Judson gave him a snide look. "Maybe I should show you what I think of you being sorry. How about we step outside and have a man-to-man talk?" His heavy breathing punctuated the air. "I've been itching to put you in your place for ten years."

So, he was still holding a grudge.

"He said he's Winter's husband." Randi glowered. "Like I believe that."

Judson pointed at Ty. "You're not her husband."

"Was," Ty clarified.

Judson jabbed his shoulder. "Outside, buddy. You and me. Now!" He stomped to the elevator.

Ty licked his lips, feeling tension creep up his spine. Sure, he'd meet Judson outside for a "man-to-man" conversation. He ran for the elevator, relieved to escape Randi's rude comments. On the way down to the main floor, he stood opposite Judson, neither of them speaking.

Ty wasn't hunting for an altercation with Winter's brother, but angry feelings had been steaming from his pores for the last fifteen minutes. He was sick of Randi. Tired of Judson's implications. But fighting?

As soon as the elevator door opened, Judson marched out like a soldier on a mission. Ty followed, adrenaline pumping through his body.

Barely outside the glass doors of the hospital, Judson pivoted toward him and pulsed his finger under Ty's nose. "I'm warning you, stay away from my sister."

"I can't agree with that. Winter and I might be getting—"

"No, you're not!" Judson yelled.

"He's a liar and a troublemaker," Randi spoke from somewhere behind Ty.

He groaned, wishing she hadn't followed them.

"And a cheat." Judson's gaze screamed of injustices needing payment.

"Not anymore." Ty braced himself. His former brother-in-law looked enraged enough to slug him. But Ty's prison experience had toughened him. Judson was fifteen years older, plus he packed more flabby weight. Ty could probably knock him flat. However, making a scene in the hospital parking lot wasn't what Winter needed. Nor would it be in obedience to that chapter on love he was memorizing.

Some of his angst fizzled, again. "How about if we just walk it off?"

"How about I punch you in the nose?"

"I don't want to fight you."

"No?" Judson grabbed Ty and yanked him away from the hospital's entrance. His manhandling upped Ty's adrenaline rush to the point where he could picture doing Judson physical harm.

"Go!" Judson pointed toward the highway paralleling the hospital. "Get away from my family. And don't come back."

"I can't do that."

"Hit him, Judson!" Randi clapped.

Ty cut a glance at her, warning her to shut up.

His ex-brother-in-law obviously meant to have it out with him if he didn't leave. Ty wasn't about to run away. He came this far. There was no way he'd let Winter grieve alone, without him nearby if she needed him. "You're making a mistake. I love your sister." He swallowed his anger. "And she loves me."

Randi gasped.

Judson faced Ty nose to nose. "My sister left you. Period. With Biblical cause. She's done with you."

He must be overly-stressed with his father's illness and impending death to be acting so belligerent. Ty's presence was, no doubt, creating fuel for his frustrations, but that wasn't any reason to fight.

"I'm a Christian now." Ty made his voice sound calmer than he felt. "I've changed."

"He's an ex-con," Randi yelled from the sidelines. "Embezzlement."

Lord, could You intervene? My temper will only take so much.

"And you plan on getting back with my sister? Bad boy turned good? That's not happening." Judson grabbed Ty's collar and pressed his thumb into Ty's throat.

He coughed. His tolerance was wearing thin. One stiff punch in the center of Judson's gut and this angry, overweight man was going down. But what if he smacked his head on the pavement and got a concussion? How would that look to Winter? Or to his future relations with her family?

In that pause, Judson shoved against Ty's chest. He stumbled backward before regaining his footing, glaring at Judson. Winter's brother had no right treating him so rudely, escorting him outside, threatening him, pushing him around. Judson wanted to settle their differences? Fine. He needed to be taught a lesson.

Ty yanked off his sweatshirt and threw it to the ground, glad it was no longer pouring rain as before. "I'm ready." He clenched his fists at his sides.

"Winter's better off without you." Judson gritted his teeth. "Dad doesn't know you're here. I don't plan to tell him. So leave or pay the consequences."

Ty's thoughts returned to the sick man on the second floor of the hospital. A knot formed in his throat. *Man.* He'd have to stifle his desire to slug the idiot in front of him, even if he deserved it. A groan rumbled through him as he realized how close he came to fighting, possibly hurting, Judson. He felt foolish. What good would it have done? Yes, his need for payback pulsed through his veins. But would that be Christ-like? Would Winter see his love for her in such an action?

Judson took a fighting stance as if daring Ty to throw a punch. Ty stepped back. No, he wasn't going to fight him.

Even so, Judson rammed his fist at Ty's face. He twisted to the left, barely avoiding the strike.

"Stop. This is insane."

"Give it to him, Judson," Randi hooted.

Ty started to move away, but Judson grabbed his collar again. "I'm warning you—leave." His breath was hot and rank.

Ty shoved Judson's hands free of his neck. He heard his shirt rip, and something snapped inside of him. One slug. That's all it would take. Then he'd walk straight upstairs to Darren's room. And, this time, no one would hinder him from going inside. He was finished waiting in the hallway.

A picture of Judson lying on the cement writhing in agony crossed his mind. But Judson deserved payback. He started this conflict. Then, Ty could almost hear Winter whispering in his head, reminding him her dad was dying, and asking him to be kind to her brother. To give second chances like she gave him.

How could he hit her brother after that?

The slug to his gut caught him by surprise. Ty reeled backward and clutched his stomach, sucking in needy breaths. Almost falling to the cement, he couldn't believe Judson hit him that hard.

"You got him good, Judson," Randi chortled.

A second swing nearly clipped him in the chin. "Stop, Judson. I mean it. Stop." He grabbed the man's fists and held them still until his own arms were shaking. "We don't need to fight like this."

"Plenty of need." Judson's chest heaved.

Remembering the last guy he fought in the early days of prison, Ty considered how he might put an end to Judson's fury.

Lord, is one punch justifiable?

No.

No? He released Judson's arms.

A picture of Jesus taking the hits, doing nothing while insults and wrongs were hurled at him caused a strange, yet welcome, peace. Fighting wasn't the answer.

But then, Judson socked him in the nose. Ty gasped at the explosion of pain and buckled to the ground. He held his nose, blood gushing into his mouth and down his chin. Did Judson break his nose? He dashed his shirt sleeve against the tide of blood.

"Had enough?" Winter's brother glowered over him.

Like a drunken sailor tottering on the deck of a ship, Ty pushed off the cement, staggered, nearly fell over, then put his fists up, ready to pummel Judson. "I'm warning you, don't do that again." Ty pointed at him, but he couldn't see straight.

With a growl, Judson barreled toward him. Ty sidestepped and shoved him. Judson thudded to the ground, landing on his elbows and knees. He rolled back and forth, groaning.

Ty lowered himself to the pavement, covering his face with his hands. His gaze met Judson's, and in that moment, with both men moaning, he saw beyond his ex-brother-in-law's display of aggression to the pain in his now, tear-filled eyes.

"I wanted to protect her back then." Judson coughed. "I couldn't."

Ty nodded, his eyes blurring. "I'm sorry."

Footsteps barreled toward them. "What's going on here?" A nurse scrutinized Ty, then Judson.

"Call security!" Randi ordered.

The nurse ran back inside the building.

"No, don't—" Behind him, someone gasped.

He glanced over his shoulder. About ten feet away, a blurry Winter stood, hands on hips, and disbelief crisscrossed her features. He turned away so she couldn't see his face a bloody mess.

"Ty?" He heard her close behind him. He lowered his face, but she bent near him. "Judson, how could you?" She put her hand on Ty's shoulder, knelt by him. "Ty, are you okay?"

"Sas?"

"Oh, Ty." Her lilting voice soothed him like a cool cloth. Seeing her again, even if she was blurry, felt amazing.

"Judson Cowan"—her tone turned to outrage—"what is the meaning of this?"

"Help me up, will you?" Her brother moaned.

Why was Judson groaning? He tripped and landed hard, but Ty had the bellyache and bloody nose to show for their fight. He felt sick. Perhaps coming to Ketchikan was one of his stupider ideas. Maybe he should have waited for Winter back in the lower forty-eight.

"Come on, both of you. Randi, help me." Winter nodded toward her brother, effectively sending her assistant in his direction. She got under Ty's arm and walked close beside him back toward the hospital. He liked that part. Her closeness. Her warmth. Maybe getting hurt wasn't such an awful thing if it meant she would take care of him.

The four of them trudged inside, toward the lobby chairs, and Ty figured the staff would think they had two more patients.

* * * *

"Nurse, could we get some ice?" Winter asked the first person in uniform who approached them.

"Certainly." The woman scurried down the hallway.

Winter dug in her pocket and handed Ty a Kleenex. He tipped his head back against the chair, pinched the bridge of his nose, and pressed the tissue against his nostrils.

A hospital security officer approached them. "What's going on here? Looks like you men were in a fight." He glared at Ty.

"It's over now, sir." Winter hoped he wouldn't call the police.

"I saw the whole thing." Randi stood as if taking charge. "This man is to blame." She pointed at Ty, and the security man's glare intensified.

"Randi, I'm sure it wasn't all Ty's fault." Winter met his sad-looking gaze. "He's in worse shape than Judson."

"You weren't there." Randi turned and spoke quietly to the security guy.

The nurse returned. "Here's the ice." She handed a see-through bag to Winter.

"Thank you." She placed the ice bag gently at Ty's cheek.

He gasped.

"Sorry. It should help with the swelling."

"How's your dad?"

She pulled tissues from a Kleenex box on the end table and handed them to him. "As good as can be expected. I'm still praying for a miracle."

"Then I will too."

She nodded, thankful for his understanding.

"What about me?" Judson moaned. "I'm in pain here too."

"Do you want to press charges?" The officer withdrew a small pad of paper from his shirt pocket and faced Judson. "Your name?"

Winter glared at her brother, telling him silently that she preferred he didn't make a stink—any more than he already had. She didn't know what the two men were fighting about. But knowing Judson's hot temper, she could guess. Past grudges, no doubt.

What was Ty even doing here?

"No charges." Judson sighed. "Just a misunderstanding."

She gave him a tight smile. What was he thinking, fighting with Ty? They were grown men, for goodness' sake. Didn't they have enough trouble in their lives with their dad so sick?

"But Judson—" Randi whined.

"Any more trouble and you both are out of here." The officer hitched his thumb toward the door.

"Yes, sir." Judson exhaled.

Ty nodded.

As the security detail walked away, Winter stood, hands on her hips again. "Now, one of you better tell me how this ruckus started."

"It was Ty's fault." Randi glared at him.

Winter eyed Ty as he wobbled to his feet. With the ice bag

gripped against his face and a wad of bloody tissues pressed under his nose, he looked like he just left the boxing ring. "Ty, sit down." She helped him return to his seat. "What are you doing here?"

"I came to talk with you. Randi and Judson told me to leave." His voice sounded nasally. "I wouldn't."

"So you hit my brother? To talk with me?"

"I didn't hit him." Ty sounded defensive, then his tone changed. "I wanted to, but he fell down first."

Judson groaned.

Winter turned sharply to her brother. "Do you have something to add, big brother?"

"I need to lie down. My knees hurt. And my chest."

His chest? He'd better not be having a heart attack. Not on top of what they were going through with Dad. She moved under his left arm, and Randi scurried under his right. Together they led him toward the elevator.

Glancing back toward the lobby, she saw Ty watching her through slanted eyes. He looked like he wasn't planning to move an inch. Just as well. He and Judson needed to stay a floor's level apart from each other.

However, there was something nice, comforting even, about knowing Ty was in the building. That he traveled all the way to Alaska to talk with her touched her heart.

Not that it changed anything between them.

Thirty-nine

All day Winter held herself together for Mom's sake. But she was losing ground. Soon, the moment would come when her composure melted in the heat of grief.

Only once, when she first arrived at the hospital, did Dad open his eyes. She felt certain he recognized her by the wet glimmer she saw in his green irises that matched her own. She was thankful he knew she came to him, but even that faded. Ever since then, he was drifting away. She didn't need the nurse to say so. She could tell he was passing from this life to another one, right before her eyes.

She didn't want to leave his side, or Mom's, for even a minute. But considering what transpired between Judson and Ty, maybe she ought to check on Ty. Did Judson break his nose? What a terrible thought.

Glancing around the dimly lit room, she saw Mom sitting close to Dad's bed, holding his hand, her lips moving in prayer. Jeremy knelt beside her chair. Pastor Gray stood near the window, reading out loud from the Psalms. Judson rested on the other bed with his eyes closed, and his wife, Tonya, sat near him. With Randi dozing in the corner, it seemed like a good opportunity for Winter to sneak away for a few minutes.

Quietly, she left the room and hurried down the hallway to the elevator.

How could her brother have hit Ty like that? A little while ago, he babbled about giving her ex what he deserved ten years ago. Then he whined and told her he was sorry for not being there for her when she needed him. How strange for Judson's protective walls to be on high alert. While she felt enraged at him for his mean behavior toward Ty, part of her enjoyed having a big brother defend her again, something she hadn't experienced since high school.

Slowly, she approached Ty, who remained seated in the lobby with his eyes closed. Was he asleep? She hated waking him up, but this break might be all the time she'd have for the rest of the night. "Hey, Ty." She nudged his arm. "How are you doing?"

His eyes jerked open. The ice bag crashed to the floor. "Oh, uh, better, I guess."

She gasped at his swollen nose. "I'm so sorry." Bending over, she retrieved the cold pack and handed it to him. "Wow. That looks painful."

"Sort of." He sounded stuffy like he had a cold. "Care to sit by me?" He set the ice bag on the magazine-laden table.

"For a minute." She dropped down on the brown seat next to his. "I really am sorry for what Judson did." She took in the swollen, purplish cast around his nose and eyes, and cringed. "I'm embarrassed by his actions, but—" Nothing she could say would take Ty's pain away or remove the incident from their memories. She could call Judson's actions foolish and immature, but he thought he was sticking up for her. Still, poor Ty. *Men.* "Do you think it's broken? You could go down to the ER and have them check."

"I'll be all right." He sniffed and looked away like he didn't want her making a fuss over him. "How's your dad?"

"The nurse warned us a couple of hours ago his time is short." She covered her face with her hands and massaged her eyes. Exhaustion made her yawn. "What did you want to talk with me about earlier?"

* * * *

The pallor of her skin, the vacant look in her eyes, the tangled red hair cascading down her shoulders, all screamed of fatigue and stress. He smiled, but the small movement shot pain up his nose. He bet his smile was lopsided too.

If only he could do something to help her. Wait. He knew what she used to like when she felt stressed or tired. Unsure if she would allow him to touch her, he smoothed his hand over her hair. When she didn't pull away, he stroked his fingers through her tresses, carefully untangling the long strands.

"What are you doing?"

"Helping you relax."

"Ty." She sounded like she might ask him to stop, but when he gently massaged her scalp, she sighed and seemed to melt into the chair.

For a few minutes, he worked rhythmically, squeezing the taut muscles of her shoulders and neck until he felt her tension ebbing away. "Better?"

Her soft purr of relaxation let him know he made a good decision, finally.

"Much. Thank you."

He couldn't resist dropping a kiss against her cheek, right in the center of her dimple.

"Ty—" She pulled away, a perplexed frown replacing her peaceful expression. "Are you ready to explain?"

His mind turned fuzzy. Explain? She stared at him like he should know what she meant. "About the fight?" He tried to read her better. "I didn't hit your brother. I came close, but I didn't. After he hit me, he charged again, and I shoved him. That's all. He flopped on the ground and hurt himself."

"I know. That's what he told me also." She turned away from meeting his gaze. "I meant, why are you here? The last time I saw you, my personal assistant was in your arms." Her eyes sparkled with unshed tears.

Oh, man.

In her rush to get to Alaska, her father's illness, and then seeing Ty bloodied by her brother, he figured she might have forgotten that incident. Now didn't seem like the right time to explain. "That's what I hoped to talk with you about." He gulped, thinking how he also needed to explain about telling Neil, Jeremy, and now, Randi, about their previous relationship.

"I can't stay long. Ten minutes, tops."

He glanced at the wall clock. Ten minutes to explain twenty-four hours of misunderstandings?

He slipped his hand around hers. "I'm sorry about your dad." He squeezed gently, relieved when she didn't pull away. "I want you to know, I'm here for you. And I love you."

"Then why were you hugging Randi?"

"I wasn't."

She pulled her hand away. "I saw you!"

"Randi hugged me. I don't know why, other than to make you think something was going on that wasn't. I didn't initiate it. Never would."

She shook her head. "Something didn't make sense. But I can't believe she'd fling herself in your arms without encouragement."

"Believe me, I didn't give her an invitation. She's got a vendetta against me."

An elderly man and woman shuffled across the hospital lobby, and by the way their arms were locked together, they seemed to be keeping each other upright. Slowly, they sat down in chairs opposite Ty and Winter.

Winter leaned closer to Ty. "That's a little far-fetched, don't you think?"

"I know she's your friend." He matched his quieter tone to hers.

"My *best* friend."

Regret pricked his heart. She used to call him her best friend, a long time ago. He reined in his emotions. "I'm going to say something, and I hope you'll be open-minded." Some of his words came out slurred due to the swelling in his face. He grabbed a tissue and wiped his nose.

"Okay."

"I'm certain Randi stashed the five hundred dollars in my wallet."

She harrumphed. "You accused me of doing that same thing."

"I'm sorry for blaming you." He touched her shoulder. "Remember, I was the one being falsely accused, and I only had one thing to go on."

"And that was—?"

"When I was in the shower that night, I heard someone enter the room." He paused, leading her back to a previous conversation. "I came out of the bathroom and found a flyer on the floor, remember?"

"Neil and Jeremy both carry them. We all do."

"But this one smelled like women's perfume or hand lotion—of vanilla—like you wear."

"Why would I want to make that awful scene in your motel room?" She stared hard at him.

He didn't want this discussion. He needed sleep. And for her to look at him with love in her gaze again. Apparently, that wasn't about to happen any time soon. "I don't know, to embarrass me?" He sighed, frustrated. "Later, I found out someone else in our group wears the same fragrance."

"Randi?"

"Yes."

"She borrows my lotion. That doesn't prove anything."

"She was the one who asked, 'Did anyone check his wallet?' She knew exactly where the money was, don't you see? Then, remember the day you and I had that fight at the shop?" He watched her face darken. "I think Randi called David."

"Speculation." She glanced at the clock and stood. "I have to go."

He stood also. "One more minute?" At her slight nod, he continued, still having trouble forming some words. "After Randi saw us together at the zoo yesterday, she retaliated by throwing herself into my arms when you stepped into the lobby. She'd been gushing about how sorry she felt for treating me badly, and her sincerity disarmed me. The next thing I knew, she was hugging the life out of me."

Winter looked doubtful. "If what you say is true, why would Randi risk hurting me?"

She checked the clock again. His time was up.

"I don't know, except she wants me off the team. She keeps telling me how more-deserving men are already in line for you. And how I'm a zero on the list."

She frowned. "She said a *zero*?"

"Yes."

"I don't know what to say, other than it's been her job to run interference for me. Tact isn't her strong point." She dusted off her slacks. "Maybe we can talk about this another time?"

"Sure. I'm here, if you need me."

"Thanks."

Love rejoices with the truth.

His chest ached with his need to tell her what he did. "Also, I, uh, told Neil and Jeremy."

She swiveled toward him. "About—?"

"Us."

Her gaze bore into his.

"I'm sorry, but Neil wouldn't let me follow you unless I gave him one good reason why. I, uh, I told him I was your ex-husband." He gulped what felt like a giant wad of toilet paper.

Her mouth dropped open, and she glared at him. "I don't believe it."

"It gets worse."

"Worse?"

He wiped his nose again and grimaced. "Earlier, I got upset at Randi, and blurted to her that I was … your husband."

"You what—?" Her cheeks turned crimson. "You had no right. You shouldn't have told anyone on my team about us."

"I know. But you didn't, not in all these years." He tried to disguise his accusation with a softer tone. "Isn't it time to share the truth?"

"That was for me to decide. Not you!"

"Paging Winter Cowan!" The intercom crackled. "Paging Winter Cowan! You are needed in room 221."

"Oh, no." She dashed for the elevator.

He'd blown it on so many levels. Should he follow her? Stay here in the lobby? Or head for the airport?

A heavy sigh rumbled through him. Then he strode to the elevator. He'd stand outside Darren's room all night, if necessary. Waiting. Just in case Winter needed him.

Forty

The wall across from room 221 welcomed Ty like an old friend. He leaned against the hard surface and shut his eyes. Sleep, that's what he needed. Eight hours of undisturbed rest would resolve a giant-sized portion of his current discouragement.

A cry pierced the hospital's silence and rippled through him. Every nerve strained at attention. Winter's voice? For several tense seconds, uncertainty nailed his feet to the floor.

When the sound came again, he launched away from the wall and rushed into Darren's room with a determination challenging anyone, including Judson, to stop him. Inside the darkened hospital room, the scene staggered his footsteps. Near her father's bed, Winter stood doubled over, sobbing. Ty's gaze crossed Darren's pale face, his rigid body, the heart monitor showing a steady flat line. The end had come.

Silently, and without making eye contact with anyone, he slipped behind Winter and gently drew her against his chest. Wrapping his arms around her, he held her. She didn't pull away, although her head and shoulders remained slumped over as she sobbed. "I'm so sorry," he whispered against her ear. "Lean on me, sweetheart. I won't let you go."

He stroked wisps of hair from her wet cheeks, and she eased against him. She still cried in his arms, but her sobs quieted as he rocked her and whispered reassurances.

After several minutes passed, he glanced at the others gathered in the room. The man holding the Bible must be the minister. Next to him, Judson had his arms around Tonya, but he stared at Ty with a suspicious glint. Troubled, Ty turned away and his gaze locked on Randi's. Her angst with him was obvious, even in the face of death and sorrow.

He sighed. They probably didn't want him here, and he was sorry about that. But nothing would keep him from Winter unless she told him to leave herself.

It was then he noticed Jeremy kneeling beside his grandmother, his arm draped over Mindy's shoulders. "It'll be okay, Grandma. We'll see Gramps again someday."

"We sure will." She patted his hand. In slow movements, like she'd been sitting in the chair for too long, Mindy stood. With shaky hands, she reached out and rested both palms alongside her husband's cheeks. Leaning in close, she whispered words no one else in the room could hear or understand, words meant only for the man she spent a lifetime loving.

Seeing this gentle woman, knowing she loved Darren for over sixty years, broke Ty. Tears welled in his eyes and ran down his face. He closed his eyes and sniffed, then he reached into his pocket for a tissue to take care of his nose, and with effort collected himself. He needed to be a strength for Winter, not falling apart himself, but the tender scene had gripped him. How he longed for the chance to love her with such devotion for the rest of his life.

He took a shuddered breath. "Everything will be all right," he whispered near her ear. "Your dad's home now. No more pain. He's waited a long time to see Jesus. Can you imagine seeing His face for the first time?" He felt her shiver in his arms. The back of her head bobbed against his chest.

"You'll always be your dad's princess." He didn't know where those words came from, but he faintly remembered Darren referring to Winter as his princess during their marriage.

His words must have touched a hurting place within her, because she turned and melted into him. Her arms wrapped around his waist, and she pressed her cheek against his chest. He held her just as tightly. She stood like that for several minutes, her face buried in his shirt, clinging to him like a drowning person clutches a lifeline. He heard her sniffles and hiccups, but her deep sorrow seemed to have subsided. He rubbed her back and held her close.

Near the machines, a nurse marked something on a chart, probably the time of death. "Folks, when you're ready, we have a private room down the hall where you can gather."

"Thank you." The minister rested his hand on Mindy's for a moment. "I'll head that way now and give you some private time to say your goodbyes." He left the room.

Judson leaned close to his dad, mumbled something, then took Tonya's hand and led her from the room.

"Goodbye, Gramps." Jeremy sniffed. "I'll see you on the other side. Maybe we can throw the football around again someday." With a backward glance, he followed his parents through the doorway.

Randi's hand lingered a moment on Mindy's shoulder, then she patted Winter. "Need anything?" Winter shook her head, and Randi left, but not before squinting at Ty, as if reminding him she still considered him an intruder.

He ignored her the best he could.

"You okay?" he whispered to Winter. "Should I leave so you can say goodbye?"

No answer came, but another ragged breath stole through

her. When she stepped from his embrace, he felt instantly at a loss. But her hand slipping into his palm pleased him, and when she didn't let go, he thanked God.

With their hands still clasped, she leaned over and kissed her father's cheek. She gasped and dropped Ty's hand. "Why is Daddy still warm? Is the heart monitor wrong? Is he alive?"

Mindy embraced her daughter. "It's all right, baby. He'll be warm for a little while." There was a catch in her voice. "Daddy's gone. And even though"—she stopped and blew her nose with a tissue—"I've been a believer for over sixty years and know I'll see Jesus one day myself, heaven became more real to me today." Tears rolled down her cheeks, but her eyes remained bright. "How dare he walk those streets of gold before me!" She chuckled, and Ty saw the hint of a smile cross Winter's face too.

"I'll wait for you in the hallway. I love you." Winter hugged and kissed her mother. Then, in a move that seemed as normal as breathing, she grabbed hold of Ty's hand again.

Outside the hospital room, they stopped where he waited alone before. No words passed between them. None were needed. Their fingers remained linked, a bond forging them together, while they leaned against the wall and waited for Mindy to finish saying goodbye to her husband.

When she joined them, her shoulders drooped, but a glow lingered in her expression. She faced death and heartbreak, yet Ty saw her inner joy wasn't diminished. Her sharp, inquisitive gaze suddenly bore straight into his. For a moment the two-edged sword of fear paralyzed him. How would Winter's mom feel about him pursuing her daughter again? Her son stood opposed to the idea. Was it a family consensus?

When Mindy reached out and grasped both of his wrists, shock rippled through him. She stared at him solemnly, then she reached up on tiptoe, and planted a kiss on his cheek.

Air whooshed from his lungs.

Was she saying she forgave him? Accepted him? She held his arms like that for a long moment, looking deeply into his eyes, as if to see the truth inside of him. He gulped. Waited. Then, finally, she whispered, "Thank you for being here, Tyler. You're good for my little girl." One of her hands slipped up near his face and she gently patted his cheek like his grandmother used to do. Then Mindy shuffled down the hall in the direction of the private room where Judson's family waited.

Ty's relief knew no bounds. His gaze settled back on Winter. Did she agree with her mother that he was good for her?

Forty-one

Surrounded by a sea of people wearing black, Ty sat next to Winter and listened to family members and close friends sharing about Darren's life. Every pew in the church was filled, others clustered near the back. Those touched by the missionary's life were given a chance to say so.

Ty sat quietly, taking it all in. What could he say about his former father-in-law? He supposed he could express his appreciation for Winter's dad allowing him to marry his daughter, even when he had reservations about Ty. But that would probably insult Judson, and the two of them had come to a silent truce since their fight.

Near the end of the service, Winter presented a moving eulogy. Her reminiscing about the close-knit ties she enjoyed with her father made Ty realize anew how much she was going to miss that man in her life.

At the reception dinner provided by Mindy's church, long tables overflowed with an abundance of food. Pleasing aromas of barbecued chicken and smoked salmon tantalized guests. Everywhere Ty looked, people were milling around, some appeared to be offering comfort, others were laughing and telling stories, revealing a cheerful atmosphere existed alongside the sadness of the day.

Ty swallowed several bites of salmon, waiting for Winter to finish talking with Mindy. He hoped they could do something together. Maybe take a walk. Or, perhaps, they could go sightseeing before their return trip to California.

When she slid into the chair next to him, his heart lurched. Oh, how she could move him. Just by being close. By that sweet twinkle in her eye. And the way she bit her lip, as if she wasn't as sure of herself as she let on, made him want to kiss her, even if they were in a crowded church hall. But he restrained himself and settled for a smile.

"You've held up well. The eulogy was perfect."

"Thank you." She smoothed out the fabric of her royal-blue skirt. "I refused to wear black. I think Daddy would approve."

Ty chuckled. "That color looks terrific on you. The braided crown is a nice touch—like a princess."

A soft look crossed her face. "Randi fixed it." She ran her hand over the loose curls at her neck. "She's handy that way."

Unkind words rolled up in his throat, tempting him to say something about her assistant he might later regret. Instead, he focused on Winter. "How are you feeling?"

"Pretty good. I'm glad to have this part of the ordeal finished."

"Can I get you anything? Are you hungry?"

"Not really. You want to get out of here?" She gave him a small smile. "Take a walk with me?"

"Absolutely." He lunged to his feet, nearly knocking over his chair. If she wanted to spend time with him, he'd stand on his head, do somersaults, anything, for a few minutes alone with her.

* * * *

They strolled for a couple of blocks, their linked hands swaying between them. Winter glanced at Ty and found him watching her. He was so kind to her all week. A strength. A true friend.

He squeezed her hand. "Thanks for walking with me."

"Sure." She smiled at him, reflecting on how different he was now. The old Ty would never have put his whole life on hold to spend this much time with her and her family. If they were together in the future, would he always be this considerate? Would he support her and stay with her, no matter what? Well, she didn't need to worry about that right now. Just holding his hand, knowing he was near and wanting to be with her comforted her. The rest she'd face later.

"What's been the hardest part?"

See, he was so sweet. He knew just what she needed to talk about. "Probably, while I know my dad's in heaven, an amazing place, realizing I won't see him again during my lifetime is hard. He was such a strength during the past ten years. Especially without, well, without a …"

"Yes?"

She wanted to swallow back those words. Resurrecting their past was foolish. Especially on the day of her dad's funeral.

"What were you about to say? It's okay." He slowed down his stride.

"Well, Dad's been there for me in this time when I haven't had a … a husband."

"Oh."

Hopefully, she didn't hurt his feelings. But his steady gaze encouraged her to continue. "I could call him any time of the day or night, and he understood my concerns, especially about the ministry. He and Neil have both been my spiritual mentors with the challenges of Passion's Prayer. But I think Dad enjoyed my two a.m. phone calls."

"I'm sorry I haven't been there for you." Ty's softly spoken words touched her heart.

"I know." She gripped his hand a little tighter. "I didn't mean to, you know, bring up the past."

"It's okay." He swung their hands back and forth, making her believe he understood. "I can't tell you how many times I've wondered how things might have turned out if I was a Christian ten years ago."

"Like you told me, rehashing what-ifs will drive you crazy." She smiled, offering him the same kindness he gave her all week.

"True." A silence fell between them. "I want you back in my life."

She hadn't meant for this walk to turn serious. "I am in your life. We're friends. And we're praying about the rest, right?"

"I know. It's just, I want so much more."

She met his gaze. His love for her was so tender. Sweet. And caring. She could see it in his smile, in the warmth of his eyes.

A couple of days ago, when her mom inquired about her relationship status with Ty, Winter told her all that transpired in the last weeks. Of course, Mom wanted to know if she still loved him. She'd reluctantly said yes, then warned her that a future with him was only a possibility. Mom made her promise to call as soon as she was sure of her own heart.

In the meantime, Mom would be praying. Which was comforting.

* * * *

Ty held himself back from blurting the question on his mind—was she ready for them to get engaged? How could he know what she was feeling unless he came right out and asked her? On the other hand, considering all she'd been through this week, maybe he should just enjoy this time together.

As they neared an elementary school, he had an idea. "Let's go this way." He veered them off the sidewalk and pulled her toward a stairway where he saw a field and playground on another day's walk. "Let's go swing and have some fun." He coaxed her up the stairs.

"Swing? Dressed like this?" She swayed her hand toward her skirt and heels.

"Where's that impetuous girl inside of you? Come on. You'll love it."

"I don't know." Her heels caught in the gravel, and he stopped her from tripping. "I feel kind of tired and old right now."

"No way." He turned her to face him. "You're young and smart and beautiful. You're still the girl who loves to swing."

"Maybe." She shrugged. "It's been years."

"All the more reason to do it now." He took her hand again and led her straight to the playground.

He hurried to one of the swings like he'd used in elementary school. Of course, now he was much taller, and the playground equipment looked short. He held out the seat toward her. He saw her skepticism, but she walked delicately across the gravel, then sat down. After a couple of pushes, he heard her giggling. "See there," he called up. "Having fun?"

"Yes."

He kept taking her higher until she was laughing outright.

"Is that enough?"

"Uh-huh."

He stepped out of the way, watching her pump her legs back and forth, somehow staying modest in her skirt, her head tipped toward the sky. She looked so beautiful and free. He wished her hair were free-flowing so he could watch it fly in the wind, unrestrained. His heart beat faster. He needed to tell her what he was feeling. *Now, Lord?* A rush of joy pumped through him.

Her swing started slowing down. "What a relief to laugh after all the tears I've shed." She grinned. "Thanks for this, Ty."

"Your laughter is music to my ears." Each time the swing passed him, he noted her dimpled cheek and sparkling eyes, and he interpreted her expressions of joy as love, not only for the experience they were sharing, but for him alone. Did she want the same things he wanted? Did she wish for a future together?

When she was low enough, he wrapped his arms around her waist and stopped the forward motion of the swing.

"What's wrong?"

"Nothing." He moved to stand in front of her and clasped her hand. "Before I lose my nerve or before another moment passes—" All thoughts of asking her how she felt, or if she were ready for this, fled from his mind. One question burned like a fire inside of him. If she answered yes, everything else would fall into place. He dropped to one knee on the gravel, his gaze never leaving hers.

"Ty, what are you doing?"

"I truly, deeply love you."

"I love you too."

Her words were balm to his heart. He played with her hand a moment, then he cleared his throat. "Would you do me the honor of becoming my wife? Will you marry me again, Sas? Live with me forever?"

She bit her bottom lip and stared back at him, but she didn't say a word. Had he shocked her?

"Please say yes." He gulped. Was it bad timing? Too close to her father's passing? "We could be married here in Ketchikan. That way your mom could attend the ceremony. Then we'd meet up with Neil and the team in California." Her silence caused his voice to break. "W-what's wrong, sweetheart? Talk to me."

Her hand trembled in his. A shadow crossed her face. His heart froze. She was going to say no.

"I love you, Ty. Really, I do. It's just … it feels too soon." Her words ripped his dreams in two. "I need more time to decide about the team—and my life."

Our lives, he wanted to correct her. He probably should have waited to ask her. He released her hand and stood slowly. Had he misinterpreted her feelings? Didn't she just say she loved him? Dirt clung to the knee of his pants, and he leaned over and dusted particles away in the awkward silence. His eyes burned.

She stepped from the swing.

"Is it because of our past? Do I still need to prove something?" He swiped his eyes. Annoying tears.

"You said you love me, and I believe you." Her lower lip quivered, and her eyes watered also. "You showed me compassion in the hospital when my dad died. I never said thanks for holding me and being so thoughtful. Thank you, Ty. It meant a great deal."

"You're welcome. I need you. I want us to be together." He rested his hands on her shoulders and gazed into her eyes, compelling her to choose reconciliation. "Don't you want that too?"

"Yes, of course."

Of course? Relief sped through him.

"I'm not saying no. I just need to be sure."

More waiting. More doubts.

"I need to spend more time in prayer. Make sure this is right for both of us, and for my team. David said—"

"David Michaels?" Hearing that man's name on the wings of his marriage proposal sent shockwaves through Ty.

"He called to offer condolences."

"And he knew I was here, didn't he?" Why was she still communicating with David?

"Yes."

Ty groaned. "What words of wisdom did the preacher have to offer?"

She stiffened. "He cautioned me not to rush into anything while I'm so vulnerable."

He sighed and glanced up at the sky, trying to keep his disappointment in check. "I'm sorry. I guess I misunderstood." He took a risk in asking her to marry him again so soon. And he'd hoped for a better outcome. "I thought you were feeling what I've been feeling."

"Don't be sorry." She leaned up and kissed his cheek. "The San Francisco conference begins the day after tomorrow, and I have Passion's Prayer to consider. I can't make a life-changing decision without thinking over how my choice will affect the rest of the team."

"Sounds like something Randi would say."

Winter shrugged. "She says you're distracting me from the ministry. In some ways, she's right."

"It's none of her business!" His angst toward Randi sizzled to the surface. "You can keep speaking and leading Passion's Prayer for as long as you want. I just want to be a part of your life. A real part of the team. I won't hold you back."

"Thank you for that." She smiled at him, but not the same as before. "I explained our past to Randi, and then to Neil, on the phone. However, the revelation didn't make Randi any more receptive to you. And Neil's going to talk with both of us when we meet up in San Francisco."

Ty kicked at loose gravel. "Did you question her about hiding the money in my wallet?"

"No. But I will. I'm praying for wisdom."

"Where do we go from here?"

She shrugged. "Take one day at a time. See where God leads us?"

That wasn't what he wanted to hear. His heart sank.

What should he do? Follow her to San Francisco for another week of meetings? Or, since the Old Clunker was fixed, should he head back to Coeur d'Alene? Bury himself in work? Maybe then he could get on with his life.

But did he want to get on with his life without her?

"Winter, I—" He swallowed back his appeal. What did she say? Pray, then take one day at a time? Okay, he'd pray.

After that, he'd figure out some way to change her mind.

Forty-two

Winter had barely seen Ty since they arrived in San Francisco six days ago. He attended all the meetings, sitting near the back, but seemed to be keeping his distance from her. He was polite on the rare occasion they were seated in the car together. But his glance held a coolness. And when the team distributed flyers around town, he made a point of working with Neil instead of her.

Neil had observed Ty's reserved manner, too, and mentioned it to her.

When they first got back from Alaska, the conversation the three of them had was awkward. Especially when Neil challenged her and Ty not to be alone, or touch, until she figured out how she felt, and they made a serious commitment to each other. She agreed with his counsel. But ever since then, she felt bereft in the absence of Ty's gentle affection. What was he thinking? Was he pouting? Angry?

This morning she got up early, put on a touch of makeup, combed her hair straight the way Ty used to like it, and slipped out of the motel room, hoping Randi wouldn't hear her exit. She was determined to get to the bottom of Ty's problem. Even if it meant she might have to go against Neil's advice and speak with him alone. For the interest of the group, and her own peace of mind, she needed to work things out with him and concentrate on building their team unity.

She strolled into the continental breakfast area, and seeing Ty reading a newspaper at a small table, she hurried toward him. "Are you avoiding me?" That probably sounded more like an accusation than a question, but the words were already out of her mouth. She met his gaze. "Are you?"

* * * *

He figured she'd eventually notice the way he was acting. Aloof. Distant. But how was he supposed to act after she refused his proposal? And then Neil told him privately he felt Ty should return to Coeur d'Alene, at least until Winter decided what she wanted to do. The team adviser's recommendation soured in Ty's gut for three days.

Time's up.

Here stood Winter, expecting answers.

He met her cool green gaze. "I suppose I have been avoiding you." Hopefully, the other guests who got up early to beat the crowd wouldn't overhear their conversation. He took in her cheek devoid of a welcoming dimple and braced himself.

"Why?"

He set the newspaper on the table. "Would you care to sit down?" He moved to pull out a chair for her.

"I just want to know why you're avoiding me." Her voice rose, and her fingers twisted together like she was nervous.

He glanced at a couple sitting not far from their table. "Shall we perhaps take this discussion outside?"

"No."

He nodded discreetly toward the other table, and her gaze followed his. "Okay. I'll sit down." She dropped into the chair, but her posture remained stiff.

"You're beautiful even when you're angry." He returned to his chair.

"Who says I'm angry?"

"I can tell. And I'm sorry for being the cause of your frustration." He picked up her hand and smoothed his fingers over her cool skin. Neil might not approve of the gesture, but they were in a public place, after all.

* * * *

She inwardly gasped at the touch of his hand against hers, the first affection he showed her since his proposal. But then, recalling Neil's admonition, she slid her fingers out of Ty's reach. "I've hardly seen you all week." She disciplined herself to focus on the subject they needed to discuss, not on staring into his glistening eyes that seemed to be pulling her closer to him.

"I know."

"Why have you been avoiding me since we returned from Alaska?" His gaze lowered, and she wanted him to look her in the eye again. "Why are you eating at different times than the team? Away from me?"

He didn't answer, nor did he look up.

"Ty?"

His sigh came long. He glanced up, then, and she was surprised by the sadness in his eyes.

"Talk to me, please? If you're mad at Neil, or me, you should communicate with us."

He jerked like he couldn't believe she, of all people, would promote getting everything out in the open. It was true, she hadn't done well in that area in the past, but she was trying to do better now.

"Neil spoke to me, and we both agree our personal ties cannot affect the ministry of Passion's Prayer."

"No?"

The contradictory look in his gaze made her ire rise. "What do you mean, no?"

"Look, I'm not here to cause trouble, Winter."

She shuffled in her chair, uncomfortable with where this conversation might lead. He used her formal name too. "What's wrong, Ty?"

"I'm heading home. Back to my shop and work."

"Why?" He couldn't just leave. How could she figure things out between them if she was traveling all over the country while he was settling back in at Coeur d'Alene?

He grimaced like he didn't want to talk about this anymore. Well, she didn't either, but they needed this discussion.

"What's going on?"

"I signed up with Passion's Prayer for one reason—to pursue you."

She gulped at his honesty.

"I want to marry you again." His eyes studied her. "If there were some way to ensure that happy ending, I'd go to whatever extreme thing it took."

What was he getting at?

"If you needed money, I'd give you every cent I could rake up. Everything, including the shirt on my back, would be yours." He looked away, then faced her again. "If hard work could make you love me more, I'd labor from dawn until dusk, then do it all over again."

If I could make you love me more? She did love him. Hadn't she told him that? Just because she wasn't sure about—

"Honestly, Winter, I've thought long and hard over this. Nothing I've said or done in these past weeks has changed your mind about me." He twirled a spoon on his plate. "You're as determined to remain single now as when I first saw you at the conference in Coeur d'Alene."

"That's not true."

His doubtful expression denied her protestation.

But she *was* closer to wanting him for a husband, she just wasn't quite there yet.

"So, until the day comes when you want to be my wife as much as I long to be your husband, I'll wait."

What could she say to change his mind? That she didn't want him to leave? That she loved him, but—?

"I'll wait for you however long it takes. But hanging around day after day, watching you from afar, not being able to talk with you privately, is tearing me up." He touched her hand resting on the table. "Neil thinks it's best that I go."

"What?" Pain ricocheted through her chest. "No, he doesn't understand. I'll talk with him."

Ty shook his head.

He was leaving? Just like that? While she couldn't imagine herself shouting, "I do," she didn't want to lose him, either. How could they reconcile if he left? "I'd like you to stay. I'll talk to Neil."

"Stay as what?"

"As my friend." She knew that wasn't the answer he wanted. "And, more."

He shut his eyes as if pondering something, then he faced her. "You have friends. In fact, the members of Passion's Prayer are so important to you that you refuse to make a decision that might jeopardize their happiness. You'll simply go without what you want."

She noticed the hardened edge in his words. *What I want?*

He leaned closer. "You should follow your heart, Sas. Stop listening to David and Randi."

Tears flooded her eyes, and she blinked to hide them. "Please, don't do this."

"I'll give you my phone number and email address." He grabbed a napkin and a pen from his pocket and scribbled numbers. "You can contact me anytime you want. I need to check on my business, anyway."

"*Your* business?" She felt caught in a mental stupor.

"Guess I didn't tell you the whole story. I own half of a company with five mechanic shops." He smiled at her, but it didn't bring her joy like it usually did.

"I was worried you gave up your business major for mechanics."

His chuckle sounded relaxed despite the tension swirling like a dust storm between them. "After prison, even though I had a degree and some business savvy, I couldn't find a job. No one would take a chance on me. Then my brother-in-law, Kyle, agreed to a partnership. He's the mechanic. I take care of the business side. We taught each other what we knew, and his one shop increased to five."

"So, you didn't need the five hundred dollars." The truth dawned on her.

"No." Ty shook his head. "I didn't."

She didn't know what to say. "Neil's worried about the rift in our group. I wanted us to talk, but I never imagined you were leaving."

He pursed his lips. "He's right. There is a rift, but I'm afraid you're too close to the situation to see it."

"I don't know what you mean."

He stared at her intensely. "You'd rather watch me walk away than address the real problem."

"Ty, I exposed my heart to my team. I told them about our past together. About meeting you in Coeur d'Alene, then keeping quiet about you being my ex-husband. About giving you a second chance on the team. I did address the problem."

"I don't mean about us." He covered his face with his hands and groaned.

"What are you talking about then?"

He leaned forward. "Sin is sin, right?"

"Yes."

"Okay, Passion's Prayer has a sin problem."

He'd gone off the deep end this time. He wasn't making sense. "What exactly are you inferring?"

"Randi."

"Let's not go there again." She crossed her arms, tired of him bringing up that subject.

"Why not? She's the one interfering, plotting, lying. She stooped to sabotage, and you didn't call her on it." His glare accused her. "Why is that?"

"Th-there's no proof," she sputtered. "What would you have me do?"

"If you wanted the truth, you'd find it." He crossed his arms too. "For the good of Passion's Prayer, if not for you and me, you should find out why she's been up to no good. Don't you want an honest ministry?"

"How dare you say that!" What did he know about her ministry?

He stood up too, slowly, deliberately. "I'm not out to get even with Randi for her conniving tricks." He pointed at his chest. "In my heart, the only thing I want is you. For ten years, I've dreamed about you and me getting back together. What does Randi want?"

"She's my friend."

"And what am I?"

She swallowed. He was her ex-husband. Someone she avoided thinking about for ten years. A man she only recently figured out she was falling in love with again. But she didn't say any of those things out loud.

"You kiss me back when I kiss you." His voice was soft and compelling. "You hold my hand like a lifeline I readily give when you need it. When we hold each other, I can tell you want everything married life has to offer." His words were like poetry, stirring her to lean in closer to him. He smoothed a cluster of her hair between his fingers. "Yet, you deny yourself the very thing you desire."

The very thing? She pulled away from him.

"What am I to you? An annoyance from your past?" His gaze drilled hers, even though his voice remained soft. "Am I a fling? A yo-yo you like one day and discard another?" He leaned over and kissed her cheek. His goodbye? "I stop being that this minute."

He picked up his plate, strode to the dirty-dishes pile, set his plate down, then left the room. Not once did he glance back at her. All they'd been through, and he was walking away?

She left the breakfast area with tears streaming down her cheeks. Her upset-tears annoyed her, but today's waterworks represented more than frustration. She was losing someone precious. Someone she wasn't ready to give up.

Was he leaving because she hadn't confronted Randi? Was her neglect sin like he said? She knew for a week that she needed to deal with his accusations about Randi. Why didn't she pursue the truth? Because she didn't want to fire her after the promises of friendship they made as teenagers?

Rushing up the stairwell, she vowed that would change today. Whatever Randi had been up to for the last month, Winter was going to find out the truth.

Hopefully, before Ty left.

Forty-three

Winter finished the call and groaned. What was Randi's game? Was she delusional? Winter thumped her fingers against the table. Should she fire her this minute? Or talk to Neil first?

How could her assistant have called David six or seven times in the last month saying Winter needed him? *Needed* him?

All this time she overlooked Randi's rough tendencies, offering mercy because of the promise she made to her when they were kids. But Randi was a grown woman. Old enough to know better than to lie and cover it up.

If only she listened to Ty in the first place.

And, if the part about David was true, what about the rest? What about the money found in Ty's wallet? Did she do that too?

The cell phone buzzed in her hand.

"Hello?" Was David calling to explain something else?

"Who's this?" a female voice demanded.

"Who's this? You called me."

"I did, didn't I?" The caller took a breath. "This is Lacey Donovan. Did you call me earlier today? And, if so, who are you?"

"Lacey?" Ty's sister? "As in Lacey Williams?" A decade had passed since she heard her voice.

"Yes." The phone went silent.

"Lacey, it's me. Winter."

"Winter?" Lacey shrieked. "I didn't recognize you." She gasped. "Was it you, then? I mean, were you the one who called me a few hours ago?"

"No, I didn't. What's this about?"

"I wouldn't have phoned if I thought it was you." A silence. "Or maybe I would have." Her sigh sounded heavy, reluctant, then words erupted from her like machine-gun fire, as if her mind, once started, needed to release every single thought. That was the Lacey she remembered. "I hate to bring this up. The trouble between you and Ty happened so long ago. My brother will be furious at me for even whispering this female's name. But a woman called me earlier, from your number, and wanted to know the name of the lady he was involved with ten years ago." She sucked in a breath. "She made it sound official, like a detective or something, and without thinking, I blurted Cindy Meyers' name. It just popped out of my big mouth."

"From this number?" Randi, again? Disgust crawled up Winter's throat.

"Yes." Lacey's breath burst over the phone, then she rushed her sentences on top of each other again. "It's been bugging me, so I clicked the number. I wanted to know if it was the police or somebody else, you know? Ty talked to Kyle yesterday and mentioned he was heading home. Said something about wanting to take a car apart. Strange guy, my brother. Anyway, I haven't been able to get this thing off my mind. Kyle said I shouldn't get involved. That I should mind my own business. But I had to find out. Winter, do you know what's going on? Who would use your phone to ask me such a personal question?"

A shudder rippled up her spine. "Our team shares two phones. It could've been a couple of people, but it doesn't make sense why either would contact you."

Deborah would never do such a thing. That left one other person.

"I'm sorry for causing any trouble." Lacey's voice softened.

"Don't be. I needed to know. Otherwise, I may never have learned the truth." She had to find Randi before she did any more harm.

"Hey"—Lacey chuckled—"I know things didn't work out between you and my brother. I hope you don't hold any grudges about my introducing you two."

"No grudges. I'll investigate this other business." She paused. "Lacey, I wish you and I didn't lose touch."

"Me too."

When they finished talking, Winter tossed the cell on the bed. Then she grabbed it again. She'd better look up that duplicate number. Sure enough. The same number as Lacey's showed up on the list from a few hours ago. What was Randi up to?

Planning to update Neil about what she'd learned, she left her room and hurried down the hall. To her surprise, Randi stood in front of the men's door, her hand poised to knock.

"What are you doing?"

Her assistant tensed. "Oh, hi. I'm delivering the mail." She waved a greeting card envelope in Winter's direction.

"Something for one of the men?"

"Mmhmm. By the handwriting, it's from a lady." Randi rapped on the door.

* * * *

Ty had just finished packing his suitcase when a loud knock sounded at the door. Did Winter come to ask him to stay?

Probably not.

He swung the door open, and seeing Randi standing there, he wanted to slam it shut. But just beyond her, Winter stood with her arms crossed, scowling. What was going on now? He probably shouldn't have walked away from her like he did. His recent anger still formed a knot in his gut.

"Who is it?" Neil joined him at the door. "Hello, ladies."

"Neil." Winter still wore that frown. *Just great.* What was she going to say to him in front of Neil and Randi?

"To what do we owe the pleasure?" Neil's face went from looking cheerful to concerned in a second. "Is something wrong?"

Winter turned toward Randi as if she were waiting for her assistant to say something first.

"It's for Tyler Williams." Randi waved a pink envelope in her hand. "It's from Cindy Meyers."

Cindy? Ty reeled back, feeling like he'd been hit. His gaze clashed with Winter's. He read her disappointment. Or hurt. Why would Cindy write him after all these years?

The envelope landed in his hands, coinciding with an explosion of fear in his chest.

"An old flame?" Randi snickered. "Cindy Meyers, huh?"

"Isn't that—?" Winter's unanswered question dangled between them.

"What's this about?" Neil's eyebrows rose.

No way was Ty going to open the card. He'd throw it away. Burn it. He wanted nothing to do with that woman ever again. His stomach twisted. "How could she even know where I am?" Did that high-pitched tone come from his voice?

"That's what I'd like to know." Again, Winter glanced at Randi.

"You've got to believe me. I don't want to hear from her for the rest of my life." He appealed to her with his gaze, but he doubted she'd believe him after the heated words they exchanged such a short while ago.

"May I have the card?" She held out her hand toward his.

What?

"But, Winter, it's for Ty," Randi said in a whiny voice.

"The card?" Winter continued holding out her hand.

Her question confused him, but he dropped the envelope in her hand, glad to be free of it.

* * * *

With the envelope resting on her palm, Winter considered what she should do next. She read Randi's displeasure. Sensed Ty's fear. "You didn't call or write Cindy Meyers?"

"No!"

"You can't believe that." Randi glared at him. "He's not trustworthy."

Winter censored Randi's cool gaze while she contemplated who the untrustworthy person among them was. Then, gripping the card between her fingers, she ripped it in half. The sound, sharp in the silent motel hallway, meshed with Randi's gasp.

Ty's gaze locked on Winter's. At that moment, a rich brilliance pulse in his eyes that she never observed before. Chocolate mixed with crushed diamonds. Devotion, perhaps? Thankfulness? Did the awareness that she finally believed in him deepen the hue of his eye color? She felt so drawn to him, magnetized by something dazzling within his tender gaze.

She turned the two envelope halves ninety degrees and ripped again. "I believe you, Ty."

She perused his handsome face, now mostly bruise-free, and delight showered over her. And, suddenly, she knew that she knew that she knew. Despite the odds against her ever reconciling with him, she loved him. And she wanted him in her life more than anyone other than Jesus. Such a consuming emotion rushed through her, it felt as if Ty kissed her. His honor surrounded her like a warm blanket, a sonnet removing every doubt she held against him.

Winter loves Ty. What God has joined together …

"Do you two need some privacy or something?" Neil's eyebrow arched.

"No. In fact, you need to witness this." She glanced at him, then Ty. "Do you mind if we come into your room? I'd rather we didn't have this conversation in the hallway."

"Certainly." Neil swayed his hand toward the center of the room.

"You too, Randi." She entered and made sure her assistant followed.

"Winter, I don't think—"

"Agreed"—Winter cut her off—"you haven't been thinking clearly."

"What do you mean?" Randi's eyes widened, but then she changed the subject. "Did you hear Neil's made contacts for Germany?"

"I've had a few emails, that's all," he corrected.

"Still." Randi's eyes glittered. "And I've talked with an agent who's interested in a memoir about your life as a missionary's daugh—"

"No!" Winter nearly shouted.

Ty and Neil both jerked at her sharpness, but it couldn't be helped. She wouldn't listen to another second of Randi's evasions of the truth.

"What's wrong with you?" Randi patted her arm. "Are you sick?"

Yes. Of your lies. "Randi, do you deny planting five hundred dollars in Ty's wallet?"

Her face blanched.

Ty made a huffing sound and stood a little taller.

"Do you deny contacting Pastor Michaels, encouraging—or coercing—him to pursue me? The day the money was found in Ty's wallet? When my dad died?"

"No, I don't deny it." Randi squinted.

"Randi!" Neil gasped.

Winter's fragment of hope that it was all a mistake died. "Why would you do that? You knew I wasn't interested in David."

"Because you deserve better than *him*." Randi jerked her head toward Ty.

Winter met his gaze. She was sorry she didn't believe him before. She never would have imagined her personal assistant could be so vindictive. "He's a good man. A godly man. Why didn't you want what's best for me?"

"He broke your heart. Winter, he betrayed you. How can you defend him?"

"Because … I love him." Saying the truth really did set her free. Despite Randi's guffaw, she grinned at Ty. He was smiling back at her. Even Neil was smiling. She returned her attention to Randi. "God and I forgave him. Why couldn't you?"

"Because I knew he'd ruin everything." Randi started crying then. "He'd come between our friendship. Just like h-he's doing now. Didn't you and I promise we'd always be friends? That we'd stick together no matter what? Now, *he's* breaking us apart."

"It's not him who's breaking us apart." Winter longed to wrap her arms around her old friend and comfort her, to tell her everything would be okay. But she couldn't.

"Our team will never be the same again." Randi sobbed. "We w-won't even see Europe."

"If we don't, that's okay. What happened to the person who wanted people drawn to God across this nation? What happened to the lady who wanted God's will to be done in every area of her life?" She laid her hand gently on Randi's shoulder.

"I'm still here."

"No, you aren't." Winter fought her emotions. "Pack your bag. I'll pay for a plane ticket to anywhere in the States." A great sadness engulfed her. This was the first firing she ever had to do.

Ty's mouth gaped open.

Neil's eyebrow quirked, but he didn't say anything.

"You're firing me?" Randi's voice rose.

"Yes. I love you dearly, but you've acted against our ministry." Winter stared hard at her friend. "You pursued your own interests instead of God's will and the good of Passion's Prayer." Her heart tore over sending Randi away, but she had to. Tears slipped down her cheeks, and she brushed them away. She needed to remain strong for a few more minutes.

"What about you and Mr. Mechanic here? Aren't you two pursuing your own interests?"

Winter ignored her question. "The day I found you in Ty's arms, whose doing was that?"

Randi sniffed back her tears. "I wanted him to l-leave." She hiccupped. "H-he tricked me into believing he liked me."

Winter glanced at Ty, saw his discomfort. "Did he apologize?"

"Y-yes. But you had two people in love with you. I wanted someone to—" Randi covered her face with her hands. "Oh, never mind. He doesn't deserve you. And I wanted things to stay the same with our team. I never meant to hurt you."

"But you did."

"I'm sorry. Don't you see, Passion's Prayer could be so much more?" Her eyes dilated and gleamed with some hidden emotion. "We just needed time for more people to hear about our team. For us to get recognized." Her voice grew louder, more emphatic. "A European ministry would jumpstart a worldwide tour for us. And a book would help us become famous. Can't you picture us on the cover of *Missions Alive* magazine?"

Winter couldn't believe what she was hearing. When did

Randi's heart change so much? And why didn't she notice before now?

"Oh, Randi." Neil shook his head.

Randi's shoulders slumped.

Winter took a steadying breath, forcing herself to finish this painful conversation. "One more thing. Lacey Williams, or Donovan, besides being Ty's sister, was a good friend of mine."

Randi's gaze held a look of panic.

"She called and told me about a phone call she received from our cell number today."

"What's this?" Ty frowned.

"Randi knows." Winter wouldn't stop until she knew the whole truth. "Tell me. Who wrote the card you delivered to Ty?"

Randi started crying again.

"Who?"

"Me." She whimpered.

Ty dropped down on the edge of the bed. "I don't believe it."

"Nor me." Neil squinted at Randi.

"Please, don't send me away." Randi sobbed. "I'm sorry. I won't interfere anymore. If you want him"—she grimaced at Ty—"I'll adjust. We can make it work."

"Neil?" Winter glanced at her co-leader. But with Randi's multiple offenses, and her obvious dislike of Ty, they needed to let her go. Besides, how could she ever trust her again?

"We can't have disunity in our ministry." Neil sighed.

"But I'll change. I promise. You'll see."

"I think you need to spend some time seeking God's will for your life." Winter drew in a breath. "Maybe it's time for something other than Passion's Prayer."

"Please, forgive me."

"I do forgive you, even though I don't understand why you did these things." She hugged Randi, knowing she'd ache for this friend who'd been faithful in so many other areas.

Randi pushed away from her embrace an the hallway.

A flood of emotions hit Winter. She longed to n her and tell her all was forgotten. That she could stay wi team, after all, but she knew she couldn't. Even so, she ba kept her tears from becoming sobs. And she didn't want to break down in front of Ty and Neil.

Needing a few minutes to pull herself together and think, she muttered, "Excuse me. I must—" Then she fled down the hall toward the ladies' motel room. If she looked Ty in the face and saw his compassion, his caring, she'd fall completely apart.

"Winter? Sweetheart?"

She heard the tenderness in his voice but didn't turn back. Besides getting her emotions under control, she had one other thing to take care of, then she'd find him and fall into his arms.

rty-four

An unsettled feeling wrestled in Ty's stomach while he waited for a taxi in front of the motel, his suitcase and toolbox on the sidewalk beside him. He had a plane to catch, but he hated leaving without telling Winter goodbye. Especially after she faced Randi's wrongs and fired her like she did. That took a lot of nerve. A lot of emotion, too. The last he saw of her she was racing down the hallway. Away from him. Which meant she still wasn't ready to be with him or for them to move toward reconciliation. She needed time. He had to accept that.

His flight would depart in two hours. Then it was back to Coeur d'Alene and his life as a mechanic. But just thinking about leaving her made him feel sick. Was waiting for her to make the next move the smart thing to do?

The fact that Neil thought he should leave had been hanging over Ty. How could he go against the team leader by staying? He asked Kyle to line up work for him back home. He had an obligation to follow through, even if his heart was tearing in two as he left the woman he loved.

What if he was leaving too quickly?

Winter announced her love for him in front of Neil. That took guts. But where did she go afterward? Why didn't she answer when he called her room and her cell? He left six messages. Plus, he knocked on her door without getting a response.

Man. He couldn't shake the idea that leaving was a mistake. But he'd purchased a plane ticket.

The cab arrived. Time to go.

Reluctance gnawed at him, but he hopped in the car. He strained to see the motel entrance just in case she ran down to say goodbye. He left enough messages stating when he was leaving that he thought maybe she'd show up by the curb. When she didn't, an ache twisted in the pit of his stomach.

Lord, am I making a horrible mistake?

Follow your heart, whispered through him.

His breath caught in his throat.

My heart—? Well, my heart wants to …

"Stop the car!"

"Seriously?" The cabdriver pierced him with a glare in the rearview mirror. "We haven't gone a block."

"I know. Pull over here."

The cabbie pulled sharply to the side of the road, and Ty tossed him a twenty-dollar bill. Grabbing his belongings, he exited the car. He took off running the second his feet hit the sidewalk. He wouldn't leave until he and Winter talked. If he had to, he'd stand in front of her motel room door until she was ready to speak with him. Their story would not end like this, with things so unsettled.

Even if he couldn't travel with the team, because Neil thought it best, he'd find a way to attend the conferences wherever Passion's Prayer went. He'd support Winter and the team however he could. And when she finally realized she needed him, loved him enough to marry him, his arms would be open wide. Occasionally, he could fly home and help Kyle on some of his bigger projects, but not today. "Following his heart" meant one thing. He had to find Winter.

Rushing back toward the motel's entrance, shock rippled through him when he saw her running toward him.

"Ty! I was so afraid I missed you." She flung her arms around his neck, kissing him.

Kissing him!

The suitcase and toolbox slipped from his hands. Without skipping a beat, he returned her kisses, her embrace, delighting in the feel of her arms clinging to him, her lips pressed against his.

A few moments later, the kiss broke.

So glad I came back. He stroked her cheek, kissed the indent of her dimple, still holding her close. Or maybe she was holding him. Either way, he'd stay this way forever if they could.

"I'm sorry I didn't believe you about Randi." Moisture filled her eyes. "I should have listened to you. And followed through on the things that troubled me about her, too."

"I understand." He was just glad things turned around. That she was here in his arms. That he didn't keep going in the cab.

"Ty, please ask me again."

He stilled. A fireball streaked across his mind, flashing red. Ask again? Scared to hope, scared to breathe, his gaze bore into hers. "Do you mean—?"

A deep crevice captured her dimple. "I do."

I do?

He pulled her against his chest again. She wanted him to ask her to marry him?

Thank You, God, for answering my prayer.

He kissed her softly, cherishing her sweet, eager response. This was going to be a day he always remembered. The day she was willing to give him—them—a second chance at love.

He took her hand in his and drew her to the side of the motel, seeking a little bit of privacy.

"Are you okay w-with this, Ty?" The hitch in her voice betrayed her nervousness.

"Oh, sweetheart. I'm more than okay with this." He clasped both of her hands and dropped to one knee. Her smile widened. "Will you marry me, Sas? Live with me forever?" He said the words the same as before, so they'd never forget. Leaning close, he waited, knowing what her answer would be this time.

Her eyes closed for a moment like she was savoring his question. Then, "Yes. Oh, yes! I will, Ty." She threw her arms around him, almost knocking him over in her enthusiasm. He laughed and held on. Standing, he drew her in his arms and kissed her deeply, passionately.

She said yes. They were going to get married again!

He heard her giggle, and her happiness pleased him. He pushed a strand of hair behind her ear, then put his arm over her shoulder, glad to know he could do this now without wondering if someone on her team would interfere. "May I ask, what changed your mind?"

"About marrying you? That's easy. I love you."

Amazing. He pulled her close again. Then he remembered something. "But you ran from me."

She rested her hands on his chest and peered into his eyes. "I'm sorry for doing that. I was falling apart. Struggling with everything I learned today. And there was something I needed to do."

"What?"

She grinned. "I called my mom."

"To tell her—?"

"That I love you." She pressed her lips against his.

Wow. If only they could get married today, then he could hold her the way he wanted to. He gulped. "Anything else?"

"I told her to get on the next plane leaving Ketchikan." She laughed. "For our wedding, of course."

"Oh, Sas." His smile wouldn't stop.

But then, an old problem she mentioned before jolted

through him. "How will our marriage affect Passion's Prayer?" This was something they needed to consider, even though a nudge of fear clenched inside him.

She snuggled closer in his arms. "I was wrong about that. Neil, Deborah, and Jeremy are fine with my decision to marry you. They love you. The five of us, together, will face whatever changes may come for Passion's Prayer."

Randi was truly out. She wouldn't be a threat anymore.

Now, Ty could be a real part of the ministry team. He and Winter were getting married. He closed his eyes and thanked God for all the amazing things He'd done to bring them together.

* * * *

Waves of joy bubbled inside Winter, making her want to dance and sing. She and Ty were going to be husband and wife again. This miracle was beyond anything she'd hoped for. And she knew, just as a harsh winter transforms into sun-drenched spring, her past, *their past*, was gone forever. *Praise Jesus!* A new season was coming—one filled with joy and love and second chances.

If only she could marry Ty right now.

"When can we get married?" He rocked his eyebrows.

She laughed at their similar thoughts. "I contemplated us heading for Nevada."

He chuckled.

She kissed his cheek. "I would marry you today."

"Me too." He met her lips for a long moment.

"But"—she pulled back and gazed into his eyes—"I think we should wait for our families. For my mom."

He nodded and smiled back at her.

She sighed, feeling so happy. Until she remembered something. "Ty, this is the last time I'll marry you."

His eyes closed, and she thought he might be praying. When

he opened them, a peace emanated from his glistening brown irises. "I know exactly what you mean." His next words came softly. "For the rest of my life, I promise to love you, pray for you, and be faithful. All I want is you, Sas." He planted a light kiss on her lips, a seal to all the words he said.

"I love you too." But then, she batted at his arm. "Are you always going to call me that silly name?"

"Always." He stepped back. "I almost forgot." He dug into his pocket. "I've carried this around for weeks." Slowly, as if he held a delicate butterfly for her to see, he opened his hand and there, resting on his palm, was her engagement ring.

"You kept it." Tears rushed into her eyes.

"I did." He brought the ring to his lips and kissed it, then he slid it onto her finger. "I always hoped one day I'd find you and convince you we were still right for each other." His palm moved to her cheek, and he stroked his thumb tenderly down her skin. "I'm so thankful in God's mercy He brought us back together."

"Me too."

"Did I mention I can't wait to marry you?" His cheeky grin let her know exactly where his thoughts had traveled.

She blushed. Soon they'd be sharing wedding vows and reuniting as husband and wife.

Ty and Winter Williams.

Finally.

What God has joined together …

Ty picked up her left hand and placed it softly over his heart, his hand covering hers. "Forever."

And she agreed.

Forever.

If you enjoyed *Winter's Past*, or mostly enjoyed it, please leave a review wherever you purchased this book. They say reviews are the lifeblood for authors, and I would consider it a personal favor if you wrote one. Even one line is great. Thank you! ~Mary

Check out the next book in this series—**April's Storm**.

What's a pastor to do if his marriage is the one in a crisis? Who can he turn to?

Between Winter's Past and April's Storm is a series of letters that Ty and Winter write to each other before their wedding ceremony.

To access these romantic letters, and to be one of the first to hear about Mary's upcoming projects, sign up for her newsletter, and receive the free pdf "To Winter, With Love."

Visit … www.maryehanks.com/FREE.html

A special thanks to…

My Purple-Pen Pals: Michelle Storm, Melinda Ridgewell, Cathy McNabb, Debby Hanks, Kathy Quinn, and Kathy Hesse, for reading my story while it was still in the rough and making it so much better.

Annette Irby, for shining up the words, making me dig deeper, and reminding me what a true hero is.

Jason, for checking mechanical stuff and reading it all again. You are quite a guy!

My brother, Lance, for creating a theme song with me. I love it! And thanks for the computer-tech help when I'm in crisis mode.

Daniel, Philip, Deborah, & Shem…for walking this journey with me. You are my dreams come true.

Family members, for letting me borrow your names.

Kathy Vancil, LeeAnn Bonds, Marylyn Cork, (my writing buddies) for encouraging me when I thought I couldn't be a writer, after all.

Suzanne Williams, for making a beautiful new series cover.

Paula McGrew, for helping with this revised edition. You are such a blessing to me.

Friends & family, students & actors, who heard me say, "Someday, I'm going to write a book!" Thanks for cheering me on.

To Jesus, the creative One, thank You!

Books by Mary Hanks

Second Chance Series

Winter's Past

April's Storm

Summer's Dream

Autumn's Break

Season's Flame

Restored Series

Ocean of Regret

Sea of Rescue

Bay of Refuge

Tide of Resolve (July 2020)

Marriage Encouragement

Thoughts of You (A Marriage Journal)

Youth Theater Adventures

Stage Wars

Stage Woes (2020)

www.maryehanks.com

About Mary E. Hanks

Mary's favorite stories are inspirational tales about marriage reconciliation. She and Jason have been married for 40+ years. They've been buffeted by their share of storms—kind of like the couples in her stories—but by God's grace have stayed together. Whenever she can, Mary likes to include her love for married romance, chocolate, second chances, and ocean settings in her books.

Mary loves Youth Theater and has written and directed over twenty full-stage productions. Her love of theater inspired her to write the Youth Theater Adventures for readers age 10-14, beginning with Stage Wars.

Besides writing, Mary likes to read, do artsy stuff, go on adventures with Jason, and meet her four adult kids for coffee or breakfast.

Connect with Mary by signing up for her newsletter on her website:

www.maryehanks.com

"Like" her Facebook Author page:

www.facebook.com/MaryEHanksAuthor

Made in the USA
Middletown, DE
27 May 2021

40533503R00196